Elysium

Elysium

Book Five
The Tyke McGrath Series

by

William Woodall

Jeremiah Press · *Antoine, Arkansas*

Jeremiah Press
PO Box 3
Antoine, AR 71922

First published by Jeremiah Press on 3/07/2014.

Printed in the United States of America.

This book is printed on acid-free paper.

ISBN: 978-0-9833298-8-6

For Nathan,

Who asked for this book.

Great is the Lord, and most worthy of praise;
His greatness no one can fathom.
-Psalm 145:3

Thoughts of a Lost Boy
By Tycho Nicholas McGrath

"To see uncritical delight in the eyes of someone you love is one of life's sweetest pleasures; all the more so when you know you're the one who caused it to happen."

"I've learned to be very careful about tossing around that word impossible. It turns out lots of things are considerably more possible than I once thought."

"It's generally not very wise to invite a poisonous snake to come live in your house, even if he seems harmless at the time."

"Magnanimity is the most beautiful thing there is; the courage to cast aside yourself for love of another, the scorning of selfishness in all its myriad forms and disguises."

"God can't do anything which is self-contradictory. You could call that a limitation on His power if you like, but you're really just playing games with words. You may ask miracles of Him, but not nonsense."

"I guess it's true what they say about how nothing lasts forever, but I've often wondered why such an obvious fact as that should make the heart ache. I think it's only the yearning for heaven, the place where all things endure forever."

"They say a man is naught but a collection of the memories he ponders most, and if that's true then I choose to remember the good and the beautiful things."

"If Joan had ever taught me anything, if Philip's sermons had ever sunk into my heart, if experience had ever shown me a single truth, it was simply this: when God asks a thing, you trust in his love and then do whatever it might be. You don't start playing twenty questions to see whether you agree with Him or not."

"Do nothing at all which isn't done for love's sake."

"In the end, a man can only say that he is what he does."

"My life has been a bridge between the things of God and the things of science; a link between truth and truth, although it took me a very long time to realize it."

"Most moral questions are really very simple things; it's usually when we're looking for an excuse to keep from having to do the right thing that we end up making them complicated."

"Quite a lot of things go on in peoples' minds which never escape their lips."

Contents

Chapter One
Sunday, December 2, 2158

"There's something I need to ask everybody," Captain Stone said.

We were all sitting around the table in Aunt Joan's kitchen for our weekly Avengers meeting on Sunday afternoon, and all six of us turned to look at him expectantly. Even though he wasn't technically a member of the group, he was a trusted advisor who often attended meetings anyway. Given that our sworn purpose is to fight evil wherever it rears its ugly head, my first thought was to wonder if Captain Stone had found some fresh trouble for us to fix. As it turned out, I was more or less correct.

"Sure. What's on your mind, Brandon?" Uncle Philip asked, swiveling his chair around to face the man.

"It has to do with Mars. You see, ever since we got back from Tharsis Tholus I've been trying to come up with a workable plan for how we might rescue some of the soldiers we had to leave behind. It didn't seem possible at first, especially since we lacked a reliable ship and couldn't even be sure that any of the rebels had survived the battle in the first place. Nevertheless, I've been directing several projects over the past few months with the aim of eventually leading a rescue mission if such a thing turned out to be feasible. I believe that time has finally come," Captain Stone said.

There was a rare smile on his face, and his fiery red hair seemed to add its own bit of dramatic flair to the announcement as it glinted in a passing shaft of sunlight from the window behind him. He looked even younger than usual that day, like a high school kid who just won the biggest game of the season.

"Really? Seems like there wouldn't be much hope left for survivors after all this time," Jesse said. I'm sure he didn't mean it to sound quite as skeptical as it did, but honestly I couldn't blame him. It *was* awfully hard to imagine that any of the rebels were still alive after being stranded in the Martian desert for six months. The Red Planet isn't a very forgiving kind of place, even after all the terraforming work that Colonel Burns and his scientists have done.

"It might seem that way at first glance, Jesse; I'll get to that part in just a minute. But first let me say that we *have* solved the transportation problem. It wasn't possible to repair the *Alabama,* unfortunately, but I've had a team of technicians working to upgrade and refurbish at least one of those old XR planes at Hilo. It's been a major undertaking, but as of yesterday, the *Susie Q* is officially spaceworthy again," Captain Stone said.

That announcement at least was met with applause and cheers of congratulations, but before long Captain Stone raised his hands for quiet and we settled down again.

"Now as for the point Jesse made, that's required some serious investment of time and energy also. It obviously wouldn't be worth making a trip to Mars unless we had some kind of evidence that there were actually survivors to be found. But Mikey and I have been working on that, and we've come to the guarded conclusion that it's very likely there are at least a few rebels left," Captain Stone said.

As usual, it puzzled me a little bit to hear the chummy way he referred to my father, as if they'd known each other since they were toddlers. Most everybody in town referred to my father as Dr. McGrath, or at least Micah. In fact I couldn't think of *anybody* other than very close family who ever called him Mikey, and even then not often.

But it wasn't really the time to get sidetracked by irrelevant issues like that.

"But how could they have survived? Do you think Colonel Burns might be holding them captive?" Jesse asked.

"Certainly not. Colonel Burns wouldn't have taken prisoners. He would have executed them right on the spot for treason," Captain Stone said coolly, and I flinched a little. I'm a molecular biologist, after all; not a soldier. Things like that are way outside my comfort zone.

"So how *could* they have survived, then?" I asked.

"Well, we're still not *sure* any of them did. But we found some interesting signs of possible occupation near the old Redoubt in the Mountains of Tantalus," Captain Stone said.

"What's the Redoubt?" Jesse asked.

"It's a secret refuge which the Martian rebels built several years ago, stocked with weapons and supplies so they could survive and defend themselves if that ever became necessary. It would have been the logical place for any survivors to go, if they could make it that far," Captain Stone said.

"How come nobody ever mentioned it before?" Hunter ventured to ask. He was just barely seventeen, four years younger than the rest of us, and he didn't normally talk much at meetings.

"Would there have been any point till now?" Captain Stone asked. He had a way of being brutally honest like that which had been hard to get used to at first, but once you got to know him for a while you realized he was never spiteful, just very blunt sometimes.

"No, sir. . . I don't guess there would have been," Hunter admitted meekly.

"All right, then. What I have in mind at this point is to head out to Mars immediately on board the *Susie Q*, scoop up any survivors from the Redoubt, and then get off the planet as quickly as possible. With a little luck, it won't take more than a few hours on the surface at most; I prefer not to give Colonel Burns any more time to notice our presence than absolutely necessary. It'll be a difficult and risky mission all the way around, which brings me to the question I actually came here to ask. I'd like for at least a few of you to consider joining me," Captain Stone said.

"*You're* going?" I asked skeptically.

"Of course. Surely you don't think I'd ask men or women under my command to take risks I'm not willing to venture myself, do you?" Captain Stone asked.

"No, it's not that. I just thought. . . " I said, and then trailed off, not quite sure what I *did* think. Brandon Stone had a long history of shattering every preconceived notion I'd ever had of an NADF officer; I don't suppose I should have been surprised by anything at all he might have said or done at that point. It just seemed odd that a high commander would get personally involved with a dangerous mission like that, you know. I'd read about such things in history books, of course, but it hadn't been a common attitude in centuries.

"I'm sure you probably thought commanders should stay safely behind the scenes and push pencils, no doubt. I've seen quite a few of that type myself, more's the pity. And maybe if this weren't such a critical and sensitive mission then I might stay home and assign a few trustworthy lieutenants to handle things. But I can't in good conscience order anyone to risk his life for nothing but a maybe. This will be a mission only for volunteers, and even though I've got soldiers with greater technical skills and combat specialties than anyone in this room, so does Colonel Burns. We can never hope to match him toe-to-toe like that. Our most valuable asset at this point is the ability to think outside the box, and unfortunately that's something none of my soldiers can give me. All of them were trained under the same teachers at the same military academy. Colonel Burns knows the way they think inside and out. At all costs we can't be predictable, and that's why the six of you came to mind instead. Besides which, I've already had the opportunity to see several of you in action, particularly Tyke and Hunter during the battles at Barbados and Jamestown. They both comported themselves with exceptional courage and resourcefulness even in the face of very difficult odds, and I've heard similar stories about the rest of you. Those are exactly the kind of people I want to have at my side during a mission like this," Captain Stone said. Such high praise was uncomfortable to hear, but I noticed Aunt Joan watching me and remembered my manners just in time.

"Thank you, sir," I said, and Hunter mumbled something likewise. Danielle reached across the table to squeeze my hand encouragingly, her diamond wedding set sparkling in the sunshine. In two and a half years that ring had never once left her finger.

"I believe in giving credit where it's due, that's all," Captain Stone said.

"So what's this evidence you mentioned that led you to think there might still be survivors?" Uncle Philip asked.

"It'll be easier to show you than tell you. If y'all have time to come up to the observatory for a little while tonight then I'll be glad to show you what we found," Captain Stone said.

"Would eight o'clock be all right?" Danielle asked.

"Perfect. Will that work for the rest of you?" Captain Stone asked.

"Fine with me," Jesse said, and Hunter sort of shrugged as if it didn't much matter.

"I think Joan and I might have to pass on this adventure. We have too many responsibilities already, and besides that it wouldn't be a good idea for us to go out in space right now; not with a new baby coming soon and all that. The others can see what you found and then decide for themselves whether to go or not. I give them my blessing, if they're willing," Uncle Philip said.

No one questioned his decision. Philip is the undisputed leader of all three hundred and seventy-six human beings still left alive on earth. We all live together in the little town of Kailua Kona on the island of Hawaii, after a man-made plague known as the Orion Strain wiped out every warm-blooded species on the entire planet just five years ago. A few of us had managed to escape to the Moon or other places, but the Earth itself was still infested with deadly spores. Some of us had been able to come home again after I discovered a workable vaccine, but we still had some vicious enemies on Mars and Venus who would have liked nothing better than to kill us and take over the world for themselves. After some fierce battles we'd destroyed their spaceships and left them stranded on their own worlds, but a handful of our own people were still unaccounted for on Mars. Those were the ones we'd been talking about.

"Thanks, Philip; I appreciate that. There's no rush; they can think about it for a day or two and let me know if this is something they want to be a part of. In the meantime, I'll see everybody tonight," Captain Stone said.

The meeting didn't last much longer, but as we walked home along the beach I couldn't help thinking about Captain Stone's request for volunteers. I could understand Philip and Joan not wanting to go on such an expedition, but Danielle and I had children to think of, too. So did Jesse, and he'd already been badly hurt the *last* time we tangled with Colonel Burns and his flunkies. I wasn't eager to sign up for a second round.

But then on the other hand, we really *did* have a moral obligation to go back for the ones we'd left behind, if there were any of them still alive and if it were actually possible. It was exactly the kind of mission any Avenger should have been proud to take on, if his heart was in the right place. My hesitation seemed unworthy of the oath I'd sworn, but that still didn't keep me from feeling it.

"So, what do *you* think about all this, beautiful?" I finally asked. Danielle hadn't uttered a peep about her own thoughts yet.

"I think we might as well go up to the observatory tonight to look at the evidence before we decide anything for sure. If it's convincing enough then yeah I think we should probably go," she said.

"You do?" I asked, kind of surprised that she'd made up her mind so easily when I'd been twisted in knots myself.

"Yeah, I do. Captain Stone has a good point about choosing people who might be more likely to see things outside the box and not be too predictable. There's nobody else who fits that description except us. Besides that, we *have* been through a lot of hard times together and faced down a lot of dangerous situations.

We're probably the best team he could hope to find, all things considered," she said.

"But what about Josie and Derrick?" I asked, referring to our eighteen-month-old daughter and ten-year-old nephew.

"Yeah. . . that's the really hard part, isn't it? But if all goes well then we shouldn't be gone longer than a few weeks or so, and in the meantime we can leave them with your parents for a little while. They like going over there anyway," Danielle said.

"Well. . . okay. What do we do with them tonight while we're up at the observatory, though?" I asked.

"Already got that one covered, too. Your Aunt Joan said she'd watch them till we get back," she said.

So that's what we did, and late that evening after the sun went down we dressed in warm clothes and drove up the mountain to see whatever there was to be seen. Jesse and Hunter rode with us in the back seat, since there was no reason to waste fuel by driving two vehicles. My father's car was already parked in the lot when we arrived, and I silently pulled up beside him.

"I didn't know your dad was supposed to be here too," Danielle said as soon as I killed the engine.

"Neither did I, but maybe Captain Stone needed him to run the telescopes or the computer or something like that," I said, and she shrugged noncommittally.

Sure enough, Daddy and Captain Stone were huddled together over the computer screen when we got inside, but they both looked up when they heard the door open.

"Well, here we all are, and just in time, too! I'm glad everybody could make it," Daddy said, getting up from his chair to give all four of us a bear-hug before he sat back down.

"Captain Stone said there were some things he wanted to show us," Danielle said.

"That's right; time to show off our detective work, Mikey," Captain Stone said.

"Sure thing. Y'all come closer where you can see," Daddy said, and we quickly gathered round the screen. I wasn't quite sure what we were seeing at first; just a reddish, dusty landscape scattered with darker red rocks.

"What are we looking at?" Danielle finally asked.

"This is the southern slope of Tharsis Tholus, about three quarters of the way up to the summit. That was the rendezvous point where the *Alabama* landed and where the battle took place," Daddy murmured.

His words reminded me unpleasantly of everything I'd seen during that battle. Colonel Burns had caught us by surprise while we tried to evacuate the Martian rebels, almost destroying our ship and nearly killing all of us in the process. I could still remember our noses starting to bleed like fountains when the flight deck lost pressure from a hull breach, and then seeing the blood start to boil on the faces of those who couldn't get suited up fast enough. We'd barely made it out of there alive, and even then only at the cost of abandoning dozens of the very people we'd come to save. The memories weren't nice ones.

"What are we looking at that place for? I'm sure any survivors would be long gone from *there* by now, no matter what happened," Jesse said.

"You're absolutely right, Jesse. Colonel Burns would have killed as many of them as possible immediately, but one of the first things we needed to know was whether anybody escaped the battle or not. For that we had to examine the battlefield itself, and there are a lot of bones, I'm afraid. Colonel Burns never took the trouble to bury them," Captain Stone said.

That was kind of a gruesome thought, actually, but I told myself I'd seen worse things. So I kept my eyes glued to the screen while Daddy fiddled with the controls until he found the exact spot where the battle had taken place. Sure enough, there were space-suited mummies lying everywhere on the red ground.

"There they are," he said wryly, and I felt a wave of pity come over me at the sight even though I knew those poor people had been dead for months already by then. Colonel Burns really could have had the common decency to bury them, one would think; even enemies in war did that much. It looked like a few of the suits had been robbed for usable parts, but I guess most of them were too damaged to be worth the trouble.

"That can't be all of them. How many did you say were left behind? Fifty?" Danielle asked.

"Forty-six, to be exact," Captain Stone said.

"There's no way that's forty-six bodies," Danielle said, and after scrutinizing the field I had to agree. They were piled and strewn all over the place, with a few of them half buried in wind-blown dirt. That made it hard to tell *exactly* how many there were, but it sure didn't look like forty-six.

"Precisely. That's our first bit of evidence for survivors. Some of the rebels must have escaped or else they'd all be lying there together right now. Count them and see how many you come up with," Captain Stone said.

"I count thirty-one," Danielle said after a while.

"I only got twenty-eight," I admitted.

"Well, just to be conservative, that still leaves at least fifteen of them unaccounted for. Maybe more," Jesse said.

"Yes, but it doesn't necessarily mean they *survived.* All it means is that they didn't die at that particular place and time," I pointed out.

"I told you we couldn't be *sure,* Tyke. I only said we had some evidence," Captain Stone reminded me.

"How did they get to the rendezvous point to start with? If they *did* escape, that's probably how they got away," Danielle said.

"Good point, my dear. That's the next thing on our list of sites to see. But to answer your question, they had land rovers," Captain Stone said.

"Don't you think Colonel Burns would have either taken those or destroyed them during the battle?" I asked.

"Maybe, if he wasn't too busy with other things. He was so intent on capturing the *Alabama* that I doubt he paid much attention to anything else," Captain Stone pointed out, and I shrugged; that was possible, I supposed.

"Here's what's left of them," Daddy said after a while, pointing out a field strewn with the wreckage of at least a dozen large rovers.

"Do you think that would be enough to carry three hundred and twenty-something people?" Danielle asked.

"It's hard to say, with them blown to pieces like that. But we're not trying to figure out if any of them are missing or not; I just wanted you to see them so you'll have at least a general idea of what they look like. Show them the Redoubt, Mikey," Captain Stone said, and Daddy quickly shifted the view about three hundred miles north to a spot on the western fringe of the Tempe Hills, at their highest and most rugged section in the Mountains of Tantalus. That still isn't saying a whole lot, to be sure; they wouldn't have seemed like much more than steep and knobby hills if it hadn't been for the fact that they looked out to the northwest across an utterly flat and featureless plain extending for hundreds of miles in every direction and ending eventually at the North Sea. All that flat nothingness made them look bigger in comparison than they really were.

But my musings were interrupted.

"There it is. And there's the rover they took. We *think*," Daddy murmured, pointing it out.

It didn't look like much to me; just a glint of metal down inside one of the many cracks and canyons in that region, something you'd never even notice unless you knew exactly where to look. It might have been a rover or it might not have been, for all I could tell. We simply couldn't get enough resolution on the image to be sure.

"So where's the Redoubt itself? I don't see anything but empty land," Hunter said.

"It's underground, dug back into the walls of the canyon down at the bottom where snoopy spy satellites can't find it. I promise you it's there," Captain Stone said.

There was nothing we could do except take his word for it, since there was absolutely nothing to see. The only tell-tale evidence of human hands was that bright little glint of metal coming from a place where it shouldn't naturally have been, and that was meager proof at best.

"So let me get this straight. You think maybe fifteen or twenty rebels escaped the battle and possibly went to this Redoubt to try to survive?" Jesse asked.

"We hope so, yes," Captain Stone agreed.

"It seems to me like Colonel Burns ought to have noticed anybody escaping in a rover, you know. There's not much cover between Tharsis Tholus and the Tempe Hills, and it's a fair distance, too. They would have stuck out like a bug on a plate, if he bothered to look for them at all," Jesse pointed out, and Captain Stone nodded.

"We already thought of that, Jesse. Unfortunately you're right; there's a very real possibility that Colonel Burns *did* notice, and then deliberately allowed them to escape for the purpose of using them as bait to draw us back there," Captain Stone said.

"And we're going to walk right into a situation like that, knowing full well that it could be a trap?" Jesse asked.

"It's one potential risk among many others that we'll have to face on this mission, Jesse, no more and no less. I've said from the very beginning that it might be dangerous; that's why this is an all-volunteer expedition," Captain Stone said.

"Yeah, I know," Jesse admitted.

"One thing I want to mention to all four of you before anybody makes up his mind whether to go or not. Under no circumstances can we allow a spacecraft of any kind to fall into Colonel Burns' hands. That's why the *Susie Q* has been fitted with a self-destruct circuit so that it can be destroyed by remote control should that prove to be necessary. If any or all of us are still alive after that, it may mean we'll be stranded on Mars for the rest of our lives, which are likely to be very short ones. That's the brutal reality, I'm afraid," Captain Stone said.

"You're painting it awfully black, aren't you?" Danielle asked.

"Only being realistic, my dear. Any or all of those things could certainly happen, and we have to be prepared for them. But I wouldn't even suggest a mission like this if I thought it was impossible. I believe there's a good chance we'll find at least a few survivors at the Redoubt and bring them safely home again without any trouble at all," Captain Stone said.

That was a much more cheerful way of looking at things, to be sure, but the specter of finding ourselves permanently stranded on Mars was enough to shake anybody's courage. I remembered enough about the conditions on that cold and dusty world to know that it was a forbidding destination even at the best of times. Our short experience on Tharsis Tholus proved *that*.

It did help somewhat that Mars was only two or three months short of opposition at the moment; that is, its time of nearest approach to Earth. That would shorten the trip considerably and also make it much easier to stay in touch with the folks back home since there wouldn't be as much radio delay. It also happened to be late summer in the northern hemisphere, which meant it shouldn't be impossibly cold. The Mountains of Tantalus are located about 35 degrees north of the equator, or roughly the same latitude as South Carolina. That's just about the northern limit of survivability on Mars; any farther from the equator than that and you'll freeze to death when winter comes. It gets so cold then that even the atmosphere starts to freeze into huge slabs of ice. Much better to stay in the tropics, if you're smart.

Not exactly the kind of place you'd want to spend the rest of your life.

But actually, in a strange kind of way I think it was that very fact which convinced me to go. In the back of my mind I couldn't help thinking that if *I'd* been the one abandoned in such a horrible place, I surely would have hoped that somebody might find the courage to come back after *me* if they could have.

Philip likes to say that most moral questions are really very simple things. It's usually when we're looking for an excuse to keep from having to do the right thing that we end up making them complicated. Maybe so. All I can say for sure is that when all the fat was sliced off the bone, it was mostly the plain old Golden Rule which ultimately settled the issue as far as I was concerned. I glanced at Danielle, and she nodded slightly.

"Danielle and I will go," I said, and it wasn't long before Jesse and Hunter added their own agreement.

"Good. I knew you'd all come," Captain Stone said, just like he'd never doubted any of us for a second.

"So when are we leaving?" I finally asked.

Chapter Two

We left the very next day, actually; Captain Stone already had everything stowed and ready before he even asked us.

Only the five of us went: me, Danielle, Jesse, Hunter, and Captain Stone himself. Our hope lay in speed and stealth, not in pitched battles, and for that a small group suited our purposes much better. Besides which, those little XR-227 planes from the old days were only built for fourteen people originally, and we didn't know how many survivors (if any) we might need to bring back with us. I noticed immediately that the *Susie Q* had been modified to carry an additional six passengers by dint of bolting an extra seat onto the end of each row. That was good as far as it went, except for the fact that it also made the center aisle so narrow that we had to turn sideways to squeeze through. It left us with fifteen slots for survivors, and I suppose in a pinch we could have carried a few more; somebody could sit in the bathroom, and others could squeeze along the walls if necessary. It wouldn't have been *safe,* exactly, but it could be done. The grubs are really good at making do with only a little when need be.

I guess I should mention that *grub* is a slangy word for *soldier,* just in case you never heard it used that way before. There are a lot of them in Kailua Kona, not to mention on Mars and Venus. Most of our techs and workers are grubs, survivors of Mars and Venus who rebelled against the tyranny and oppression in those places. Captain Stone is the high commander of all such rebel forces, even though he defers to Uncle Philip on most things.

Anyway, the grubs had done a good job refurbishing that old ship; it looked almost like a new one, inside and out. I don't doubt they upgraded and repaired as much of the mechanics of the thing as humanly possible, too. Nevertheless, fifty year old equipment is still fifty year old equipment; it's not new, and it won't take as much abuse as a new one might. That was something we had to keep firmly in mind. There wouldn't be any gravitational slingshot maneuvers or harsh takeoffs in the *Susie Q;* she was a grand old lady who had to be respected.

That said, the five-day trip out to Mars was fairly dull. We spent most of it irradiating every square millimeter of the ship and ourselves with an intense ultraviolet lamp to kill any stray Orion spores which might have been carried onboard. The very last thing we wanted was to spread the infection to a whole new world. The techs back in Kona had promised us that the lamps would work just as well as nitric acid to kill spores, and be much less messy to boot. They were tedious to use, true, but still a vast improvement over what we had to endure on the way to Venus.

Other than that there were no serious problems to have to contend with and everything on the ship seemed to work exactly the way it should have.

We set down on the smoothest and flattest place we could find at the edge of the northern plains, and Jesse timed the landing so we'd have a whole day to explore before we had to be back to the ship. It was a fairly rough landing in spite of the relative smoothness of the terrain, and I could hear Jesse muttering about tearing up the landing gear if we weren't careful. But we must not have, because he didn't say anything else about it once we were down.

In the old days we would have needed space suits to go outside on the surface even for a few seconds, but Mars had already changed a lot since the old days. Colonel Burns' scientific team had been busily modifying the atmosphere ever since they first arrived, although that was unavoidably a much slower process than it had ever been on Venus because there'd been so little atmosphere to work with in the first place. They had to go the biological route, using genetically engineered bacteria to attack the red hematite soil, releasing oxygen and leaving behind iron dust. Not the most ideal solution in the long-term, but in the meantime it had produced a thin atmosphere of 95 percent oxygen and 5 percent assorted other things, including 3 percent carbon dioxide.

The air pressure was still dangerously low, to be sure; only about 200 millibars even at sea level, which is only about one-fifth of the pressure on Earth. Almost all of that was pure oxygen, of course, so we *could* take off our masks and breathe for a while if we liked, at least down there at the lowest elevations. But not indefinitely. Three percent CO_2 is roughly a hundred times the amount we would've been breathing back home on Earth, and that's on the very verge of reaching poisonous levels. It wasn't quite enough to do us any serious harm immediately, true, but it was enough to make us feel constantly drowsy and short of breath, not to mention raise our heart rate and blood pressure to unhealthy levels.

The environment was dangerous in other ways, too; that oxygen-rich atmosphere meant we had to be *extremely* careful about sparks and fire, because anything flammable could be dangerously explosive under those conditions.

But discounting all those hazards, we wouldn't die just from exposure as long as it wasn't too cold outside and as long as we didn't venture too far above the lowlands. Unlike on Venus, the mountains and the high plateaus of Mars were not at all places you'd want to visit without a space suit. Up there the pressure quickly fell to deadly levels, and that's why we had such a horrifying experience at Tharsis Tholus; we'd been *way* up beyond the safety zone.

Our landing spot that day was roughly ten thousand feet above sea level, nowhere near as high as Tharsis Tholus, and as a result the pressure gauge read close to 150 millibars when we landed. Plenty enough not to need a space suit, but still much too thin for us to breathe without an air tank and a face mask for more than a minute or so.

Oh, I suppose if we'd been Incas from the high Andes then we could have handled it pretty well, or even if we'd lived in the Rockies or the Sierras for a while. The body responds to low oxygen pressure by producing more red blood cells than usual and enlarging lung capacity, so that after a while you become adapted to those kinds of conditions and they don't affect you as much anymore. But it does take a while; your body can't adjust instantly, and that's why a person who's accustomed to sea level conditions (such as ourselves) can't simply drive up to a village high in the mountains and expect to run a marathon like the locals do. You're liable to wind up sick or even dead if you try it. There's a real and measurable physical change that has to take place first.

I guess you could say walking around on the Martian surface was something like going for a long hike in the Himalayas while wearing a paper sack over your head, and none of us had had time to adapt to that kind of environment yet.

It'll get better eventually, of course. Give it a few more decades and you'll be able to breathe without an air tank all the time, even in the mountains. But for the moment, I guess it could have been worse.

It was strange to use the air lock without any kind of protective gear on. We weren't wearing anything but ordinary street clothes, with a warm jacket over the top. I have to confess that I was just a bit nervous about opening the door, in spite of what the air gauge read. I remembered the incident at Tharsis Tholus all too well, and I was sure Hunter in particular hadn't forgotten it either. The last thing I wanted was a repeat of *that* experience. But Jesse seemed to have no doubt about it, so I took a deep breath and cracked the door.

It was a crisp and chilly 45 degrees when we first set foot on the reddish dirt at nine o'clock in the morning, headed for a high of around 70 later that afternoon. It really does get pretty warm on Mars sometimes, at least during the summer. I couldn't resist the temptation to unlatch my mask and take a breath of Martian air, even though I knew I'd have to be quick about it. The short whiff that I got smelled dry and dusty and vaguely metallic, like rusty pipes. Not to mention noticeably and uncomfortably thin, and it didn't take more than a few seconds before I was ready to put my mask back on.

We crunched our way eastward across flat hardpan desert scoured clear by the wind except for a few pebbles and larger rocks here and there. Almost everything we saw was some shade of red; dull crimson dirt, pinkish sky, rocks that varied anywhere from burnt ochre to butterscotch, and the towering spires of the Mountains of Tantalus themselves in the distance, a reddish smudge against the horizon. It was an easy walk, even if not a terribly interesting one. The gravity was only a little more than a third of what it would have been on Earth; just enough weight to be surefooted but still wonderfully light. There was a mild breeze blowing from the west, and even though it was chilly enough to have a bit of a bite to it, the exercise soon warmed us up.

"So what if they're not here?" Hunter finally asked.

"We'll cross that bridge if and when it arrives, okay?" Captain Stone said, which of course was another way of saying he didn't know. We didn't have the time or the resources to mount a planetwide search operation, especially right under Colonel Burns' nose. If there were no survivors at the Redoubt, then it was likely we'd have no choice but to turn around and go home empty-handed.

We made it to the canyon about three hours after leaving the *Susie Q,* and by then the sun was already climbing towards noon. One of the nice but also aggravating things about Mars is that it has a day and night cycle which is only about 40 minutes longer than Earth's. It's nice because it feels normal, physically speaking; 40 minutes is not enough extra time in a day for your body to notice.

But it's aggravating for timekeeping purposes, because even if your body doesn't notice the change, your clock certainly will. Trying to stay on a 24-hour day when the sun disagrees with you is highly annoying and inconvenient. It doesn't matter so much if it's daylight or dark for weeks on end, like it was on Venus or the Moon. But on Mars it's just enough off kilter to be jarring, and there aren't many good options for dealing with it.

You can ignore the difference, of course, and in that case it'll be 40 minutes earlier by the sun every single day; sort of like daylight savings time on steroids. Or you can adjust the length of your day to accommodate reality and then you'll be out of whack with Earth time, and even worse, out of whack with the calendar before long. Or if you don't like *those* options, then you can always keep two completely separate clocks and calendars, with all the possibilities for mistakes that that involves. No matter what you choose, it's still a headache.

According to the files at Southern Command, the Martian colonists had decided to split the difference. They used the simple expedient of setting aside 40 minutes every midnight which wasn't allowed to intrude on the 24-hour cycle; that was as close to pretending it didn't exist as possible. It would have gradually ended up adding ten Earth-days to the calendar every year as that extra time accumulated, so they dropped the last day of each month except February and December. That arrangement kept things in line so the time and date were never more than a few hours different from Earth; no worse than a time zone switch.

Our watches were set for the correct time of day at the Redoubt, and it felt like a normal summer afternoon when we finally arrived at the canyon; warm enough that I was ready to shed my jacket by then. There was no sound except the faint whistling of the wind across the desert, and no obvious signs of life.

"So where are they?" I asked, staring at the canyon.

"I told you; down at the bottom. They have to keep things concealed from Colonel Burns, you know," Captain Stone said.

No doubt they did, but that made it hard for *us* to find them, too.

We soon found a gully which led down into the canyon, and then gingerly picked our way along it until we reached the bottom. Like many such places on Mars, it bore unmistakable traces of flowing water at some point in the past. It was hard to say how long ago that might have been; it could have been only a matter of days, for all we knew. The Martian weather cycle had started to reestablish itself as the atmosphere thickened and the temperatures rose, and that meant rainfall at least now and then, sometimes heavy. The thought made me kind of uneasy, actually; I didn't feel like getting caught in a flash flood at the bottom of a canyon if I could help it.

I glanced up at the sky just in case, but there wasn't a cloud to be seen at the moment. I told myself not to worry about it unless I had reason.

The walls of the canyon were only about as far apart as three cars parked end to end, and in most places they were sheer cliffs, rising almost two hundred feet from floor to rim. Not terribly deep or impressive compared to certain others, maybe, but by the time we reached the bottom it felt like we were on a journey to the center of the earth. It was awfully cold too, down there where the sun never had a chance to shine. It didn't take me long to decide I still wanted my jacket after all, and I zipped it up a little closer around my throat.

Captain Stone seemed to know which way he was going, so we let him take the lead and the rest of us followed. Danielle and I brought up the rear, holding hands partly for warmth and partly just because we wanted to. I'd seen several prettier (and uglier) places than Mars, but I'd rarely had a chance to share them with her except by telling stories after the fact. This was in some ways a rare treat.

We hiked for about two hours along the rock-strewn floor of the crack until we reached a somewhat wider area where the walls drew apart just a bit, and a wider and longer gully came down from above. That's where we found what must have been the glint of metal we'd seen in that satellite image at the observatory; a dusty land rover.

"I *knew* that's what it was," Captain Stone said in satisfaction, patting the fender with one hand.

"Yeah, but where's the Redoubt?" Jesse asked.

"Just a little bit farther. Not very much," Captain Stone said.

The canyon narrowed again past the place where the rover was parked, and it was during a particularly constricted section that we stumbled into the booby trap.

It shouldn't have surprised anybody, I don't suppose; I'm sure Captain Stone suspected there might be things like that in the vicinity. That's no doubt why he went first in line. But the Martian rebels must have been awfully clever about the way they set it up, because I think they caught even *him* off guard. In any case, we suddenly found ourselves in the midst of a rain of falling rocks, some of them awfully sharp and heavy ones. And even though the gravity was low, a rock that would have weighed a thousand pounds on Earth will still weigh 380 on Mars. That's plenty enough to either kill you or do some serious damage, thank you very much.

Everybody scattered without thinking; you don't have time to make plans during something like that, you've only got time to dodge boulders and try to stay alive. But there was nowhere to escape the deadly barrage, and one by one it got us all. I felt something hit me on the back of the head, and for a few seconds I blacked out.

When I woke up I was covered in wet blood from a gash on the back of my head, and I was half buried in rocks and dirt. The air was full of red dust, gradually settling out even as I watched.

I think if we'd been on Earth, the weight of the rocks would have been too much for me to get out from under, at least without help. As it was, I still had to struggle to shove aside some of the bigger and heavier ones. I soon discovered cuts and scrapes and bruises everywhere, and when I tried to stand up I found I couldn't put weight on my left ankle. I couldn't tell what I'd done to it, whether it was broken or just badly twisted or what, but whatever it was, I could only hobble on one foot.

Danielle was buried nearby, and even though she'd been knocked senseless by another falling rock, it didn't look like she was any worse off than I was; just a bunch of cuts and scrapes. No doubt we'd both be too sore even to lift a finger by the time tomorrow rolled around, but in the meantime it was nothing life-threatening.

I soon realized that *we* must have had it fairly easy, though. We only caught the tail end of the rocks, last in line as we were. The others must have had it *much* worse, and no sooner did I grasp that fact than I hobbled forward to look for them, leaving Danielle as comfortably arranged as possible on the rocky ground.

Hunter had been right in front of us, and he was the one I found first. He was lying on the ground under a massive boulder, with his head turned to one side and a thin trickle of blood running out of his mouth. At first I thought he was dead, but when I got closer I could see him gasping for air like a beached whale. His oxygen mask had been knocked off when he fell, and I quickly replaced it so he'd get enough air. I suppose if I'd taken very much longer to find him then he probably would have suffocated.

But that was the least of his problems. I didn't know if I had the strength to move that huge chunk of stone off his body, and I wasn't actually sure if I should try. As I've said before, my specialty is molecular genetics, not medical science or first aid. What little I knew about *those* subjects I'd mostly picked up from Joan, and she'd never taught me what to do in case somebody gets crushed by a falling boulder. That's not exactly a common medical emergency, you know. All I knew was that he looked really bad, and way down deep I felt the first cold prickle of fear that he might not make it.

There was nothing else I could do for him without help, so I stumbled on ahead to see if I could find Jesse or Captain Stone. Jesse must have been buried under so much rubble that he wasn't visible, but presently I spotted part of Captain Stone's hand sticking out of a pile of rocks. I knew it was him right away because the skin was so pale. Like many people with red hair, Captain Stone is white as milk and couldn't tan even if he tried. He doesn't even have any freckles.

I started moving rocks from around his hand as fast as I could, following his arm downward into the pile until I reached his body. He was buried pretty deep, but he was still alive and even awake; he'd just been covered with too much debris to get out.

"Are you okay?" I asked him as soon as we could speak.

"I think so. Don't feel too good but I don't think there's any major damage. What about everybody else?" he asked.

"Danielle's okay but still knocked out, I've got a twisted ankle I think, and I can't find Jesse under all these rocks. Hunter's got a boulder on top of him which is too heavy for me to move; he's in pretty bad shape but I didn't know what to do," I said. The truth was probably even less kind than that, actually; out in the middle of the Martian desert, with no help at hand, it would be a miracle of the first degree if Hunter survived long enough even to make it back to the spaceship. He might not even last long enough to get out of the canyon.

"Come on, then. Show me where he is," Captain Stone said, crawling out from under the last bit of dirt. He had a few cuts and scrapes, but he must have been in better shape than I was. He didn't limp when he walked, and he made to Hunter long before I did. Indeed, by the time I came in sight of him he'd already pushed the boulder away by himself.

Hunter's body was a bloody mess underneath it. As I've said before, a little blood doesn't bother me, but *lots* of it does. The kid's clothes were soaked with it, and so were the rocks all around him. But before I had a chance to get sick, I saw Captain Stone lay both his hands on Hunter's head and look up with his eyes closed, for all the world like he was praying. Which maybe he was, for all I could tell; I suppose it wouldn't have been such an unreasonable thing to do, under the circumstances.

He hadn't noticed me yet, and I hesitated, not wanting to interrupt. When he was done he stood up to head back in my direction.

"He'll be fine, I think. The boulder didn't do as much damage as it looked like at first. Just a few cuts and bruises," he said lightly, after he saw me.

"It didn't?" I asked, too shocked to think of anything else to say. Then I glanced past him to see Hunter trying to pull himself up into a sitting position next to the bloody boulder, unbelievable as that seemed.

"No, it looked a lot worse than it really was. Don't worry about him anymore; he'll be all right. Let's go find Jesse," he said.

Now I might be a lot of things, but I'm not an idiot. I'd seen what kind of shape Hunter was in with my own two eyes, and even though I was willing to admit that it might have looked worse than it really was, I knew perfectly well he had some serious injuries if nothing else. There had been way too much blood for it to come from only a few little cuts and bruises.

But on the other hand I knew Captain Stone wasn't crazy, and I couldn't imagine why he'd lie about such a thing or how he could possibly be mistaken, and besides that I could actually see the kid sitting up right there in front of me. I had no idea what to think or believe, honestly.

If he hadn't reminded me of the still-urgent need to find Jesse then I might have tried to get to the bottom of things right then and there. But as it was, I frowned and decided maybe it wasn't the best time to push the issue. Questions could wait, and if Hunter was really all right then I should probably be thankful for that and save my curiosity for later.

Nevertheless, I had no intention of forgetting about the incident.

We found Jesse buried under the heaviest part of the rock fall, but strangely enough I think that's exactly what saved him. He was trapped in a kind of pocket between two huge boulders, either of which would have crushed him like a bug if they'd landed on top of him. But one of them had landed right beside him, and the other had landed in such a way that it was leaning up against the edge of the first one, creating a cave of sorts about the size of the space underneath an office desk. Jesse was able to take shelter under that, and even though he was buried nearly ten feet deep in the rubble, he was actually hurt less than any of us.

Before long all five of us were gathered together again back at the rover, bloody and battered but all of us still alive, at least.

"So what do we do now?" Hunter asked, and again I couldn't get over the fact that he was actually still alive. His clothes looked hideous, torn and blood-soaked from neck to groin, but the boy himself seemed to have come through his death-defying ordeal with nothing worse than a few cuts and scratches.

"We wait right here," Captain Stone said decisively.

"Just wait? That's all?" Jesse asked.

"That's right. The folks inside the Redoubt will notice that one of their booby traps was sprung, and sooner or later they'll come to investigate. That's exactly what we want, and besides that it'll also keep us from running afoul of any more security measures like that landslide. The next time we might not be so lucky," Captain Stone said.

"What happened back there, anyway? I never saw a tripwire or anything like that," Jesse asked.

"I'm sure they used an invisible x-ray laser to cross the canyon at some point, and then when one of us crossed it and broke the connection, it sprung the trap. Very simple, very clever, and when it's done properly almost impossible to detect until it's too late. That's why we need to wait right where we are," Captain Stone said.

So wait we did, for what felt like hours even though my watch said it was really only about thirty minutes. But when a young soldier in rust-colored camo stepped out from behind a rock with his laser pistol drawn, none of us were much surprised.

We'd found the survivors after all.

Chapter Three

"Who are you?" he asked. He looked young and thin, with pale green eyes and short stubbly hair the color of fresh hay. On the shoulder of his uniform there was a sewn nametag which read *Jacob Trewick, Rgr.* Whatever that meant.

Captain Stone seemed completely unruffled by the gun, stepping forward a bit and pulling off his oxygen mask so the boy could see his face.

"Don't you recognize me, Jacob?" he asked.

"Captain *Stone?*" the boy asked, eyes wide. His voice sounded thin and tinny because he was so far away, but there was no mistaking the astonishment in his tone. I suppose it wasn't so unusual that a rebel soldier would recognize his high commander, but it did seem a bit remarkable that Captain Stone would remember the face of an ordinary grub. He might only have been reading from the nametag, of course, but that wasn't how it felt. He'd called the boy by his first name, and that implied personal recognition.

"Indeed so. We're here to take you home, soldier," Captain Stone agreed, slipping his oxygen mask back on.

"There are only ten of us still left, sir; I'm afraid that's all," the boy said, lowering his weapon.

"Then it was worth the trip, wasn't it?" Captain Stone asked, and even though it seemed slightly out of character for a soldier, the boy laughed.

"You didn't forget about us, after all," he said, half to himself.

"Certainly not. But take us inside now, and let's see what the situation might be. We have things to talk about, and several of my associates need medical attention," Captain Stone agreed.

"Yes, sir," the boy said, holstering his gun and turning to lead us past the rock fall and deeper into the canyon. He must have had some way of switching off the booby traps, because we didn't encounter any more of them before eventually arriving at a place where there was a slight overhang of rock, and in the shadows underneath it the unmistakable outline of an airlock door. I was glad it was no farther, since my head still ached and my ankle was killing me with every step.

Ten minutes later we were all inside a warm and well-lit room which reminded me of the foyer deck on the *Alabama;* a place to change clothes and shed air tanks and deal with all the other aspects of going outside. As soon as that was done, we were led down a lengthy corridor past dozens of rooms and passages; judging from the size of the place, it looked like the Redoubt must have been built to hold hundreds of people. The handful of rebels who were left must have rattled around in all that space like marbles in a shoebox.

But soon enough the five of us were seated around a large metal table in what looked like a meeting hall, joined by the last ten survivors of the battle at Tharsis Tholus.

"Is this everybody?" Captain Stone asked.

"Yes, sir," another soldier said. He seemed to be the leader, because he sat directly across the table from Captain Stone and also wore the gold pins of an officer, although in a slightly different arrangement.

They all told us their names, most of which I promptly forgot. The only ones that stuck in my mind were Sergeant Jones (the leader), and the one we first met in the canyon beside the rover, Jacob Trewick. I probably wouldn't have remembered him either if it hadn't been for his nickname, Buzz. He had an odd little patch of black hair on the back of his blond head, and seeing the two colors together like that sort of reminded me of a bumblebee. Hence the nickname, I guess. He was the youngest of the survivors, and (from what I gathered) a scout and a ranger by training. That's why he'd been the one to come find us.

"How long will it take before everyone can be ready to leave?" Captain Stone asked.

"No more than two hours, sir. It'll take that long to shut down the Redoubt properly and gather the things we need to take," Sergeant Jones said. I half expected Captain Stone to tell him not to worry about shutting down the Redoubt, properly or otherwise, since I couldn't think of any conceivable reason why anybody would ever need it again. But maybe those kinds of things are ingrained in people's minds sometimes, because he didn't object.

"All right. Let's get started, then," Captain Stone said, rising from the table. Everyone else did too, and before long the survivors were quickly and efficiently scattering everywhere to do whatever it was that needed doing. A girl named Nona something-or-other stayed to treat our cuts and bruises and to wrap my ankle with tape, a small courtesy which I greatly appreciated. Then she gave us fresh clothes to replace our torn and bloody ones, and even served us refreshments. Only cheese and crackers with reconstituted fruit punch, to be sure, but I was in no mood to be fussy.

"Don't leave your old clothes here. We don't want Colonel Burns to get hold of them, just in case he ever finds this place," I warned the others.

"Why should we care about that?" Hunter asked.

"Because they're covered in blood stains, that's why. That's just as good as giving him a genetic sample to work on. Given enough time, he might even be able to figure out the vaccine for the Orion Strain. Don't make it easy for him," I said.

"You don't think he's already got a genetic sample anyway, from when they had us locked up in Atlanta?" Jesse asked.

"He might, but why take a risk when we don't have to?" I countered.

Nona had overheard all this, of course, and she spoke up for the first time.

"Do you think we should burn them, then? We have an incinerator, even though we don't use it very much," she offered. I was about to say yes, but then Captain Stone shook his head.

"Is it shielded in such a way that the heat isn't detectable from outside?" he asked.

"I think so, sir, but I couldn't say for sure," Nona said.

"Let's not, then. We don't want to risk alerting Colonel Burns that we're here. I'd rather just carry the clothes with us back to Earth than take a chance on *that,*" he said.

So we stuffed the nasty clothes into sacks to take home with us, and then carefully washed our hands with hydrochloric acid to destroy any genetic material that might be washed down the sink from the blood on our hands and potentially be recoverable later.

"Do you think we should go clean up that rock that fell on Hunter? There's quite a bit of blood out there, too," Jesse asked, and I nodded.

"Yeah, we probably should, just in case," I agreed.

So we took a tank of acid along with a spray nozzle back out to that place, after checking with Sergeant Jones to make sure all the booby traps were disarmed. Then we sprayed everything down thoroughly. I know it might have been overkill, but with people like Colonel Burns you simply don't take any chances when you don't have to.

By the time we were finished with that, the ten survivors had everything shut down and ready to go, and together we left the

Redoubt as a group. It was close to five o'clock by then and we only had about two hours of daylight left, but it helped that there was an elevator which took us directly up to a concealed opening on the surface. According to Sergeant Jones, it was only about an hour and a half walk from that point to reach the place where the *Susie Q* was parked, and I was awfully glad the grubs were familiar enough with the area to know all the shortcuts. That saved a lot of time.

The air was starting to get chilly again even up top, and in spite of the shortcut I couldn't help wishing we'd been able to land the *Susie Q* at least a *little* closer. My ankle was killing me, in spite of the tape. The gash on the back of my head didn't feel all that great either, to be honest, but at least I didn't have to put any weight on *that*.

"Are you hurting, baby?" Danielle asked, glancing at me.

"No, I'm all good," I lied, not wanting to sound like a whiner. She saw right through it, of course, and only laughed at me.

"All right then, tough guy; whatever you say. But if you change your mind, put your arm around my shoulder and maybe it'll help take a little weight off that ankle," she said.

"I will, if it gets to hurting too much," I said. I wanted to take her up on the offer, but I was determined to wait a while first even if it killed me. There's such a thing as pride and dignity, you know.

I'm sure she thought I was being silly, and who knows, maybe she was even right. After I hobbled along for another hundred yards or so I decided dignity was for the birds; pain is a much deeper issue.

"Danielle, I think I'll take that shoulder now, if the offer is still open," I finally said, and she smiled a little.

"Yeah, I thought so. Come here then," she said, and you know, it really did help. It was clumsy, true, but at least I could get along without having to suffer near as much.

"It seems like this whole thing went off pretty well, after all," I said after a while.

"Let's not count our chickens before they hatch, baby. We're not home yet," she pointed out.

"No, but there's no reason to think we won't make it back all right. We slipped right in here under Colonel Burns' nose and rescued the survivors, and with just a pinch of luck we'll be back out in space before he even knows we were here," I said.

"Hopefully. I'll feel a lot better about things once we're off Mars," she said.

"What, you don't love these wild and scenic landscapes, this grand adventure to the far ends of the universe?" I asked facetiously, and she laughed again.

"Yes, my love, but only because you're here," she murmured, and squeezed my hand.

"Likewise," I agreed.

We talked like that for the rest of the way, and presently we should have been approaching the *Susie Q* if Sergeant Jones had picked his shortcut properly. He was walking up ahead with Jesse and Captain Stone, and when they all three stopped suddenly I wondered what they were doing. Jesse was pointing at something on the ground and talking to Captain Stone, but we were too far away for me to hear what he was saying.

"Come on, beautiful, let's go see what's happening," I said, and she must have been just as curious as I was because she didn't say a word as we headed over there. As soon as we got within range, I heard something ominous.

"But it was right here; I *know* it was. Those are the tracks from where we landed, for pity's sake. It's *got* to be here," Jesse said.

"Except for the obvious fact that it isn't," Captain Stone said dryly.

"Well. . . let's follow the tracks for a while. I guess I *might* have been off just a little bit," Jesse said doubtfully.

"What's going on?" Danielle asked.

"The *Susie Q* is missing, that's what. She ought to be sitting right here in front of us, but it's like the ground opened up and swallowed her without a trace," Jesse said.

"The Bermuda Triangle of Mars," I said.

"It's not funny, Tyke. If we don't figure out what happened to that ship then we're stuck here, and I for one don't want to live my whole life on Mars," Jesse said.

"Nor I. So let's follow these tracks a bit and hope our shortcut led us partly astray," Captain Stone said.

So that's what we did, picking our way along the hardpan and trying to keep in sync with the tracks. They were awfully faint and hard to make out, even coming from such a heavy piece of machinery as a spaceship, but I think we did a reasonably good job of following them. But Jesse and Sergeant Jones really couldn't have been all that mistaken in their navigation, because soon we reached a place where the tracks ended completely. In fact I was almost sure I recognized the spot as the place where we'd first set foot on Martian soil, even though everything we'd seen so far looked so much alike that it was awfully hard to be sure.

Then we noticed the *other* tracks.

"Uh-oh. Look at that," Jesse said, pointing them out. They looked like the tracks of landing gear, and there seemed to be several of them. They definitely hadn't been there when we first landed, and that was a bad sign.

"Colonel Burns must have been here," Captain Stone said decisively, and that statement was enough to strike fear into the bravest of hearts. Especially when I remembered what Captain Stone had said at the very beginning, about destroying the *Susie Q* rather than allowing her to fall into the Colonel's hands.

"You really think so?" Jesse asked. He was doing a good job of staying calm and detached on the surface, but I knew him well enough to notice the tinge of fear in his own voice, too. He understood what Captain Stone's words meant just as well as I did.

"There's no other explanation for these tracks. He must have detected us when we entered the atmosphere and sent out a team to intercept the *Susie Q* as soon as it landed. By the time they got here we must have been long gone already, so they simply took the ship and left. We wouldn't have left any footprints for them to follow across the hardpan, and the *Susie Q* would have been the biggest prize anyway. Colonel Burns wouldn't have cared if his men shot us or if we died later on from exposure and starvation in the desert," Captain Stone said, and it sounded like a horribly likely scenario when he put it that way.

"So what do we do, then?" Hunter asked, and that was indeed the question.

"For now we go back to the Redoubt. It'll be dark soon and there's nothing we can do at the moment anyway," Captain Stone said.

"Do you think we should activate the self-destruct circuit?" I asked, forcing myself to say the words.

"Not quite yet. I'd like to try to recapture the ship ourselves first, if possible. We won't destroy her unless it becomes clear there's no hope of getting her back. The first thing we'll have to do is figure out where he's taken her," Captain Stone said, and I tried not to let it show how relieved I was to hear that.

"Any ideas about where that could be?" Jesse asked, not even bothering to cover up his own relief.

"Colonel Burns has a settlement at Phoenix on the Golden Sea, about five hundred miles east of here. That's my best guess unless we find out otherwise," Captain Stone said.

"How do we get there?" I asked.

"We'll have to take the rover, even if some of us have to take turns riding on top. It'll be awfully crowded, I'm afraid; those machines are only built to carry ten passengers at the most, and there are fifteen of us. We'll have to make do, though; there's certainly no way we can walk that far," Captain Stone said.

"We walked nearly a thousand miles on Venus," I pointed out.

"Yes, but you could *breathe* on Venus, Tyke. Here you can't," Captain Stone reminded me.

That was the one stubborn reality I didn't have an answer for, of course. When push comes right down to shove, you've got to have oxygen to stay alive, and there's just not enough of it on Mars to cut the mustard for very long.

So walking was out of the question; we'd die from altitude sickness within days or maybe even hours if we tried such a foolhardy stunt as that, and there was no way we could carry enough air to last us that long. Let alone the fact that without thermal suits we'd freeze like popsicles at night.

Much as I hated to admit it, Captain Stone was absolutely right; we had no choice at the moment except to beat a hasty retreat to the Redoubt and work out some other kind of attack plan.

So that's what we did, much to our chagrin, and by the time we reached the elevator again it was far past sundown. Phobos provided a little bit of moonlight to keep it from being *completely* dark; we didn't have to contend with the kind of impenetrable blackness they have to endure on Venus, at least. It was also beginning to get bitingly cold, and I for one was glad to see the Redoubt again.

Everybody was in a somber mood when we got back inside. The survivors quietly switched the lights and the heat back on, along with all the other systems they'd shut down only a few short hours ago, and Sergeant Jones told us to find a room we liked and bed down for the night. There were plenty to choose from; all of them identical little cells which reminded me of the tiny cabins we'd had to live in on the *Eastern Star* when we first got back to Earth. Each one had a number on the door like a motel room might have had, I guess so people could keep track of where they were. Danielle and I ended up with room number 27.

"Do you really think we'll get the *Susie Q* back?" Danielle asked soberly, after we shut the door.

"Of course we will. No way do I plan on spending the rest of my life here at the Martian Motel," I said staunchly, trying to sound as sure of myself as possible.

"I'm glad we weren't there when they came to take the ship, at least. I guess we can be thankful for that much," she said.

"Definitely. But tell you what; let's go back down to the kitchen and see if we can find the others. Captain Stone might have told them some more details about what he's got in mind, and besides that I'm hungry," I said.

"Good enough," she agreed.

So we left the room and headed back to the kitchen, not only to see if there was anything to hear but also to scrounge up some food if there was any to be had. It was long past suppertime.

There was nobody there except Hunter and Jesse when we got there, sitting at one of the metal tables and mechanically eating what looked like ravioli or some kind of chunky soup.

"Come eat if you're hungry," Hunter said, waving at a pot on the stove. Danielle and I grabbed a bowl full of whatever it was, and joined the others at the table. I took a bite of my food and decided it was probably some kind of cheese ravioli, although honestly it was so bland I couldn't decide for sure. But it was food anyway, and for the moment that was all I cared about.

"So have you heard anything?" I asked between bites.

"You mean about plans? No, not much. Captain Stone was in here a little bit ago and he said Sergeant Jones promised him the rover is in top-notch condition, so apparently we'll be leaving tomorrow morning sometime, before Colonel Burns has time to set up any sneaky little plans of his own. I think they're afraid he might change his mind and decide to come after us, instead of just letting the desert kill us off," Jesse said.

"Makes sense, I guess," I agreed, not liking the idea.

"Captain Stone did say it'll take us several days to get to Phoenix, though. It's all mountains and hills to the east of here, and we can't cross that. We'll have to make a wide circle to the south and follow the Red River along the edge of the plains, and that might take as much as a week," Jesse said.

It sounded like a good plan to me, but then again I really didn't know enough to form a worthwhile opinion on the subject anyway. I knew the grubs traveled in rovers pretty regularly, sometimes even for long distances, so I figured as long as we were reasonably cautious and didn't encounter any unexpected hazards, we ought to be all right during the trip.

It was the part about what might happen after we reached our destination that worried me.

Chapter Four

Captain Stone wasted no time whatsoever in putting his plan into effect. No sooner did morning arrive than he had us packing supplies into the rover and arranging things for a journey. The Redoubt was well stocked with anything we might need, of course, being intended as it was to provide food and other goods for up to five hundred rebel soldiers during a siege of several months if necessary. We had no shortage of supplies, but I have to admit the rover was weighed down almost to the breaking point by the time we finally set out. It was never meant to hold fifteen people plus all their gear and provisions. But it was a tough little thing, as it had to be I suppose, and it was certainly a lot faster than walking.

Before we left, I took the opportunity to examine a map of the entire Tharsis region so I'd have a general idea of where everything was. Most of the area seemed to be a smooth and featureless plateau, and even though it contains a good number of the highest and most notable peaks on the planet, most of them are so wide and broad-shouldered you'd barely notice them from the surface. In fact, you could stand on the very summit of Mount Olympus, the tallest mountain in the solar system at 69,822 feet, and all you'd actually see would be a flat and featureless plain extending in all directions. You might think of them as huge bulges in the ground instead of the sharp and needle-like peaks you're probably imagining. In a strange kind of way, they're simply too enormous to see. You can spot them easily on a satellite map, but not in person.

Tharsis Tholus is one of the notable exceptions, of course; *that* one looks just like the huge volcano that it once was, towering above the surrounding plateau and visible for almost a hundred miles in every direction. No doubt that's why it was chosen as a rendezvous point; it's awfully hard to miss.

The little colony of Phoenix was indeed about five hundred miles to our east, and a little bit south. It was built a little bit upstream from the mouth of the River of Fire as it flows into the Golden Sea, in a broad valley nestled right between the foot of the Tempe Hills to the north and the Caprock Plateau on the south. The grubs had named it the Valley of the Sun, and it's actually a sort of double valley through which ran the River of Fire to the south and the Red River to the north, with numerous overflow channels that connected the two of them here and there before they finally reached their mutual sandy delta about fifty miles east of Phoenix.

The River of Fire itself is a translation of the Japanese word *Kasei,* which means fire-born or some such thing. The grubs had never hesitated to use English translations for words that were hard to pronounce or which simply sounded more interesting or colorful that way. Nor do I blame them, I don't suppose; the astronomers had done the same thing not so very infrequently, after all. The stream is almost 1200 miles long from its source in Echo Lake; one of the lengthiest rivers on the planet, all told. It's also swift and strong, and it had carved a canyon through the Caprock Plateau over a mile deep in places. Not long after emerging from that canyon it plunged over Angel Falls in a series of three stair-step cataracts which added together were over two thousand feet high.

That was pretty much all I could glean from the map, other than the fact that the stone and the dirt in the Valley of the Sun were supposedly darker and redder than elsewhere. On Mars, that's really saying something. And even though this was hardly a tourist expedition, I confess I did hope we'd get a chance to see the Caprock Canyon and Angel Falls. They seemed to be among the few things worth visiting on this cold and dusty planet.

I have to admit it was certainly a boring journey in the meantime, though. There was nothing to see except the hardpan desert stretching monotonously to the horizon in every direction, with nary a wrinkle or a mole-hill to break the sameness. Days weren't too bad, but nights were bitterly cold and we usually had to resort to wearing thermal suits or even sleeping inside the rover. There were no living things to be seen, not even so much as a cactus or a creosote bush, and that made things even more dull.

Well, maybe that's a bit of an exaggeration. There were thin, crunchy lichens on the ground here and there, growing in ragged mats anywhere from a few inches up to several feet across. Cryptobiotic crust, they call it. And wherever there are plants, there are bound to be things that feed on them, too. Thus we also encountered ants; *lots* of them, tiny little red ones that normally minded their own business, except when we lay down on the ground to sleep. *Then* they wanted to crawl inside our thermal suits and even inside our clothes; I suppose to get at our dried sweat and dead skin cells. That was a real bonanza feast for them. They bit and stung, too, leaving itchy welts all over us, and they were so small that even the tiniest opening was enough to let them in.

I knew Colonel Burns and his scientists had had no choice but to introduce tough and adaptable species like ants and algae first, before they could move up to anything bigger and better. That's exactly what any biologist would have done as he built an ecosystem from scratch. I would have done the same thing myself, if I'd been sitting in a lab somewhere and thinking about the best way to terraform a new planet. That didn't mean I had to enjoy living with the little pests, though. For a while I got to the point of hating bugs almost as much as Jesse used to. We couldn't even escape them by sleeping in the rover, because they'd climb the tires and find their way inside there, too.

We didn't find a way to get rid of them till Hunter had the bright idea of parking the rover in the shallows of the river, where the ants couldn't reach us. However inventive they might be about getting through cracks, water stymied them.

The Red River of Mars wasn't quite what I expected. It was very muddy for one thing, and that gave it a deep reddish color I couldn't remember seeing anywhere else. Chunks of ice came floating downstream occasionally, and wherever the water was still or shadowed it tended to be coated with even more ice. Besides being cold, that portion of the desert was also unbelievably windy, with numerous dust devils the size of garbage trucks sweeping down out of the Tempe Hills and leaving long tracks in the dust. Some of them were so big they reminded me of tornadoes, and the ones like that were downright scary. I don't think I've ever seen dust devils on such a grand scale before. Whenever one of those came along we had to hunker down and wait till it passed, and afterwards we sometimes ended up having to dig the rover out of a drift of crimson dirt several feet deep before we could go on.

But in spite of all that, there was still luxuriant algae growth in the river because of the elevated carbon dioxide levels, growing in thick mats which were almost impossibly green against the orangey-red background. It really wasn't a very pretty place at all.

"Kind of ugly, isn't it?" I said one day, looking out at it. Jesse and I were taking our turn riding on top of the rover, and even though our thermal suits kept us pretty warm I could easily imagine how cold it would have been without them.

"Yeah, but they say when it's done it'll be nicer," Jesse said.

"I'm sure it will," I agreed.

"Captain Stone said the breathable atmosphere gets almost five feet deeper every single day," Jesse said.

"Really? That much?" I asked.

"Yeah, really. I didn't believe it either at first, but he swears it's true. All that nasty algae you see out there in the river is specially modified to produce lots of oxygen, at least during the summer. All this will freeze over when fall comes and nothing will happen for a few months, but then it'll start back up again next year. In about thirty-five Martian years you'll be able to breathe without supplemental oxygen almost anywhere on the planet, except on the tallest mountains," Jesse said.

"How many Earth years is that?" I asked.

"Not quite sixty-four. But still, that's not really all that long in the greater scheme of things, you know," he said.

"No, but I doubt you and me will live to see it," I said.

"Speak for yourself, buddy. I'll still be a young buck when I'm eighty-four years old," Jesse said.

"Yeah, I bet you will be. All the ladies in the nursing home will probably beg you for every dance," I said, and he laughed.

"Well, hey, they might," he said.

"I'm worried about what'll happen when we get to Phoenix," I said, not really in the mood for jokes.

"I guess we'll just have to wait and see what the circumstances are. It's hard to make any serious plans without knowing anything," Jesse said.

"No doubt. But I think out of all the places we could've got stuck, this is probably the worst," I said.

"Oh, come on, Tyke, you wouldn't go *that* far, would you?" he asked.

"Maybe," I said.

"You'd rather be stuck on Titan with the A'rum?" he asked.

"Well. . . except for *that,* " I admitted.

"You'd rather be stuck on the Moon where you know it's only a matter of time till the air leaks away?" he asked.

"Not for the long haul, no," I said.

"Well, I don't know what Venus was like so I can't say much about that, but surely two out of three ain't bad, is it?" he asked. He was trying to cheer me up, of course, and I grudgingly had to admit he was right. Mars wasn't really all that bad, except maybe in comparison with the mountain-isles of Venus. Those had been truly beautiful, even though sharing a planet with Luke Bartow hadn't been all that appealing. But then again, sharing a planet with Colonel Burns wasn't all that appealing, either, and Mars had a lot fewer compensations to make up for its demerits.

Maybe in the future it would be better, when the air thickened up and it didn't feel like you were constantly on the verge of suffocating, when real plants could grow and it wasn't so dastardly cold all the time. No doubt it was already ten thousand times better than it had been just a few years ago, but it still didn't look like much. Terraforming is like that; all the hard and heavy work that has to come first is almost invisible, and you don't start to see major changes in the landscape till later on when the process is so far along that it could practically finish itself. Colonel Burns and his crew had actually done a labor worthy of Hercules, and in my clearheaded moments I saluted them for that. But no amount of scientific appreciation could reconcile me to the thought of having to live at the Redoubt for the rest of my life.

What I really wanted with my whole heart was to be back in Hawaii, of course, but since I couldn't have *that,* I supposed I might as well grin and bear whatever I had to. At least I had my girl with me, and that was more than Jesse or Hunter could say.

I tried to cheer myself up with the thought that I'd been stranded before, in places much worse than anything I'd yet seen on Mars. Places like the Altai crater swamps and Desolation Island on the Moon where I was liable to get eaten by mutant monsters or vampire roaches at any moment, or in the middle of the Shangri-la desert on Titan where I could have instantly frozen to death from the tiniest rip in my thermal suit. Even Venus had been far more dangerous at times, such as when Hunter and I had to stagger our way across the sizzling-hot bottom of the Cytherean Sea. And yet things had always turned out all right somehow, even though it was hard to believe it in hindsight.

Knowing all that gave me at least a little hope that things would turn out all right this time, too. But I was none too sure of it.

We had to wear air tanks constantly for three days while we crossed the very highest part of the plateau, but things gradually got better again after that as the elevation dropped. As soon as it was safe to do so, Captain Stone insisted that we start breathing without our tanks for as long as possible every day, so as to acclimate our bodies to the thinner air.

We all hated that, especially at first. I don't know how the others fared, but it gave me a constant headache and made me perpetually sleepy all the time. Not to mention the fact that all of us fainted at least once or twice and had to be revived with supplemental oxygen. But Captain Stone was relentless, telling us we might live to thank him for it someday. And you know, it did get gradually easier to breathe as time passed, although I'm not sure whether that was from my own adaptation or whether it was from the dropping altitude or some combination of both. I still hated it, though not quite as much as I had to start with.

But finally we reached the spot where Captain Stone said we had to halt, about two hundred miles upstream from Phoenix.

We were standing at the edge of a cliff about five hundred feet high, looking down at the upper portion of the Valley of the Sun. The Red River was right below us, having come down off the plateau through a deep gorge where we couldn't follow. The River of Fire and the cliffs on the far edge of the valley were too distant to make out even from that high up, even though I knew they were there.

"Seems like there's a theme to a lot of these names. Tempe and Phoenix and all that," I mentioned as we stood there.

"There is. The Valley of the Sun is where the original Phoenix on Earth is built. Colonel Burns is from Arizona," Captain Stone said absently, staring out across the valley.

"Really? I didn't know that," I said.

"I don't know that it matters much, except to explain his taste in names. But the first thing we've got to do is slip into Phoenix and do a little reconnaissance to see if we can't find out where he's taken the *Susie Q*. I doubt very much if he would've taken her to the airfield; that's too obvious. But unfortunately, he might have a dozen hiding places anywhere on the planet," Captain Stone said.

"No guesses?" I asked.

"I was never stationed here. I don't know a lot about this place," he said.

"The ones from the Redoubt don't know anything?" I asked.

"Nothing that matters. Only Sergeant Jones had any rank, and even he not much. Colonel Burns tells no one anything unless strictly necessary," Captain Stone said.

"So then how will we find out anything?" I asked.

"That remains to be seen. The rover can't get past this cliff, so the ten from the Redoubt will set up a base camp here while the rest of us go into Phoenix and see what there is to see. They'd be recognized; we won't," Captain Stone said.

"We won't know where anything is, though," I pointed out.

"Yes we will. Sergeant Jones has sketched a map of the town and nearby areas for each of us. Make sure you study it just in case you need to know," he said, handing me a folded sheet of paper. I glanced at it briefly and then stuck it in my pocket to examine more closely later.

"How do we get down there, then?" I asked, nodding at the valley below us.

"We'll have to be lowered by cable," Captain Stone said, and at that I almost choked.

"What?" I asked.

"I do believe you heard me the first time, Tyke. We'll have to be lowered by cable. There's no other way unless we want to spend days hiking along the canyon rim looking for another path which might not even exist. That's time we don't have," he said.

He was right, of course, but that still didn't mean I had to like it.

Nor did I, when it came time to be lowered down. I had to sit in a kind of basket thing made of cable, with straps to hold me in. It took over an hour to lower me down all the way to the bottom, and I kept my eyes tightly shut the whole time till I felt my feet touch the ground. Then I let out a long sigh of relief and lay down to hug the dirt.

"Oh, come on, Tyke, surely it's not *that* bad, is it?" Hunter asked. I was the next-to-last one down, with only Jesse left to bring up the rear, and the others were staring at me with varying expressions of amusement or pity on their faces. I quickly got up.

"Nah, no big deal," I lied, brushing the dirt off my clothes and pretending it had all been a joke. It hadn't been, not really, but as long as I was the only one who knew then it didn't matter. In any case, we were down out of the plateau and into the upper portion of the Valley of the Sun, and even though it was still a considerable distance to Phoenix, all we had to do at that point was follow the rivers downstream.

So that's what we did, and you know it really didn't take all that long to get within pretty close range. It was flat and downhill almost all the way, with only a few areas of broken ground where dry flood channels connected the two rivers. But on the third day we started climbing again, which I thought was strange at first.

"Are we going *up?*" I asked, when the slope had been noticeable for quite some time.

"Yes, for a little while. Have you not been studying your map? There's a big block of the Caprock Plateau cut off and sitting between the two rivers like an island, about a hundred miles long and seventy wide. That's where the airfield is located, and even though I don't *think* that's where the *Susie Q* will be, we need to at least check first before we do anything else," Captain Stone said.

I really *hadn't* been studying my map as much as I probably should have, but the Caprock Plateau must have been an utterly flat, utterly featureless plain of windswept stone, if the detached piece of it we had to cross was any guide. There were occasionally little ridges of red sand sculpted into knee-high dunes by the wind, but that was all.

It was Danielle who first spotted the airfield.

"There it is," she said quietly, pointing to the east. It was barely visible at the edge of the horizon, maybe two miles away, and the only reason we saw it at all was because of the tower. All of us were wearing rust-colored camo to blend in with the surroundings, of course, but we moved with extreme caution after that, not making any sudden moves and being as stealthy as possible.

Captain Stone made us crawl when we got closer, which brought back vivid memories of the spaceport at Barbados. Thankfully we didn't have to go near as far this time, and eventually Captain Stone had us hidden behind one of the little red dunes where we could observe the airfield while keeping concealed ourselves.

Just as we all suspected, the *Susie Q* was nowhere to be seen. The airfield itself appeared to be deserted, with no visible activity going on.

"Don't they ever come up here and do anything?" I asked.

"Only when they need to fly a mission, which isn't every day. It would be a waste of resources to keep the place staffed when it isn't being used," Captain Stone said.

"So why are we hiding, then?" I asked.

"Because Colonel Burns knows we're on the planet, that's why. He might have posted guards up here, out of an abundance of caution. There's no more reason to waste our time, though; the airfield is no more good to us now that we know the *Susie Q* isn't here," Captain Stone said.

"So what do we do now?" Jesse asked.

"We'll slip around the edge till we reach the eastern side. There ought to be a road somewhere over there leading down into Phoenix," Captain Stone said.

"Maybe we'll get to see Angel Falls," I muttered.

"I'm sure we will; I'm told you can see it from almost anywhere in town. But in the meantime let's not worry about things like that, okay?" Captain Stone said.

The airfield was less than a mile from the Caprock Canyon, and that's the way Captain Stone took us, hugging the edge of the cliff so as to cut down on the likelihood of meeting anybody. The canyon walls themselves weren't very high at that point, of course; the really deep part was already far behind us upstream. I was kind of disappointed that we didn't get to see that section, but I figured maybe we could catch it on the return trip, if we happened to come back that way.

As it was, we stood barely thirty feet above the swirling water of the river, and we could already hear the thunderous noise of the falls not far up ahead. In fact, it wasn't long till we could see them too, or at least the top of them and the empty space beyond, dropping down to the lower valley. It was an awesome sight, and I tried to get a little closer so I could see better.

That's when I heard Captain Stone's warning.

"You probably ought not to get so close to the edge, Tyke; sometimes the rock is crumbly," he said.

"It's all right. I'll be careful," I said. I was already closer to the edge than anybody else, and my heart was sitting right in my throat just thinking about it. But I was determined to prove my mettle after that humiliating experience at the cliff a few days ago, no matter how much it scared me, and besides that I really *did* want to see better. Which just goes to show that pride can make a fool of you, I suppose, as if I didn't already know that from abundant experience.

To make a long story short, the edge of the bank crumbled under my right foot, and before I knew it I was plunging headfirst into the water.

Chapter Five

I didn't know and had no time to ask Jesse what the terminal velocity might be after falling from the top of Angel Falls, but I was absolutely certain it wasn't within the survivable range. If I got swept over the edge then I was dead meat, no two ways about it. And in the meantime I might add that the water of the River of Fire certainly doesn't live up to its name. In fact I think it might better have been called the River of Ice from the way it felt.

But it so happens that I'm a good swimmer even if I'm nothing else, and I was determined not to give up without a fight. The very first thing I did was to tear off my air tank and face mask and kick my boots off, letting all of it sink in the river without a second thought. I might suffocate if I made it to shore, but I'd never make it even that far with so much heavy weight dragging me down.

The first cataract I couldn't do anything about; I was too close to the edge to even think about stopping before it swept me over. But that one at least was only about a hundred feet high; plenty enough to scare the bejesus out of me but not really all that dangerous as long as I didn't land badly. It was hard to land any way at all except how the current tossed me, so I didn't even try, conserving my strength for the next round. I landed in water and plunged deep under before popping back up again, and then almost before I knew it or even had time to snatch a quick breath I was swept over the second falls and tumbling through the air all over again. That one was almost twice as high as the first one, but still survivable under Martian conditions at least. But I was lost and disoriented by the constant falling and the roar of the water and the thick white mist and foam all around me. I could have sworn I heard people screaming somewhere in the distance, but maybe that was only my imagination.

But the mother of all cataracts was coming up at some point not too awfully far ahead of me, and I didn't dare go sweeping blithely over *that* one. I'd be crushed like a bug under somebody's boot heel. So you better believe I put forth every iota of effort I could squeeze out of my bruised and frozen body, swimming hard against the current and a little bit at an angle to try to reach shore. It wasn't enough to keep the river from pushing me downstream, but I hoped it might be enough to slow me down a little.

And you know, I did hit *something* after a while. I didn't know what it was at first, but I wasted no time scrambling up on top of it. Turns out it was only a reddish-black rock about ten feet across, and when I turned around I saw that it was right at the very edge of the final cataract. Another half a second and I would have been lost. I was so close to the drop-off that I could even see over the edge of it. But I was too cold and exhausted at that point even to be scared in hindsight, and all I could do was lie down flat on my back and gasp for air. I felt like I might pass out at any second, and I probably would have if I'd had to keep swimming for much longer.

But my body must have adjusted to Martian conditions at least a little bit by then, because I didn't quite faint. Gradually the blackness retreated from the edges of my mind and I was able to breathe more or less normally again. And even though he wasn't there to hear it, I silently thanked Captain Stone for forcing me to endure all those training sessions without my air tank. He'd probably saved my life.

The rock was warm from the sun, and once I recovered my breath I kept lying there for a while to let the heat bake the deathly chill out of my bones. Presently I started to feel almost human again, and when I sat up to look around I noticed that the river was full of scattered reddish-black rocks of all shapes and sizes in that particular region, so maybe it wasn't so surprising after all that I happened to encounter one of them. Several were within jumping distance, or at least I thought they were, and that gave me an idea.

On Earth I can jump about six feet if I start out standing in place. I know that because Jesse did track and field for years and even though I never particularly liked athletics, I did go to practice with him now and then just to be sociable. On Mars I should be able to jump something like fifteen feet because of the lower gravity, and there were at least five rocks within that range. With any luck, I *might* even be able to hop from rock to rock till I reached shore.

Of course, if it turned out I'd miscalculated or if I slipped and fell then I'd be over the falls in a flash, with about twenty seconds to live before I hit bottom. They say skydivers whose parachutes fail and other people who fall from high places will black out before they hit the ground, but I'm not sure if I believe that or not. I think it's one of those comforting thoughts people like to believe because the reality is so horrible to imagine. Either way, I wasn't keen to find out.

On the other hand, I couldn't stay there in the middle of the river forever, either. It *might* get cold enough after dark to freeze the water, of course, and after that I could simply walk to shore. But the problem with *that* idea was, I didn't know if I could survive the cold long enough to wait. I wasn't wearing anything but light clothes, and wet ones at that. They'd have a chance to dry out somewhat before dark, but probably not completely.

I sighed and shook my head. They say ogres used to offer their victims a cruel choice before they killed and ate them, as to whether they'd like to die fast or die slow. This was sort of like that. I could either jump the rocks and risk a quick death by falling or I could wait for the river to freeze and risk a slow death from the cold. I might not have an ogre standing over me grinning in pitiless brutality while he enjoyed watching me agonize, but I can promise you the choice was every bit as cruel nevertheless.

One of the worst dangers in situations like that is to become so paralyzed by fear of doing the wrong thing that you end up doing nothing at all, and usually that's a kind of passive choice even in its own right. It certainly was in my case, since doing nothing would only mean I'd be waiting for the river to freeze. I didn't have the luxury of not deciding, or even of putting it off for much longer. Not choosing was only a choice by default.

It didn't take me long to decide that if push came right down to shove, I'd rather fall than freeze. Partly because I hate cold and partly because it crossed my mind that even if I did cross the ice, I'd still be stuck outdoors overnight with no shelter, and that was a serious danger in its own right. If I made it to shore now, while the temperature was still tolerable, then I *might* be able to find a cave or some other place to hide out for the night.

The closest rock was maybe ten or twelve feet away, sort of upstream and to the south. It looked pretty flat and dry on top, and it had more or less the same surface area as the one I was standing on. I could make it. . . I hoped.

I think that first jump probably took more courage than anything else I've ever done in my entire life. I could vividly imagine landing a foot short of that other rock and plunging right back into the river again; I knew exactly what the icy water would feel like as it soaked me to the skin in an instant, and even worse I could envision exactly what it would feel like to shoot out over the falls and see that yawning gulf of empty space below my feet.

But that didn't happen, and even though I swayed a bit I managed to land on the rock and keep my balance. I went weak-kneed with relief and had to sit down for a minute to regain my composure, but once I did I was a little bit more confident the next time. It took eleven jumps in all to reach shore, and I'm proud to say that I only fell in the water once during that whole time. But that was near the end, and I was far enough out of the main flood by then that the current was nowhere near as strong as it had been before. I was able to swim far enough to catch hold of another rock and pull myself up almost immediately. My confidence was shaken and I was soaking wet again, but other than that I was all right.

I finally set foot on the south bank of the River of Fire about four o'clock that afternoon. I couldn't tell exactly what time it was because my watch had stopped working. It was supposed to be waterproof, so maybe I smashed it against a rock or something along the way. But I could judge fairly well from the sun, which was just beginning to set behind the huge bulk of Sacramento Island to the west. I could see the first lights of Phoenix already twinkling down in the shadowed valley far below, but how in the blessed world I'd ever make it down there was another thing altogether. The road was on the other side of the river, and I certainly didn't feel like trying to jump any more rocks.

Then I happened to remember the fact that there's often a kind of hollowed-out space behind waterfalls, where the backsplash from the river gradually erodes the stone. So I walked upstream to the base of the second cataract to check, and sure enough there was an area of jumbled boulders behind the cascade. With a little care I was able to cross all the way over to the north shore with nothing worse to show for it than getting thoroughly wet and chilled again.

I had to climb a short but steep slope to make it up to the road, but once I did I started trotting back upstream again to look for the others and let them know I wasn't floating downstream as a lump of fish food.

Then I heard voices up ahead which definitely weren't anybody's that I knew, and I quickly scrambled behind some rocks to hide till they passed.

Just in time, too, because no sooner did I get myself concealed then a group of people came around the next curve in the road, and to my horror I recognized the others, yes indeed, but all four of them were chained together with those white plastic leg irons that seemed to be NADF standard issue, and escorted at the back by two armed guards holding laser rifles. Danielle was crying and Jesse looked like he wanted to, and the others had a kind of shell-shocked numbness on their faces. I suspected all that was from watching me go over the falls and drown right in front of them, because when you stopped to think about it, how could they believe otherwise? They knew how high the drop was and how swift the current, and they didn't know about the rocks downstream. It was all I could do not to run out and tell them I was still alive.

But I bit my lip and stayed put, because I knew if I showed myself then I'd soon be chained in a set of leg irons right along with them, and that wouldn't help anybody. I waited till they passed and then for a good while afterward before I came back out on the road again, and then I set off purposefully downhill.

I wished there could have been another way to get down into the valley, but I didn't know of any and didn't have time or resources to look for one. All I could do was trot along as fast as I dared without getting out of breath and hope nobody saw me.

As the road descended lower and lower into the valley things started to change, especially as I started getting into the outskirts of Phoenix. We were practically at sea level by then, but I suppose it still got too cold at night even down there to grow much of anything. In any case, there were none of the farms and fields I remembered seeing on Venus. Here there were rows and rows of greenhouses full of vegetables, and occasionally a few tufts of grass were starting to grow among the buildings where it stayed warm enough overnight.

But even more amazing than the buildings were the trees; the first ones I'd seen on Mars. They were spruce and fir, mostly; evergreen taiga trees that grow in cold and desolate places. The grubs must have planted them as soon as the air thickened up enough to let them survive, which meant they were somewhere between five and ten years old. None of them were especially large yet, and they'd been planted far enough apart to keep them from becoming a fire hazard, but there's just something about greenery which is very restful to the eyes after you've seen nothing but desert for so long. Mars may never be a tropical paradise even after they finish with it, but under the circumstances I was ready to embrace the North Woods wholeheartedly.

In fact, I think the lower portion of the Valley of the Sun is one of the few places on Mars that I actually liked, and I could see why Colonel Burns might have picked it for his settlement. The rock really *was* even redder than usual, dark and blood-like, which was kind of startling and vaguely Christmasy next to the evergreens. Everything is sheltered from the biting winds that howl across the plateaus above, and that fact alone made it highly attractive to *me*, at least; especially dripping wet as I was when I first saw the place. It's also one of the warmest spots on the planet, with plenty of water from the rivers and easy access to the sea. Not to mention Angel Falls, of course; that really is a beautiful backdrop, at least when you're looking at it from below. I suppose if I had the whole planet to choose from for a settlement, then the Valley of the Sun is probably the same spot I would have chosen myself.

The style of architecture reminded me of Jamestown on Venus; not very fancy, but clean and graceful in a way that suggested a kind of settled tranquility. The only major difference was the fact that everything was made of red stone instead of black, and the buildings seemed to be crowded a little closer together. That might have been to help conserve heat, I suppose, but that's only speculation.

But my approval was short-lived when I remembered with whom I had to deal. Colonel Burns might simply be doing the practical and smart thing, knowing (as I'm sure he did) that human beings like to live in pretty places and that if they're given that kind of setting then it will improve morale and therefore also loyalty and productivity. So I doubt the trees or the location or the architecture had anything to do with a disinterested love of beauty by any means. I might have thought slightly better of the man if I believed he actually harbored a noble sentiment like that in his soul. But in fact he reminded me of Colonel Bartow in a lot of ways, cold and calculating as a cash register.

I still had my uniform of rusty Martian camo, even though I'd lost my hat and my boots in the river. The hat I might possibly slide by without for a little while, but not the boots. I'd have to find a way to replace *those* pretty quickly if I intended to roam around Phoenix for long; otherwise some passing officer would eventually notice and say something.

I ducked off the road into one of the greenhouses with the purpose of seeing what I could find, and immediately found myself in a warm, humid environment full of cornstalks planted in long rows. I found a pair of black rubber boots in there amongst the agricultural implements, which didn't look *quite* like the everyday footgear the grubs wore but close enough that I hoped nobody would notice the difference if they didn't pay too much attention.

I had to wear them without socks, which is something I've always hated. It's all right for a while, but it gets really nasty once your feet start to sweat. But there was nothing to be done about it, so I slipped them on without a second thought and then headed out. I couldn't find a hat, but there was nothing to be done about that, either.

I didn't really know where I was going, other than following through with a vague idea of looking for the others if possible. I couldn't ask for directions since that would have instantly marked me as someone who didn't belong there, and that was the one thing I had to avoid at all costs. My map was ruined from the unexpected swim, and all I had to go on was the little bit that I remembered. I wished I'd listened to Captain Stone and taken the time to study it more thoroughly while I still had the chance. But I hadn't, and now I was regretting it.

I *thought* the jail was down near the river, if memory served, and since that seemed to be one of the more likely spots the others might have been taken, I decided to try that place first.

Chapter Six

One of the stranger and more notable things about Mars is the fact that it's hard to hear anything. If Angel Falls had been located on earth, the sound of it would have been a terror for miles. But as it was, in Phoenix you could barely hear it at all except as a thin, distant-sounding murmur, even though it was barely a mile upstream. Peoples' voices sound high-pitched and tinny, like what you'd hear through a set of cheap earbuds held at arm's length with the volume turned way up. You don't notice any of that when you're wearing a mask and talking through radio transceivers, but I was reminded sharply of it while walking the streets of Phoenix. The place seemed unnaturally silent, which made me feel edgy and ill at ease, like you tend to do when the birds and the insects suddenly get really quiet for some reason but you don't know why.

I knew it was only the thin air, of course; there were plenty of birds to be seen in the valley, and if I watched closely I could even see some of them singing. I just couldn't hear them very well unless I was really close. It was nice to see living creatures more substantial than ants for a change, actually, even though I don't think the birds could have survived without human help. I noticed several feeders as I went along.

The jail in Phoenix is built of red stone, just like everything else in town. And just like the one at Jamestown, I don't think it ever got used very much. But *unlike* the one at Jamestown, it didn't have windows in the cells. I'm sure that had more to do with the weather than anything else; on Venus it didn't matter if there was nothing between a cell and the outdoors except a few bars, because it never got uncomfortable outside. On Mars it does.

That left me temporarily stumped as to how I could find out if the others were inside or not, let alone speak to them. I was at a loss for what to do at that point and afraid to be seen loitering with no apparent purpose, so I turned away and slowly headed back the way I came, trying to think of some kind of plan.

I knew full well that I couldn't just aimlessly wander the streets, though, because sooner or later somebody would notice that, too. What I really needed was a place to lay low while I worked out some way of getting inside that jail.

For lack of any better options I went back to the same greenhouse where I found the boots and slept on the ground that night among the corn rows where I could stay warm and hopefully wouldn't be seen. I guess I wasn't, because nobody raised an alarm.

There's a lot of dust in the Martian atmosphere, whipped up by the constant wind that blows across the deserts, and that's the reason why the sky looks pink or tawny so much of the time. Otherwise it would be blue, just like Earth's. But all that dust also creates some of the most incredible sunrises and sunsets I've ever seen, red as blood sometimes. Sleeping in a cornfield isn't all that comfortable, so I woke up with ample time to view the crimson dawn over the Valley of the Sun. The valley runs eastward, so the red light shone right down between the canyon walls and made all that red stone almost seem to glow. It was an amazing sight, and in spite of everything I stood there on the frosty hillside to gape at it for a while.

I still didn't know what to do about the others, or even myself for that matter. I had half a mind to go directly to see Colonel Burns myself and try to negotiate with him, even knowing as I did that there was no hope of bargaining with the man.

I had enough sense not to do something *that* foolhardy, of course, but nevertheless I had to do *something*, and pretty soon, too.

What I actually did was to hide myself in the thick bushes that lined the riverbank so I could watch the front door of the jail and maybe get some inkling of how the place was run, hopefully to figure out some kind of stratagem. Just like in Jamestown, it seemed to have only one guard; any more than that would have been a waste of resources, after all. I was able to deduce that much after the shift change at three o'clock, when I noted the fact that only one fresh guard went inside the building and only one left. Once I was sure I only had one enemy to deal with, the first stirrings of a plan started to form in my mind.

But first I needed a weapon of some kind, and a rock or a stick wouldn't do.

I was finally able to swipe a stunner from a lone soldier I caught working late at one of the greenhouses. They had big plastic tubs of ammonium nitrate fertilizer stored in there to use for the plants, and with a little chemical finagling I was able to decompose some of that to produce nitrous oxide gas and thereby contaminate the air supply inside the building. After that it was only a matter of slipping outdoors to wait for the dude to pass out from the odorless fumes, while making sure to hold my breath and not inhale any of them myself when I went back inside. I even snatched his hat and his watch while I was at it, tossing my dead one into the trash.

It was way after dark by the time I was able to accomplish all those things, but I figured that was all to the good anyway. Then came the really tricky and dangerous part.

I went back to the jail armed with my new weapon, going right up to the front door to press the buzzer just like I belonged there. My whole plan depended on nobody suspecting anything until it was too late, so at all costs I had to act natural.

The guard looked out the peephole and must not have thought it was strange to see a young man in rusty camo standing outside. She opened the door with a bored expression, and then before I had time to talk myself out of it, I yanked out my stunner and nailed her. She fell backward with a frozen look of shocked surprise on her face, and I quickly dragged her away from the door and shut it behind us. Then I stood staring at her for a second.

You've really done it now, I whispered to myself, but there was nothing for it but to plunge ahead at that point. I was committed, like it or not.

I relieved the guard of her security badge and her hand laser, then swiftly searched the entire building to try to find the place where the others were being kept. Besides a jail, the building also served as a storage facility for everything from spacesuits to medical supplies, and everything imaginable in between. It was a lot to search, and the longer it took the more nervous I got. Somebody might find that unconscious soldier at the greenhouse or else the stunned one downstairs at any time.

I finally found the cellblock where the others were being held, and seconds later I had the door open. All their eyes went wide with shock when they saw me, but Danielle was the first to recover. She jumped up with a glad cry and ran to grab me tight.

"Tyke? Is it really you?" she asked, looking me up and down like she couldn't believe her eyes.

"Yeah, it's really me," I said.

"I can't believe it. I thought I'd never see you again," she said, squeezing my hand.

"I was afraid I'd never see you, either," I said.

"But *how?* We saw you go over the falls; I know we did. Believe me, that's something I'll never forget as long as I live. How did you survive?" she asked.

"I'll tell you later, but right now come on; we've got to get out of here before anybody finds us," I said.

"Wait just a minute, Tyke. We've got to grab a few things or we'll never survive if we have to leave the city. They confiscated our packs," Captain Stone said. That was excellent good sense, and even though we didn't have time to make a careful selection, we all tried to grab various assorted things along the way which looked like they might be useful. Thermal blankets, painkillers, plastimetal canteens, rope, and whatever else we could easily stuff in our pockets.

We'd already reached the street in front of the building when I heard rough voices yelling for us to stop, and I glanced back to see five soldiers racing after us with weapons drawn. I felt the heat when a laser beam fried the hair above my left ear, and that's when I knew they were shooting to kill. Captain Stone must have known it too.

"Follow me!" he cried, and then ducked off the road into the bushes that grew on the slope leading down to the riverbank. We were halfway down the slope when I heard Danielle scream and saw her fall to the ground out of the corner of my eye. My heart skipped a beat, but there was no time to stop and check to see where she'd been hit. I slowed down long enough to grab her, and if it hadn't been for the light gravity I'm not sure I could have carried her.

Within thirty seconds we were down on the riverbank, and Captain Stone pulled us into a shallow cave out of sight of the soldiers. The darkness and the thick vegetation concealed us more effectively than anything else we could have hoped for.

Our safety wouldn't last more than a few minutes, of course. The riverbank would soon be crawling with soldiers, and when that happened there wasn't the faintest chance they'd overlook us.

"Jesse and Hunter, keep watch at the door while we make sure Danielle is all right, but only fire if they see you. Give them the weapons, Tyke," Captain Stone ordered as we entered the cave.

"They're clipped to my belt," I said, and Jesse quickly grabbed the laser and the stunner before handing one of them to Hunter so they could take up positions at the entrance as Captain Stone had ordered.

But I barely paid attention to all that, anxious as I was to see how badly Danielle might be hurt. I carefully put her down on the rocky floor to check her over, switching on a flashlight at its dimmest setting so I could at least see what I was doing in the pitch darkness. It was barely brighter than a candle at that setting, but I didn't dare turn it up any higher for fear of giving us away.

That's when I noticed she wasn't breathing.

My heart came right up into my throat, and I quickly felt the side of her neck, where my worst fears were soon confirmed. No pulse, either. There was no bleeding anywhere, after the manner of a laser wound, but I swiftly found a hole in the back of her camo suit.

I couldn't let it end; not like that. I immediately started CPR, but all my efforts produced no response. Finally I gave in to despair, and laid my head on her chest and wept.

"Move, Tyke," Captain Stone said finally, and even through my tears and broken heart, there was a tone in his voice that no one would have disobeyed. I moved aside and let him get down next to her. He put both his hands on her head, just like he'd done with Hunter in the canyon, and whispered something under his breath that I couldn't make out.

Then he spoke louder.

"Wake up, child," he told her.

Danielle breathed deeply and opened her eyes, and at the time I didn't ask or even care what had just happened, or how; I simply fell to my knees and grabbed her in my arms and held her as tight as humanly possible.

Then we heard heavy footsteps in the bushes outside, and garbled yelling.

"We've got to go before they find us. Switch off that light, Tyke," Captain Stone said briskly. I grabbed Danielle's hand and followed him down the bank to the river's edge, with Jesse and Hunter close behind us. Then we had no choice but to stop.

"Into the water," Captain Stone hissed, and no one questioned him. There was enough turbulence to mask the sound of our splashing, and within seconds we were swimming downstream through the ice-cold water. The current was still strong, though nowhere near what it had been up above the falls, and it quickly swept us far beyond the city within just a few minutes. Captain Stone brought us ashore in a small clearing on the southern bank surrounded by pine trees. All around us was nothing but silence.

I finally let go of Danielle's hand, wondering gloomily how much worse things could get. We hadn't accomplished anything at all as far as finding the *Susie Q* or getting home was concerned, and the whole debacle had almost turned into a major catastrophe.

And it still might, if we didn't find shelter soon. All of us were soaking wet and chilled to the bone, and it was highly questionable how much farther any of us could make it right then. Colonel Burns might nail us yet, if the bitter cold didn't kill us first.

"What do we do now?" Hunter asked quietly, trying not to shiver and failing miserably. But if he thought Captain Stone was ready with a miracle plan to save us all, then he was disappointed.

"I don't know. Let's try to get as far downstream as we can," Captain Stone finally said, with a tired edge to his voice.

So that's what we did, hurrying along as fast as we could through the dark woods. None of us were foolish enough to think the grubs had given up looking for us. We had to make the most of the darkness while it lasted. It wasn't near as cold at night down in the valley as I'd been used to up on the plateau, but it was plenty cold enough to be utterly miserable in wet clothes, even with thermal blankets wrapped around us. The only positive thing I can say about the ordeal is that at least there wasn't any wind.

I don't know how many miles we trudged that night, but it had to have been at least twenty. We stumbled into a cave at the base of the canyon wall in the first glow of a blood-red dawn, hopefully to keep hidden from whatever search parties Colonel Burns saw fit to send out. We collapsed on the rocky floor in utter exhaustion, huddling as close together as we could under our thermal blankets to conserve a little body heat.

It was about noon when I woke up, with a fierce headache and what felt like the first symptoms of a cold. My throat was sore and my nose runny, and I generally felt like crud. I suppose that might have been from making a forced march in the freezing cold all night long, but there was no telling. I *hoped* that's all it was; the last thing I needed was to get sick on top of everything else.

Most of the others were still asleep, but after a while I noticed Captain Stone sitting by himself on a rock near the entrance and looking outdoors with a far-away expression on his face. I quietly got up from my rocky bed, feeling aches and pains in practically every joint and muscle I possessed, and stretched a few times to work some of the stiffness out of my body. Then I went over and sat down next to him.

"How long have you been up?" I asked.

"Not long. Maybe thirty minutes or so," he said.

"What happened last night?" I asked abruptly.

"I guess you mean with Danielle?" he asked.

"Yeah, and Hunter too, now that I think about it. They both ought to have died, and then somehow you did something to change it. I'm grateful, but I sure would like to know how you did it," I said, and he looked at me keenly.

"Do you really wonder so much, after all you've seen?" he asked at length.

"What do you mean?" I asked, unable to figure out what he was talking about.

"You remember Cadron Pool, don't you?" he asked, referring to the holy spring on my grandparents' ranch in Texas which could heal any sickness or injury.

"Of course. But what about it?" I asked.

"That place is only a shadow, Tyke. A reminder, if you will; a reflection of something greater," he said.

"I'm not sure what you mean. A reminder of what?" I asked.

"I can't tell you everything, but far away in a secret place there's a fountain of water, clear as diamond and colder than ice. Only a very few people ever find it, but anyone who does and then has the courage to drink of that water will live far beyond his years, young and beautiful till the end, with the power to heal all the hurts of the world and to wipe away for just a little while the curse of the Fall," he said somberly.

It was the first I'd ever heard of such a thing, but under the circumstances I wasn't inclined to doubt him. Seeing is believing, and I'd seen plenty.

"You drank from that fountain?" I said, and it wasn't quite a question.

"Yes, when I was sixteen years old. Ever since then I've looked exactly as you see me now, and if I choose I can do things like you saw yesterday," he agreed.

I'd never actually asked Captain Stone how old he was; he didn't look much more than sixteen *now*. I'd always assumed he was simply a young-looking twenty-something, like all the other grubs I'd ever seen. But now I couldn't help but wonder.

"How long ago was that?" I finally asked.

"A hundred and forty-five years," he admitted, and even though I was already braced for something like that, it still shocked me.

"Really?" I asked, unable to think of anything else to say.

"Really and truly, Tyke. Nor did I have the benefit of skipping over any of those years with a tachometer like your parents did. I remember every single day of that century and a half," he said, and as he gazed at me I swear he looked every bit as ancient as he claimed to be, at least in his eyes. I think I've mentioned before that they were a bright and startling blue, the same color as Uncle Philip's, but now they looked deep as the wells of the sea, the repository of long memory that belied the young face from which they gazed. It humbled me, in a strange kind of way that's hard to explain.

"Thank you," I murmured, and then looked down. I've noticed that sometimes you have a tendency to do that, in the presence of greatness. It tends to make you feel very small and unimportant. I didn't stop to wonder what I was thanking him for; Danielle and Hunter perhaps, or my own life because of the breath training, or even the simple fact that he'd chosen to taste that water and thus had the power to help and heal when no one else could have. Maybe it was partly for all those things.

"I'm glad I could help," he said.

"It must have been really lonesome now and then," I ventured to say, and I saw a fleeting shadow of pain pass over his face at that.

"You have no idea. I think the hardest part was having to watch all the people I loved pass away while I still lived on without them. That hurts. But I chose my path willingly and I don't regret that. I've kept the faith and done what was asked of me. That's all that really matters in the end," he said.

"You talk like it's all in the past," I said.

"It mostly is. My time is almost up at this point, Tyke; I can feel it in my bones. I don't know exactly how much longer I've got left, but sooner or later this gift of mine will fade away. When that happens then I'll start to age again, and my power to heal things will be gone too. You'll surely live to see me as an old man someday, if we both survive that long," he said.

"I'm sorry," I said.

"No, don't be sorry. Be glad, and praise God for the chance to glimpse one more little facet of His love. I've been looking forward to the end of my work for a long time, honestly. That's when I'll finally be given my heart's desire," he said.

"What's that?" I asked. I guess maybe it was a cheeky thing to ask, but I was dying of curiosity by then. But he only smiled, a real one that reached all the way to his eyes.

"You'll find out soon enough. But in the meantime, please don't mention anything we've talked about to other people," he said.

"Why not?" I asked.

"Because it tends to make people look at me the way you're looking at me right now, like I'm an angel with a flaming sword on top of a tall pedestal. The burden is already heavy enough, without adding that too," he said.

"Okay then. I promise I won't say anything," I agreed.

"I appreciate it," he said.

"I'd love to hear the story someday though, about how you found the fountain. If you're willing to tell," I said.

"I'll tell you one of these days, whenever we get home. There's not time right now," he said.

"So couldn't you just. . . I don't know, blast Colonel Burns with lightning bolts or something like that?" I asked, and he sighed.

"It doesn't work like that, Tyke. I can only make whole what was broken, not destroy anything. Would you take someone to Cadron Pool and try to use it to give him cancer, or to boil him alive? Even your worst enemy?" he asked.

"Of course not," I said, appalled at the very thought. It seemed like blasphemy even to suggest such a thing.

"Then remember that. I can't do anything at all which isn't done for the sake of love, and neither can you," he said. That cast things in a somewhat different light, and I decided it was a good lesson to keep in mind.

"I'll remember," I promised.

"Do that. But as long as we're telling secrets, I guess there's one other thing you probably should know," he said.

"What's that?" I asked.

"It's no accident that you and I are sitting here together right now. Part of my gift is to know the meaning of dreams and visions, and it so happens that a long time ago your grandma Lisa had one about you, even before your father was born. She told me about it later, and I've known ever since then that part of my task would be to look after you and certain others as best I could. I never knew *everything,* mind you, but I knew enough to understand that I'd find you in Jamestown, on the island of Eleuthera in 2158. That made absolutely no sense to me for a long time because I thought at first it was talking about the island of Eleuthera in the Bahamas, and there's no such place as Jamestown on *that* island. They didn't even name the one on Venus till about fifteen years ago, but as soon as I heard about it I started bucking hard for a spot in the colony. They sent me out with the very first survey team, back when the whole planet was nothing but dead rock and gravel, so things were pretty rough there for a while. Anyway, the vision makes perfect sense when I look back on everything *now,* but sometimes hindsight is a lot plainer even for me," he said.

"What other people did you have to look out for besides me?" I asked.

"Children of my friends, mostly. Wolf Bartow, Jonah Anderson, Levi Black, Zach Trewick, a few others. I'm sure you'd recognize some of their far-flung descendants, if you thought about it," he said. I'd never heard of any of those people, actually, but the names were suspiciously familiar.

"Danielle?" I asked uncertainly. *Black* had been her maiden name.

"Yes, among others. Levi was her grandfather's grandfather, and a dear friend of mine at one time. Hunter and Leah came from Wolf, and Tommy and Amie from Jonah. Buzz came from Zach," he said.

"But surely those people must have had more descendants than just those few, especially after all this much time," I pointed out.

"They did. But some were lost, and others killed, and a few chose to walk in darkness. I couldn't save them all, Tyke. Only a handful," he said softly, as if the memory saddened him.

"I'm sorry," I said. Grief is easy to understand, even if I'd never known most of the people he was grieving over. Finding out that Hunter and Danielle and even I myself held a rather larger place in his heart than I'd heretofore suspected gave me a lot to think about, too.

"It's all right. I helped as many as I could over the years," he said.

"So how did you know my grandmother? Was she a friend of yours, too?" I asked.

"No, she was my sister," he said succinctly. That threw me for a loop all over again, but when I considered the matter I decided I ought not to have been surprised. It explained all kinds of little things I'd never understood before, like the way he always called my father Mikey and how close those two had been ever since the beginning. I'd heard Daddy talk about his Uncle Brandon several times on Saturday mornings at the lab, and of course I'd vaguely known for a long time that that was Captain Stone's first name. I'd just never connected the dots before.

"So you're my great-uncle?" I asked.

"So I am. If you like, you can call me Brandon. Captain Stone seems a little bit stuffy for a family member, doesn't it?" he asked.

"But why didn't you ever tell me before?" I asked.

"I thought about it, but then I decided to wait a little while till I knew you well enough to be sure you could keep a secret. I wouldn't have told Mikey so soon if he hadn't recognized me right off the bat. He almost scared me to death when we first met up in Kailua Kona, actually; I thought he was about to spill his guts and tell everybody who I was right then and there," he said.

"But he didn't, though," I said.

"No, and it's a good thing, too. It would have been hard to explain all that to my soldiers," Captain Stone agreed. Well, no, I supposed I should call him *Brandon* now; he was right about how formality between family members is very bad manners.

I thought about all the things he must know and remember after living so many years, and for a second time felt very small sitting next to him. I've often reflected on the fact that you seldom really know people even half so well as you think you do, but sometimes the secrets they keep are almost mind-boggling.

I suppose I might have been even more astounded by Brandon's revelations if I hadn't been forced to believe so many other strange things over the past few years. But still, I can't deny that it was a lot to think about.

Katrina McClendon used to like to say that we should never allow our assumptions to dictate what we see or what we believe, because that will make fools of us. Instead, we should always try to see things as they really are, and be ready to alter our assumptions whenever necessary to fit reality. Easier said than done, of course, but a very sensible piece of advice nevertheless.

There was a time when I might have flatly dismissed everything Brandon had said as pure fantasy, simply because it didn't fit in with my preconceived notions about the nature of reality. But I've learned to be very careful about tossing around that word *impossible*.

It turns out lots of things are considerably more possible than I once thought.

Chapter Seven

Even though a thousand more questions still burned in my mind, we didn't have any more time to talk that morning. I heard somebody stirring behind us, and turned my head to see Jesse sitting up to stretch. And since I'd promised to keep Brandon's secret, we couldn't very well keep discussing it in front of the others.

"So what's the plan for today?" Jesse asked, coming up to stand beside us. He looked bleary-eyed and tired, and I could hardly blame him.

"The plan for today is to hide out in this cave and rest as much as possible so hopefully Colonel Burns won't find us. Then tonight we'll head out for the ocean," Brandon said.

"What's down there?" I asked. It was the first I'd heard about any specific destination, and I was curious.

"Nothing particularly. But the *Susie Q* is being kept on the Isle of Xanthe, and if we intend to recover it then we'll have to go collect the rest of our members first. That means we'll have to circle around and head west again eventually, but we don't dare go back through Phoenix," Brandon said.

"How did you find that out? And where's the Isle of Xanthe?" I asked.

"It's down at the southern tip of the Golden Sea, maybe a hundred miles offshore. And as to how I found out, suffice it to say that I still have a few friends here," Brandon said.

"Like who? I thought all the rebels ran away," I said.

"Not rebels, *per se*. But there have always been a certain number of people who were sympathetic to the goals of our movement even though they wouldn't go quite so far as to join us themselves. One of those told me. At great personal risk to herself, I might add. She was in the middle of trying to think of a way to break us out of jail when Tyke came along and solved the problem," Brandon said.

"It wasn't that guard I stunned, was it?" I asked.

"No, it wasn't that one. But I'm sure my informant will be glad to hear that we escaped on our own without needing any more involvement from her," Brandon said.

"Sounds like a fair-weather friend," I muttered.

"Don't be ungrateful, Tyke; she didn't have to help us at all," Brandon scolded.

"Why did she, then, if it was so dangerous for her and she didn't really want to join us in the first place?" I asked.

"Because she knew if she didn't, all four of us would have been executed at noon today," Brandon said coolly, and my jaw dropped.

"Really?' I asked in a small voice.

"Yes, really. Colonel Burns had already ordered it," Brandon said.

"It's a good thing you have friends in high places, then," I said.

"Indeed it is. Be thankful for small blessings," Brandon said, and I could only nod mutely.

We lounged and rested at the cave for the rest of the day, and then spent another wearisome night trudging along the river valley. It wasn't quite as bad as the night before since we were dry, at least, but it was still cold. Wrapping thermal blankets around our shoulders helped a little, but not as much as you might think. The fabric of those blankets is paper-thin, which is nice in some ways because it can be folded up into a package no bigger than a small napkin, but it's not so nice in other ways because it's not stretchable or form-fitting the way a cloth blanket would be. That means it lets in cold air as you walk, anywhere that it's not actually touching your body. They're good for sleeping under, but they make a pretty lousy substitute for a jacket.

Brandon didn't stop at sunrise this time, and we pressed on till we reached the seashore about ten o'clock that morning.

It was my first glimpse of the Golden Sea, and in spite of the pretty name I can't honestly say I was all that impressed with it. The water was extremely salty and acidic from dissolved minerals and carbon dioxide, and it was cold and bitter to the taste. It was also a muddy yellowish brown color, which I suppose is why they call it the Golden Sea. The files at Southern Command had mentioned that in the early springtime there were terrible storms that came howling down across the frozen surface from the north pole, lashing the coast with hurricane-force winds and also storm surges if it was after the time when the ice had melted. That's the main reason they were careful to build Phoenix so far from the ocean.

Even in late summer the Golden coast was still blustery and cold, with the wind driving whitecaps against the rocky red shore. We turned south to pick our way along the coast as best we could among the boulders, slow and difficult as that was. Very rarely did we see anything resembling a sandy beach, just endless rocks that seemed to go on forever. We were always cold, wet, and footsore, with no prospect of things changing anytime soon.

Brandon's plan was to turn west again after we got far enough from Phoenix, then cross back over the Caprock Plateau and come out on the eastern canyon wall of the upper Valley of the Sun, more or less directly across from where the grubs were waiting for us. Then we'd have to see about getting to the Isle of Xanthe, but that was far in the future. Surviving long enough to make it back to base camp seemed unlikely enough at the moment.

We had almost nothing to eat at first except algae and pine nuts, which I can promise you is far from the most delicious combination of foods I've ever tasted. But presently we found that the sea wasn't quite as lifeless as the information in those old NADF files had led me to believe; there were little yellow crabs that lived in the pools and among the rocks, and even a few small shrimp. More species the grubs had recently introduced to the Martian environment, no doubt, like the ants we'd had to contend with on the plateau. The shrimp had an acrid, bitter flavor which made them almost inedible as far as I was concerned, but the crabs didn't taste too bad.

We had to eat everything raw, of course, since we didn't dare try to start a fire. There was too big of a risk that it would get away from us and burn up everything flammable within reach, including our own bodies.

On the positive side, we were low enough in elevation to breathe indefinitely without supplemental oxygen; a major advantage since our air tanks were either lost or confiscated. The Caprock Plateau was another story altogether; I had serious doubts about whether we could actually survive a trek across *that* with no air tanks, but it wouldn't have done any good to say so.

We were only a little bit north of the Martian equator at that point, but there were still occasional icebergs floating in the sea offshore. The little creeks and rivers we crossed now and then were considerably warmer than the ocean, so that's where we took our baths and got our drinking water.

There were occasionally little crevices and caves along the shore, and that's usually where we spent the nights whenever we could find one. If nothing else, they provided at least a little bit of protection from the biting wind that never ceased.

Here and there in sheltered spots we came across gnarled and wind-bitten little trees which I guess had escaped from cultivation in the valley and gradually extended their range along the coast. They didn't usually amount to much, but sometimes when we couldn't find a cave to sleep in we had to make do with a thicket of spruce saplings huddled up against the bottom of a cliff wall. That always made me a little bit uneasy, actually; like sleeping in a tinderbox or a gunpowder factory.

The fifth day out from Phoenix we encountered a storm, at least of the cold and rainy variety. It swept down unexpectedly from the north, catching us out in the open with nowhere to take shelter, and soon we were all soaking wet again. There was a strong and gusty wind blowing in off the sea, and even though we put on every scrap of clothing we possessed, nothing seemed to help. It was still wretchedly cold, with the dark gray clouds spitting stray pellets of sleet amongst the rain.

High summer on Mars, I thought bitterly.

About noon we did find a cave to take shelter, and even though it was still freezing inside it was at least dry and there was no wind. I sat on one of the boulders near the entrance to look out at the wintry mix falling on the whitecapped sea, and wished for the millionth time that we were back in Hawaii.

"Today is Christmas, you know," Danielle said, coming up behind me to put her arms around my shoulders.

"Is it?" I asked, without much interest. I hadn't had much reason to check the date recently, and at the moment I was too cold and surly to care.

"Yeah it is. I just now looked at the calendar," she said.

"That's nice," I said, and she sighed and sat down beside me, snuggling as close as she could to help stay warm. The temperature was steadily falling even inside the cave, and outdoors the rain had mostly switched over to sleet.

"You know something Joan always likes to tell me?" she asked.

"What's that?" I asked.

"She likes to say that life is only as hard as we think it is. If we focus on all the things we don't have then it'll be nothing but misery, but a thankful heart is happy anywhere," she said.

"Yeah, that sounds like something Joan would say," I agreed. I knew perfectly well what she was getting at, but I didn't feel like taking the bait.

"I said that for a reason, Tyke. I know things are not the best in the world right now; doesn't take a genius to see *that*. But I think we'd all be happier and have an easier time if we could find something to be grateful for," she said.

"I don't see much to be grateful for right now, beautiful. We're stuck on a freezing planet millions of miles from home, we may never see our daughter again or even survive this expedition ourselves, and to top everything off it's *raining,"* I said.

"I know all that just as well as you do. But like I said, today is Christmas. Can we not remember *that* much at least, and act like it still means something to us?" she asked.

I wanted to say something bitter about how I didn't feel like celebrating anything in a wet cave on Mars, especially not without Josie and Derrick. But I knew how much it would disappoint her if I said such a thing, so I made an effort to get myself under control.

"We *could*, I guess," I admitted grudgingly. Not very enthusiastic, perhaps, but it was the best I could manage at the time.

"Then let's do it. I know I saw some little spruce trees not too far back there. We can go cut one of those and bring it back, and then we'll see what we can do about decorating it and everything else," she said.

I almost dug my heels in again when I heard *that* suggestion. The very last thing in the world I wanted right then was to go back out in the weather again, much less to cut down a Christmas tree, of all things. But it would have been awkward for me to change my mind after I'd already agreed, so if that's what Danielle wanted then I was willing to give it a shot.

"All right, then. Let's go find one before the sleet gets any thicker," I said.

So that's what we did, and it wasn't actually all that far to the little clump of spruce trees she'd been talking about.

"Let's just get a small one; we can't drag anything very big inside the cave," she said, and I nodded. Most of the trees were twisted and gnarled from the constant wind, but some of the smaller ones were in better shape. I found one just about half my height which seemed more or less symmetrical, and then glanced up at her.

"Will this one do?" I asked.

"It's perfect. Now let's get it back to the cave before we freeze to death out here," she said.

I got down and went to work with the hand laser, and in spite of the circumstances it reminded me weirdly of other Christmases in North Carolina at the Andersons' farm, when we used to go cut a tree up on Sugarloaf Mountain and drag it back home through the snowy woods. Dragging this one home to a cave on Mars through the driving sleet wasn't *quite* the same, to be sure, but that's what it reminded me of.

And you know, the memory of happy days did cheer me up a little, almost in spite of myself. We set up the little spruce in the middle of the cave and decorated it with bits of yellow crab shell and red hematite pebbles, and we folded up one of the thermal blankets in the shape of a silver star.

And silly as it may sound, we gathered around our little spruce and sang Christmas hymns in praise of God, in that bleak and desolate place which had never heard such a thing since the day the universe was made.

I suppose Danielle must have had a point about choosing to be thankful if you want to be happy, because as we sang and celebrated the holy day I did find that happiness crept up on me unawares, in spite of all our troubles and worries, in a place and time I never would have expected to find it. We had no gifts to give each other except pine nuts roasted by hand laser, but we laughed and enjoyed that, too.

"You were right, beautiful," I said to Danielle later that night, turning my head to give her a kiss before we settled down to sleep. It was still sleeting outside, mixed with a little bit of snow. It would have been awful to be out walking in that stuff, but we were snug and warm under our blanket. As long as we could lie there safe and dry, I didn't care if it snowed all night long.

"Of course I was right," she agreed, and I laughed.

"Do you know, this is the first snowy Christmas I've ever had since I was ten years old? I mean, I know this is mostly sleet instead of snow, but close enough," I said.

"I don't ever remember any snow in Tampa," she said.

"No, it was in North Carolina, at the farm where y'all stayed last year. It snowed so much that year that me and Jesse and Chris went out and dug tunnels underneath it like moles, all the way from the house to the barn. You remember when we got snowed in by that blizzard on the Moon and ended up having to dig tunnels down to the river to catch catfish? That's what gave me the idea for that," I said.

"I don't guess I ever knew that," she said.

"It was pretty sweet. I always did love that place," I said.

"Which one? North Carolina or the Moon?" she asked, and I laughed again.

"Well, I *meant* North Carolina, but now that you mention it I'm pretty fond of the Moon too. After all, I never would've met *you* if we hadn't both gone there to live, now would I?" I asked.

"Oh, we might have sooner or later. I like to think we would've ended up together somehow, one way or another," she said.

"How come? You couldn't really miss me if you never knew me, and vice versa," I teased.

"You might be surprised," she said.

"What's that supposed to mean?" I asked.

She took so long to answer me that I thought she must have fallen asleep, but I guess she was only thinking. When she finally spoke up, it wasn't at all what I was expecting.

"Do you know you're the first boy who ever talked to me just because he cared how I felt, and not because he wanted something from me?" she finally asked.

"Uh. . . no, I don't guess I ever knew that," I said, kind of embarrassed.

"It's true, though. You saw me grieving over Derrick in that cave on the Moon after we crashed, just like everybody else did, but you're the only one who took the time to ask me how he was or even to talk to me at all. I don't think I ever told you how much that meant to me, but I knew right then you were the one I wanted for mine someday," she said.

"Well. . . it's not like you had a lot of choices or anything," I said, trying to make light of it.

"I was being serious, Tyke. I loved you at least a little bit ever since the first time we ever spoke, and that's the honest truth," she said.

"Me too," I said in a small voice.

"What?" she asked.

"I said me too. When you smiled at me that day I thought you were the most beautiful girl I'd ever seen," I said.

"Really?" she asked.

"Yup. Cross my heart," I said.

The conversation had drifted into solemn territory, but for once I didn't mind so much. It had been a while since the two of us had had a discussion like that about matters of the heart, not because we didn't still feel them but because life tends to get in the way, I suppose. There was always so much going on back in Kona that it was easy to get wrapped up in work and kids and suchlike; we talked all the time, about all kinds of practical things, but rarely about each other.

Now here we were, as far from home as I could ever wish to be, in a cold and dripping cave in the middle of an ice storm on Mars, talking again. And even though it was in many ways the strangest and most uncomfortable Christmas I'd ever spent in my entire life, I think reconnecting with Danielle like that was one of the sweetest gifts I've ever received.

Chapter Eight

The next morning we woke up to a world coated in a mixture of ice and sleet and snow, glistening brightly in the sunlight.

"Do you think we can travel, with everything iced over like that?" Jesse asked, staring out at the glistening boulders.

"We may have to. We can't afford to wait here for it to melt; we don't have enough food for that," Brandon said.

"I don't think I ever saw sleet in the summer before," Hunter said.

"It's not all that surprising, you know. If it's cold enough then water will freeze, regardless of what season it is on the calendar. Simple as that," I said.

"Yeah, I guess so," he agreed.

"I think it's starting to melt, though. Maybe if we wait a few hours it'll be safer to walk out there. I wouldn't want to fall and break an ankle on that stuff," Danielle said

So that's what we did, and by early afternoon most of the ice had melted. I say *most* because we still found plenty of slick patches even after we left the cave, and that called for extra caution as we gingerly picked our way ahead. But even though we all had a few close calls and Jesse fell flat on his back at one point, nobody broke anything.

We didn't make much progress that day, but at least by evening the rocks were more or less dry again. The ice storm was officially over.

A few days later we finally turned west away from the shore to climb through the low and jumbled hills that led up onto the Caprock Plateau on its eastern side. The hills didn't amount to much, and at last we found ourselves on that same old familiar and featureless plain, with nothing to see but the occasional drift of dusty crimson sand.

It was hard to breathe up there and only got harder the higher we climbed, and I once again had cause to thank Brandon for his forced breathing exercises. I would have been curious to view a complete hematocrit analysis to see how many extra red blood cells my body had produced by then as it adjusted to high-altitude living, but since my lab was millions of miles away I had to be content not to know for sure. It seemed to be enough, because even though I felt constantly sleepy and short of breath, I never actually fainted. If we'd had to run or jump or do anything strenuous then it might have been a different story, but as it was we took things easy and made our way across the plain at a slow pace that all of us could manage.

It should have taken us about a week to cross the entire width of the Plateau at the speed we were going, and I suppose if we hadn't encountered any problems then that would have turned out to be a more or less accurate estimate. But the Red Planet still had a few surprises in store for us up its nasty little sleeve, and it wasn't long before we ran into the first one.

We were on our third day of trekking across the Caprock and probably approaching the very center of it when we first saw the dust storm. It looked like a brownish-red wall hanging in the air off to the northeast, stretching all the way from horizon to horizon and as far upwards as the eye could see; a massive, monstrous thing blotting out half the sky, full of blue-white streaks of lightning. It blew up suddenly with no warning, quickly approaching as all of us kept glancing at it uneasily.

"I hope that thing blows itself out before it gets much closer," Danielle said, eyeing it.

"I doubt it will. Dust storms can move pretty fast," I said.

"So it's a pretty safe bet it'll catch us, then?" Jesse asked.

"It's practically a sure thing. You saw how fast it popped up over the horizon, didn't you?" I asked.

"All we can do is keep moving. Let's tie ourselves together so we don't get lost from each other, and keep your mouths covered with a rag so you can breathe. That's all we can do," Brandon said.

So that's what we did, and it was none too soon, either. Less than half an hour later the duster was on top of us, surrounding us with thunder and lightning and swirling dirt so thick it was literally hard to see your hand in front of your face. I don't know how the others did, but I coughed and choked on dust even with the rag over my mouth, and before I knew it my eyes and mouth were caked with mud that I had to keep blinking and spitting away.

Not only that, but the dirt started piling up around our ankles and we had to keep pulling our feet out and stepping high to keep from getting buried. We could vaguely see the sun as a lighter patch in the dust, and as long as it was still daylight we could at least tell what direction we were headed by following it. But after sunset it turned black as pitch, without the slightest glimmer of light to pierce the darkness.

Flashlights were useless under those kinds of conditions, but in spite of all that we didn't dare stop moving. We would have been buried in dirt within twenty minutes if we had. We had to keep high-stepping just to stay on top of the dunes. After several hours of struggling through the dirt we were all exhausted, and the storm showed no signs of letting up anytime soon.

Here and there on the Caprock there are cracks and canyons of various sizes, and eventually we came across one of these. Only a narrow and shallow one, to be sure, no more than three feet wide and five feet deep, and I wouldn't have seen it at all till I stepped off the edge and fell into it if Jesse hadn't stopped right in front of me and caused me to run into his back.

I couldn't hear anything over the howling wind, but when Jesse put his lips up to my ear I could barely make out words.

"Jump down!" he yelled hoarsely, and even though that didn't make any sense at all, I turned to Danielle and Hunter behind me and passed along the message to them. Then I inched forward till I came to the edge of the crack, and noticed it just barely in time to turn an embarrassing fall into an awkward jump.

The first thing I noticed when I got down there was that the wind stopped. The air was still full of dust, of course, but for the most part the storm blew right across the top of the crack without slowing down. Only a little bit of dirt sifted down from above.

All of us were in bad shape by then. Jesse's skin and lips were chapped and bleeding from the sand-blasting effect of the storm, and the rest of us were no better. I hadn't noticed it out there while it was still going on, but now that it had stopped it hurt like fire. My ears were packed with dirt and so were my clothes, and I quickly got rid of it to the extent that that was possible. Then I spit out as much mud as I could and wiped my eyes clean, thinking to myself that I'd never been so thirsty in my entire life. Not even at the bottom of the Cytherean Sea on Venus had I been so thirsty.

Brandon let us each have a little drink of water, and even though it tasted like mud I was never more thankful to get it than I was that night. We didn't dare drink very much, and I was far from satisfied with the miserly sip he let us have. But at the same time he gave us the water he contrived things in such a way that he was able to lay at least a finger or a thumb on everybody's face, and I wasn't surprised when shortly afterward our cracked and bleeding lips subsided to normal. Maybe the others chalked it up to simply getting out of the wind, but I knew better.

Or maybe they knew or suspected more than they let on. I've discovered that quite a lot of things go on in peoples' minds which never escape their lips. But whatever they might have known or not known, they didn't see fit to mention anything.

"How long do you think the storm will last?" Hunter asked after a while. His voice was hoarse from dust, so that he barely sounded like himself anymore.

"The ones in the summer don't usually last more than a day or two. They're not near as strong or as bad as they used to be before the polar cap melted, but they can still be pretty intense while they do last," I said.

"We can stay here in this crack at least for the rest of the night. It'll be safer than anywhere else we could find. But one of us will have to stay awake at all times to make sure we don't get buried if the wind shifts. If it starts blowing parallel to this groove instead of crosswise then we'd be covered up before we knew it," Brandon said.

"What do we do tomorrow?" Jesse asked.

"First we'll see if the storm is still going on or not. If it's not then we'll go on with our trip, and if it is. . . well, we'll see about that tomorrow," Brandon said. It didn't sound like a very hopeful plan to me, but I didn't know of anything better to add to it. We were at the mercy of the wind at the moment.

"How much water have we got left?" Danielle asked.

"Enough for about four days, and it'll be hard to do without it in this dry air, even as cold as it is. But let's not worry about that right now; we need to get some rest while we can. So I'll take the first watch, and y'all sleep for a while," Brandon said.

We all settled into whatever semi-comfortable spots we could find, and I found one with my back up against the wall of the crack, with Danielle snuggled up in front of me so we could share both our blankets. It was *almost* warm enough to be comfortable that way, if the rock underneath us hadn't been so cold. I could see Brandon sitting against the far wall, head bowed and lips moving silently in prayer. As well he might, considering the danger we were in.

"I can see now why you don't like for me to come along on these adventures," Danielle said quietly after a while. I'd thought she was asleep already, but apparently not.

"It took you this long to figure that out?" I asked jokingly.

"Well, no. . . I knew it already. But things like this have a way of reminding you how cruel the world can be sometimes," she murmured.

"Yeah. . . I guess it is," I admitted.

"So thank you for loving me enough to want to protect me. It might irritate me sometimes when I forget why you're doing it, but I want you to know I treasure it up in my heart and it doesn't go unnoticed," she said.

"Uh. . . you're welcome," I said, feeling foolish, and she laughed.

"Oh, Tyke. You have such a way with words," she said.

"Not so much, I'm afraid," I said.

"I was being ironic, silly boy. I just wanted you to know I love you for loving me, that's all," she said.

"I know. I love you too," I said.

"You see Captain Stone over there praying?" she asked.

"Yeah. He's trying to be inconspicuous about it but I can tell," I said.

"You know what he did the other night at the jail, don't you?" she asked. It was the first time she'd ever mentioned it, and I'd started to think she didn't remember the incident.

"You mean when you got hurt?" I asked.

"I was more than hurt, baby. I was dying; I know I was. I remember feeling the heat from the laser when the beam hit me, and I found the hole in my shirt later on, but there wasn't a mark on my body anywhere. That's not possible, unless God stepped in and set aside the normal rules for a few minutes. But I've been thinking about it a lot since then, and I *know* Captain Stone had something to do with what happened. I haven't asked him, but I know it anyway," she said.

"Yeah, we talked about that for a little while. He made me promise not to tell anybody anything because he said it made life hard on him, but since you know already I guess I can tell you that much at least. He put his hands on your head and made you well, just like that," I said.

"I thought so," she said. I thought she'd ask how that was possible or want all kinds of details, but for some reason I guess she didn't.

"I wonder a lot about him sometimes; where he came from, who he really is. Normal people can't do those kinds of things," she murmured.

"Well. . . he *is* my great-uncle, you know; he told me that, too. He said we should start calling him Brandon if we liked," I said.

"Really?" she asked.

"Yeah. If you ask him about it he might tell you the whole story himself. He hasn't even told *me* all of it yet," I said. I didn't mention what he'd said about knowing her distant grandfather, or anything else he'd told me.

"Maybe I will, when all this is over. He's pretty awesome," she said, and in spite of the utter silliness of it I actually felt a twinge of jealousy.

"So he's your hero now, huh?" I asked, and Danielle saw through me instantly, of course, just like she always does. But she only laughed again.

"No, Tyke. You are," she said, and I could have kissed her for that. In fact that's exactly what I did, and then we settled down to try to sleep while the storm raged above and the red dirt slowly sifted down to cover us with a fine layer of dust.

By the time morning came our blankets were coated with about two or three inches of the stuff, which I suppose probably helped to keep us warm overnight. I woke up to the sight of what looked like a blanket of red fleece stretched over everything, and when I stood up the dust fell off my body in clouds that made me sneeze.

The storm seemed to have blown itself out overnight, and the entire Caprock Plateau was coated with the same fine red dust that covered us down in the crack. There was a considerable amount of it still floating in the air, but not near as much as yesterday. I could see maybe a hundred feet or so before the dirt became impenetrable.

That was a good thing, because if we'd had to stay hunkered down in that crack for very many days then I'm sure we would have run out of water, and after that it doesn't take too long at all to die of dehydration.

As it was, we were able to get up and be on our way again as soon as everybody was awake. We left five glaringly obvious sets of footprints in the red dirt which would have been hard for a blind man to miss, and I worried about that at first.

"You don't think we should try to cover up our tracks?" I asked, glancing back at them.

"It wouldn't help. There's no way we can make the surface as smooth as it is everywhere else. We'd just be wasting our time," Brandon said.

"But doesn't that give somebody a perfect way to track us?" I asked.

"For a while, yes. But the wind will erase them sooner or later, and that's the best we can do. In the meantime, I hope everybody back in Phoenix is too busy digging out from the dust storm to pay much attention to anything else for a while. It came from that direction," Brandon said.

"I hope so," I agreed.

That must have been the case, or maybe something else came up and distracted Colonel Burns for a while, because we never saw hide nor hair of any pursuit for the rest of the time we were on the Caprock. Then three days after the storm we came suddenly to the sheer drop-off at the western edge of the plateau, looking down on the upper vales of the Valley of the Sun. Below us was the River of Fire, and somewhere about a hundred miles to the west was the other side of the valley and hopefully our base camp.

"So how do we get down *this* time?" I asked. I knew we didn't have any rope long enough to lower ourselves down, and to tell the truth I was glad of it. Me and heights just don't get along.

"We'll have to walk along the edge till we find a place where we can climb down. There's no other way," Brandon said.

That turned out to be harder than we anticipated, for several reasons. For one thing, the edge of the plateau was cracked and broken in several spots, making it hard to find a safe way forward. And then for another thing, we were almost out of water. The entire Caprock slopes downward from west to east, and that meant there were precious few creeks or water sources there on the western edge. It was maddening to be dying of thirst while constantly walking in full view of a river down in the valley which we couldn't reach.

Nevertheless, we eventually found our way down through a steep cleft in the rock and by dint of some careful climbing. As soon as we got down to the bottom I ran to the bank of the River of Fire and buried my face in the water in spite of the cold, drinking down huge gulps as fast as I could swallow them.

"You better slow down, Tyke; you'll give yourself a stomachache," Jesse said. He was right beside me drinking from the river himself, but at a much slower pace.

"I don't care if I get a stomachache as long as I can get some water," I said. But even though I *said* that, I did slow down a little. Not that it helped at that point; I still ended up with a vicious stomachache anyway. But that was a price I was perfectly ready to pay for the infinite blessedness of quenching my raging thirst. The water was still cloudy and reddish and had a muddy flavor from the recent dust storm, but I didn't care two cents about that either.

We had to partly swim and partly wade the river to get across, but that didn't involve anything worse than another dunk in cold water. I think all of us were used to that kind of thing by then.

There was nothing whatsoever in the valley to eat, and the last of our pine nuts had run out the day after the dust storm. All together we spent six long days without food before we made it back to base camp, with nothing but water to keep us going. That may sound like a long time to go hungry, and I suppose it is, but I reminded myself it was nothing I hadn't had to endure before.

But at long last we finally reached the Red River Gorge and the spot directly below where our base camp should have been, and then I had to endure another episode of dangling form a cable for couple of hours while the grubs pulled each one of us up to the top. Just like last time I kept my eyes squeezed tightly shut and pretended I was only sitting in a swing hanging from a tree limb.

But at last we were there, and that was good enough.

Chapter Nine

Brandon didn't waste any time resting. The second we all arrived, he immediately gave orders to break camp and get ready to head out for the Isle of Xanthe before Colonel Burns decided to move the *Susie Q* elsewhere. He pointed out that next time we might not be able to find out where she was, and that was a scary enough thought that it got us all moving with alacrity, even those of us who'd just come from a forced march across the desert.

There isn't much to tell about the next few days. Most of it involved following the course of the valley upstream, since the cliff walls of the Caprock blocked our way eastward pretty darned effectively. There was nothing to see but more of the same old flat and dusty plateau, with one notable exception. Two days after we set out, the reddish spire of Tharsis Tholus came into view for a little while to the west before dropping back below the horizon again after only a few hours.

It wasn't much to see, not from that distance, but it did give Hunter and me an opportunity to regale the others with the amazing and courageous tale of what happened to us during the battle there. At first I was actually kind of shy about mentioning such things in front of the grubs, knowing they'd been through a lot worse than anything we ever had, but Brandon soon corrected me on that.

"Don't be afraid to tell them what happened, Tyke. Men live by the stories they hear; they thirst after heroes and greatness, and they like to feel that their sufferings are worth something. So inspire them. Lift them up. Paint them a picture of the wonderful things you've done and how they were a part of all that. I promise they'll love you forever," he said.

I remembered him telling me something very similar back on Venus, so I decided to loosen up and maybe even embellish the tale or brag a little when it seemed called for. But then again I didn't want to seem like a complete gloryhound either, so I took care to listen to everything the grubs had to tell, too. Buzz was particularly talkative once he decided we really wanted to know, maybe since we were so close to the same age.

"I don't think I was very brave, honestly. I was pinned down under enemy fire when the *Alabama* took off, with no mirrorsuit and a rifle battery which was two-thirds empty. Then Captain Stone came on the radio and told us to retreat; to save as many as we could and he'd come back for us later. So I wrapped myself up in a thermal blanket with the shiny side out, and then ran for the field where the rovers were parked. It's a miracle I ever made it, but some way or other I did. Sergeant Jones was already there, trying to collect as many survivors as he could. I was the last one he picked up before we tore out of there, but nobody ever came after us, though," Buzz said.

I strongly suspected Brandon's promise to come back and rescue them had had a lot to do with why there hadn't been any pursuit. Colonel Burns and his officers had surely overheard that promise, and it had probably been more than enough to convince them to let Sergeant Jones' little group escape as bait. Otherwise they would have been hunted down and slaughtered without mercy. Brandon had practically admitted as much, while we were talking at the observatory.

No doubt our fearless leader had known exactly what he was doing, manipulating Colonel Burns with words in a last-ditch effort to save as many lives as possible. And he'd succeeded, too, with a plan which never would have crossed my mind even to try. It had been a brilliant strategic move, purely aside from the kindness of the thing.

I glanced at him curiously as he sat in the front seat of the rover, wondering what other hidden depths might come to light at some point. But I kept my musings to myself, and after a few minutes went back to swapping battle stories with Buzz.

Other than socializing, there wasn't really much for us to do except ride in the rover for those few days and stare at the passing scenery while we recuperated from our recent ordeals. I was perfectly all right with that, though. It was fantastic to have as much food and water as we wanted for a change; it was luxurious to be really warm at night, and no amount of boring terrain could have knocked a chip off my satisfaction right then.

The rover was a lot speedier than walking would have been, and soon we were high enough that we had to put oxygen masks back on in spite of all the high-altitude adaptations in the world. Your body can only do so much. Unfortunately, there was no other way forward except to cross the heights.

As I said before, the River of Fire begins in Echo Lake, which is technically part of the Valles Marineris canyon system even though it's not connected to it. That's a series of cracks and faults running east-west across the southern portion of the Tharsis Plateau, beginning at the Labyrinth of the Night and ending up (eventually) near our destination at the southern end of the Golden Sea. The various canyons are over a mile deep in places, quite often several miles wide, and mostly filled with freshwater lakes which are the source of quite a few major rivers in that part of the world.

We had to thread our way gingerly along the high ground between the canyons for several days, and that was dangerous in spite of appearances; the edges are notorious for collapsing on a regular basis. I knew *that* from my recent experience at Angel Falls.

But Brandon and Sergeant Jones navigated the danger competently, and as we dropped down off the high ground we were finally able to take off our breathing masks again. We followed another river whose name I never knew down through the hummocky Yellow Hills and finally back to the coast again, although much farther south than before.

The Golden Sea looked pretty much exactly the way I remembered it, except that in this region it was much shallower and dotted with a million little rocky islets near the coast, and there were none of the scraggly little spruce trees we'd seen farther north. No doubt for the simple reason that they hadn't had a chance to spread that far yet, but without them the place looked even more barren and inhospitable than it usually did. We stood on a narrow plain of ochre dust between the water and the hills, where the wind blew constantly and the dirt occasionally swirled up in a way that reminded me unpleasantly of that dust storm on the Caprock.

That portion of the Golden Sea coast is a sort of massive delta region where three or four huge rivers come together to empty into the ocean at more or less the same place, along with dozens of smaller streams. We had to pick our way southward through all that muddy mess until the coast gradually curved around to the east, and finally we halted in a spot which the grubs called the Ares Channel. It looked no different than any other place we'd seen lately, at least not to me, but they seemed sure of it.

"Xanthe is right there across the sea, maybe a hundred miles. This is the narrowest place to cross," Brandon said.

"So how do we get across, then? The rover won't make it, and we can't swim that far. Nor do we have a boat or any way to build one," I said.

"We'll have to walk it, I'm afraid. There's no other way," Brandon said.

"*Walk* it?" Jesse asked, sounding every bit as shocked as I felt myself.

"Yes. The water is only a few feet deep, in spite of how it looks. We might have to swim here and there a little bit, but never very much. And we've got thermal suits to keep us warm," Brandon said.

"But how do we sleep? There's no way we can walk a hundred miles through water in only one day," Hunter pointed out.

"We won't be able to sleep. Sergeant Jones brought drugs from the Redoubt which will keep us awake for as long as necessary," Brandon said.

I had serious doubts about whether that was really wise; sleep isn't one of those things your body can do without for very long. It's a physiological requirement, and if you don't get it then lactic acid and other waste products start to build up in your muscles and organs. Sooner or later the consequences are fatal.

"Do you really think that's a good idea?" I asked at length, when nobody else said anything.

"No I don't, Tyke; but we don't have all that many choices at this point, you know. We've got to get across the channel," Brandon said. That was undeniably true, of course, so I shrugged a little and didn't say anything else.

We slept one last night there on the shore, and at the crack of dawn the next morning Sergeant Jones passed out a little yellow pill to each of us along with a swig of water to wash it down with. Then we got started.

Brandon was right about the water not being very deep; it only came up to my chest for the most part. Too deep for the rover to cross, but not quite too deep for a human being to walk. I'm sure if there'd been any current at all then we wouldn't have been able to do it, but as it happened, that region of the sea was placid as a cow chewing cud. Here and there it got a bit shallower or a bit deeper, and in those places we sometimes had to swim for a while; sometimes as much as a hundred yards or so. I'm glad it was never more than that, because trying to swim while dressed in a thermal suit is almost like trying to swim in a choir robe or a pair of coveralls. It gets exhausting after a while.

But that didn't happen too often, and for the most part we slogged ahead without too many problems for the rest of the day. There was no reason to stop after sunset since we couldn't sleep anyway, and I do have to admit *that* part was a little scary. Phobos gave just enough light to let us see where we were going, but not much more than that. We kept on all night long, and I never felt the slightest bit sleepy. Whatever drug Sergeant Jones had given us, it certainly did its work efficiently.

We had to stop and take another pill at sunrise, and then it was just another weary day of sloshing through ice cold water again. It went on like that for days, and by the time the fifth morning rolled around I was beginning to notice the wear and tear on my body from four sleepless nights. I was bone-tired even though I was wide awake, and the muscles in my legs especially were aching and burning from overuse. I was stretched almost to my uttermost limit in spite of all the pep pills in the world, and when the crash finally came I knew it was likely to be a harsh one. You can only borrow energy for so long before you have to pay the price for it, and my body was putting me on notice that I'd already accumulated a pretty steep tab.

We had to swim across another wide channel on the afternoon of the sixth day, and I think that was the hardest part of the whole trip. It was supposedly the last day of our crossing, and Brandon expected to finally reach the shore of the Isle of Xanthe within no more than twelve hours or so if his reckoning was correct. That was fabulous news to look forward to, but it didn't help us in the meantime.

I swam like a tired bear, actually doing more floating than swimming because I simply didn't have the energy for anything more than that. Even my arms were beginning to hurt at that point, and my legs had progressed almost to the point of numbness. But I think I would have made it all right, speaking for myself.

Others must have been worse off than I was, though, because about a third of the way across the channel, disaster struck. I heard someone give a strangled cry somewhere behind me, and glanced back over my shoulder just in time to see one of the grubs slip underneath the water. I guess he didn't even have the energy to fight or splash anymore like drowning people usually do. He was so far spent he just slipped below the waves with only that last muffled cry of despair to mark his passage.

I was too far away to even think of getting there in time to help, but three of the grubs who were swimming close by tried to save him, diving under the water where he disappeared to try to pull him back up. But they were only a hairsbreadth less exhausted than he had been, with the result that the murky sea quickly claimed three more victims like dominoes falling in a line, while the rest of us could only watch in stupefied horror.

"No more! We can't help them; just swim!" Brandon commanded, and I suppose even the grubs who might have wanted to disagree with him wouldn't have thought of disobeying a direct order like that.

But still, it was a somber and silent group of us who finally sloshed ashore on the Isle of Xanthe seven hours later. Of the ten survivors we'd come to rescue, only six were left. We'd lost almost half of them in the space of a single day, in one terrible accident.

Just like that.

We collapsed on the rocky shore, and I know I at least was in agony by then. But all I could do was lie there and suffer, since the medicine Sergeant Jones had given us that morning still wouldn't let me sleep. Lying still was a thousand times better than walking, no doubt about it, but unless you've ever been sleep deprived for a while I don't think you could possibly understand what it feels like after that long.

After a few minutes I noticed Brandon come up beside me on his knees, looking more haggard that I could ever remember seeing him. He put his hands on my head, one on each side, and at the time I didn't even have the strength to ask him what he was doing. They were warm, and I remember thinking that was odd after he'd just come up out of the ice-cold sea right along with the rest of us.

"Sleep, Tyke," he whispered, and that's pretty much the last thing I remember.

Maybe the pills had finally reached the limits of their power to keep us awake, or maybe Brandon used his power on me. In any case, I soon fell into a deep and dreamless sleep that seemed to last forever, and I don't think I could have woken up if my life depended on it.

When I finally *did* wake up it was mid-afternoon, and when I looked blearily at my watch I saw that I'd slept for over eighteen hours straight. I still felt awful, but considerably better than I had the day before. I struggled up into a sitting position and took a long drink of water from my canteen. I was uncomfortable in all kinds of ways at that moment but thirst was by far the worst. It was only about half full and I drank every bit of it.

I got up and walked around a bit to work some of the soreness out of my body, noting that several others were doing the same thing. The island was a flattish plain strewn with rocks and boulders of hematite here and there, pretty much exactly like the country we'd been traveling through on the mainland. I wish I could say something nicer about the place, but it is what it is. Brandon, as usual, was off to himself at the edge of the camp, seemingly lost in thought while he watched the sea foam spray against the rocks.

"So what's next on the agenda?" I asked, going up to him. He never seemed to mind being interrupted, so I'd long ago decided not to worry about it.

"We're only about a half-day's walk from where the *Susie Q* is supposed to be hidden. As soon as we recuperate a little bit then we'll go see about getting her back," he said.

"Any idea how?" I asked.

"I'm not sure yet. My informant in Phoenix said there were only three soldiers assigned to guard it, last she heard. But that might have changed since then, especially since Colonel Burns knows there's always a possibility of leaks. He may even have moved the ship elsewhere by now," he said.

"I don't understand what good he thinks it'll do him anyway. It wouldn't hold enough soldiers to do anything effective against almost four hundred of us back in Hawaii, and it's not like he could even visit Earth at all without a biohazard suit. Not unless he wants to end up dead in a few hours from the Orion Strain. What's it gain him to have such a little ship?" I asked.

"Probably nothing immediately. But I can think of circumstances when it might be very much to his advantage to have a way to visit Earth at some point, even if he has to wear biohazard gear. He could send a team to pick up electronic components and other things which he can't manufacture here but which he'd need in order to build a larger vessel, for one thing. Given enough time, he could accomplish a lot with that one little ship," he said.

"That's true, I guess," I admitted.

"Which, purely aside from getting home ourselves, is one more excellent reason to make sure he doesn't get to keep it," Brandon said.

"Well. . . assuming it's still here, how do we go about taking it?" I asked.

"It'll probably involve some fighting, if nothing else. We also need to keep the guards from alerting Colonel Burns, if at all possible. He'll send reinforcements immediately, and even though it'll take them at least an hour to get here, that's still not much time. If we dither and dally too long they might still catch us before we can get out of the atmosphere. They'd shoot us down rather than let us escape, I can promise you that," Brandon said.

"How much time do you figure we've got?" I asked.

"We need to get it all done and launched in no more than thirty minutes. Any more than that and we run a serious risk of getting caught, depending on how fast Colonel Burns can get his reinforcements in the air. I'd rather not cut it any closer than we have to," Brandon said.

"Me neither," I agreed.

We rested for another entire day there by the seashore, until most of us felt at least reasonably strong again. Then, before we left, Brandon took us down to stand at the edge of the water to pray for the ones who were lost in the crossing. None of them ever washed ashore, so that was the best memorial service we could give them.

But there came a time when we found ourselves lurking behind a jumbled collection of boulders and looking down on what was surely the *Susie Q*, seemingly not much worse for the wear since the last time we'd seen her.

There was a dirt runway and two prefab buildings of plastic and steel, along with a gaggle of solar collectors and antennas and such.

I don't know what the facility was used for when Colonel Burns didn't need a place to hide spaceships, but I'm sure it must have had some kind of function or they wouldn't have built it in the first place. I suppose it might have been a mining camp or something like that, since nobody can dictate where mineral deposits will occur. That's my best guess, at least. It might have been Colonel Burns' private vacation retreat, for all I know.

But whatever it was, it was still too close to Phoenix for comfort. We might have had to circle around the long way to get there, but as Brandon had said it was barely an hour's flight from the airfield above Angel Falls. That cut down our margin of safety almost to the bone.

There was no other choice except to give it our best shot, though. It was either that or else activate the self-destruct sequence before we headed back to the Redoubt for the rest of our lives, and I for one still couldn't stomach *that* idea. I don't actually think I could have faced the idea of swimming back to the mainland at that point; I would almost have preferred to get fried in a laser battle.

Which I knew might very well turn out to be the case, unfortunately.

We all had laser rifles; standard issue NADF models exactly like the ones Colonel Bartow's troops had used on Venus, manufactured of plastimetal alloy and producing a beam the color of a ripe red apple. It seemed to me that a red laser wasn't the most ideal choice on a place like Mars where almost everything has at least a reddish tinge to it, and I mentioned something about it to Brandon when he handed one to me.

"You don't think all this red rock and red dust and all that will make the lasers not work as well?" I asked.

"I'm sure it won't help, Tyke. But since we'll be firing at soldiers and buildings which are *not* red, I don't think it'll matter too much if a stray beam fails to put a hole through a piece of hematite. I'm a lot more worried about whether they've got mirrorsuits or not," he said.

"Well. . . true," I admitted.

"As soon as we've got them pinned down in the building, we'll run to the *Susie Q* and get on board. That'll be the most dangerous part of the whole thing, because as soon as they realize what we're doing they might try to disable the ship by firing at it. If they manage to cause enough damage that we can't take off, we're finished. We won't have time to cross back over to the mainland before Colonel Burns' reinforcements can get here, and there's nowhere on this little island where we can hide for very long. So we better make this count," Brandon said, and I nodded. The only time I'd ever used a laser rifle before was during that pitched battle with Olivia Deming on the roof of Colonel Bartow's house in Jamestown, but I figured even a little experience was better than none at all. If things like *this* kept happening, I might have to invest some time at the gun range.

Then I reminded myself that I dearly hoped this was the last battle I ever had to fight.

Chapter Ten

We crept up on the facility as closely as we dared without running a serious risk of being spotted, keeping an eye out for guards. So far we still hadn't seen any, and that was a problem. You can't exactly attack somebody if you don't know where they are.

"They've got to be either inside the buildings or else inside the *Susie Q* itself. There are no other places to hide," Hunter muttered under his breath. He was stationed next to me on one side and Danielle was on the other, but he was starting to get impatient with the long wait.

"True, but we can't get too hasty. If we do the wrong thing it could wreck the whole plan," I reminded him. He grumbled a little bit at that, but I guess he understood the reasoning. He just didn't like it much. Not that I could blame him, since I didn't particularly like it myself. When you're all keyed up and ready for action, the hardest thing imaginable is to do nothing at all.

I guess we should have remembered that our opponent might do something completely unexpected, because that's exactly what happened.

"I don't like this. It's too quiet, and we haven't seen a soul since we got here. I bet you anything you like that it's some kind of trap. Colonel Burns probably didn't know for sure if we'd show up or not, but he might have planned a nasty little surprise for us just in case we did. That's what I think," Danielle said.

"She's probably right. That old unguarded spaceship thing is a classic strategy," Hunter said.

"Yeah, I know that. But you know why people keep using such an obvious plan? Because it works, that's why. The *Susie Q* is the bait, and when we go out there to try to take it then we'll spring the trap. We know it full well, but we can't *not* go out there either. So we're stuck both ways," I said.

"No we're not. We only have to spring the trap without getting killed, that's all," Danielle said.

"I wonder how many rats used to think that exact same thing every night," Hunter muttered.

"Any rat smart enough to wonder about a question like that would've been smart enough to poke the trap with a stick first before he ate the cheese. Then he wouldn't have had any problems," I said, pretending to answer him at face value even though I knew perfectly well what he meant.

"So maybe we should take a lesson from the rats, then. What's our stick to poke the trap with so we don't get killed before we eat the cheese?" he asked.

"Maybe half of us could go out there first, while the rest of us stayed hid in the rocks. If they thought that was all of us, then we might get them to give away their position and then our backup could surprise them," I said.

"I'm sure Brandon has thought of that," Danielle said.

"He probably has, but I think I might go talk to him anyway, just to see if there are any plans in the works," I said.

Brandon was down at the far end of the rocks, and I crept all that way carefully and quietly till I could squeeze in beside him.

"Have we come up with a plan yet?" I asked.

"Not yet. I've sent out three scouts on reconnaissance missions to see if they can find out anything, though. They should be back shortly, and then maybe we'll be able to make some decisions," Brandon said.

"Hunter and Danielle and I were talking about it just now. We thought maybe sending half of us out there first might spring the trap, if there is one, and then give the rest of us a chance to surprise the guards," I said. I didn't really expect him to jump on that plan with both feet, but I felt obliged to mention it at least.

"That's too obvious, Tyke. They'd either pretend to attack our advance force with just a few of their soldiers till they drew out our full number, or else they wouldn't do anything at all till they were sure they knew where all of us were. All these people have been to military school, you know. You can't use textbook ploys if you want to surprise them," Brandon said, but not unkindly.

"Oh, all right," I said, feeling deflated.

"No problem. You have to learn somehow," he said.

"So where did the scouts go?" I asked, mostly to change the subject.

"One of them went to check out those buildings, another one went up there to make sure there's nobody lurking behind those rocks on the hill, and a third one went to see how close he could get to the *Susie Q*. That one also happens to be a pilot, in the unlikely event that he gets an opportunity to actually take possession of the ship," Brandon said.

"You think he will?" I asked.

"No, I'm almost certain he won't. But stranger things have happened, and it would be a shame if we wasted our best chance just because our scout couldn't fly," he said.

Just then there came a shout from behind the building, and the red flash of laser fire. One of the grubs came running out from behind the nearest building, dodging irregularly back and forth to make himself harder to hit, and as soon as he got a little closer I recognized Buzz. Not all that surprising I don't suppose, considering his background as a ranger; that kind of work was his specialty.

"Give him some cover," Brandon ordered, and immediately all the soldiers nearby started firing at the place where the other beams were coming from. I'm sure it helped, but apparently not quite enough. The boy was maybe two thirds of the way back to our rocks when a laser shot caught him squarely in the neck and he stumbled and fell face-down on the dirt.

Brandon never hesitated. He leaped over the ridge and ran down there to lay his hands on the fallen scout's head, just like he didn't even notice the fact that he was right in the middle of a battle zone. Then he yanked Buzz to his feet and pulled him stumbling along till they were both under cover behind the rocks again.

I noticed the gaping hole in the collar of the boy's camo jacket, right below that patch of black hair that gave him his nickname. He'd almost certainly received a fatal shot out there, just like Danielle back in Phoenix. They always aimed for the head or the heart when they meant to kill. No doubt Buzz hadn't been *quite* dead yet when Brandon reached him, any more than Danielle had. Believe it or not it's almost impossible to kill somebody *instantly*, but it didn't take a genius to know that he'd probably been dying. Not now, though. From what I could see through his holey jacket, he didn't even have a mark on his skin.

The grubs might not have known for sure what happened or how, but they knew immediately and beyond doubt that Captain Stone had saved that kid's life at the risk of his own. I hadn't been close enough to see what he might have done at the Battle of Jamestown or afterward, nor at the spaceport on Barbados or even at Tharsis Tholus. Xanthe was the first time I'd actually seen him up close and personal in a real battle situation, and watching him dodge through those laser beams to drag Buzz back to safety made a lasting impression on me. Maybe it mattered to some extent that Buzz was one of that small group of individuals who were specially dear to his heart, but honestly I think he would have done the same thing no matter who it was.

I think it was then that I really began to understand why all the grubs loved him so much and would have followed him anywhere. They mattered to him as individuals, not just as numbers on a list or beans in a pod.

I suppose I should have noticed it before, if I'd thought about it. He knew every one of his soldiers by name. He'd taken the time to manipulate Colonel Burns into letting at least a few of the remaining rebels escape, even while locked into a vicious battle himself. He'd never thought twice about the danger before he ran to help Hunter in the canyon or Danielle at Phoenix. Maybe I'd been too close to those experiences to understand, but this was different. It was something beautiful to see; the kind of thing you remember for always and which inspires you to be a better and braver person from then on.

But I didn't say anything, knowing he wouldn't have liked it, and besides that we soon found ourselves locked in a fierce firefight which didn't seem to be slacking off anytime in the foreseeable future.

"We've got to make it to the *Susie Q;* all they're doing is pinning us down till reinforcements can get here," Brandon said after a while.

"But how?" I asked.

"Let's focus our fire on one source at a time and then we'll eliminate them one by one," Brandon said.

So that's what we did, and with all of us firing at the same place we soon wiped out what had to be the first guard, and then the second and third. There were five altogether, and as soon as the last one had stopped firing we made a run for the *Susie Q.* The hairs on the back of my neck were standing up the whole time, and I half expected to feel a hot laser burn somewhere on my body at any second.

But that didn't happen, and soon enough we reached the ship and climbed aboard. There was plenty of room for all of us; a sad reminder of how many we'd lost along the way. Then Jesse came out of the cockpit looking scared.

"They've changed the access codes; I'm afraid we're not going anywhere," he said. My heart came right up into my throat at that news, but Brandon only smiled.

"They may *think* they have, but we foresaw that particular possibility months ago. I had the techs write a hidden emergency override sequence into the computer code just in case we needed it. Try this," he said, and gave Jesse a sixteen-letter combination.

That seemed to work, and before we knew it the *Susie Q* was up and running again, and all of us had hastily buckled into our seats. Jesse took off and gained altitude as fast as he dared, but that seemed painfully slow.

And in fact it *was* too slow, because we'd only reached a fraction of escape velocity when we saw Colonel Burns' reinforcements appear over the northwest horizon. The guards had done their work and delayed us just a bit too long.

"Keep going. We don't have the firepower to engage them," Brandon said grimly.

"I'm pushing her as hard as she'll go," Jesse said.

"Push harder. Don't worry about evasive maneuvers or anything like that. Our only hope is to get out of the atmosphere before those jets get close enough to shoot us down," Brandon said.

It was a slow, nail-biting process; you'd be amazed how much time during a battle is taken up with just waiting. We gradually got higher and our pursuers gradually got closer, and at some point not long before we broke out into space they must have gotten just barely within range to start firing on us, or at least they must have decided they had to try while they still could. All I know is, the air around us was suddenly filled with red fingers of light.

"Put suits on, just in case they burn a hole in the hull and depressurize the cabin," Brandon ordered, and we hastened to obey since there was nothing else to be done anyway.

Lasers don't have an infinite range, of course, any more than bullets do. Dust and various other particles eventually scatter the light and make the beam ineffective past a certain distance. It varies somewhat based on conditions; you can fire a deadly shot at a much greater distance in space than you could in the middle of a dust storm, for example. Colonel Burns' jets were already straining at the very upper limit of how high they could fly and we were getting farther away from them every second, but the air was mighty thin up there. That unfortunately meant their weapons had a greater range than they'd had while we were lower down.

But eventually there came a point when they had to give up the ghost and let us go, like it or not. We cheered and whooped and clapped our hands when we saw them turn back in defeat, but maybe we shouldn't have gotten so excited quite so soon.

Everybody was asleep when the first sign of trouble came, hours later. The cabin lights were turned off and I woke up thirsty for some reason; an oddity in its own right since that's not something I usually make a habit of. But I quietly got up and went to get a drink of water to soothe my parched throat, not really thinking much of it. On the way down the aisle I kept catching occasional faint whiffs of a foul, acrid odor which seemed to come from nowhere in particular. At first I thought I was imagining things, but it kept getting stronger as I neared the back of the ship until I smelled it constantly.

But there was nothing to be seen or heard or felt, and nothing seemed out of the ordinary. It smelled vaguely like something was burning, but since it was abundantly obvious that nothing actually was, the strange odor left me more puzzled than anything else.

I got my drink of water and went back to my seat, and the smell faded almost to the point of becoming unnoticeable. I was sleepy and didn't want to think too much at the time, and I almost dismissed it as one of those inexplicable phenomena that occur now and then which nobody ever gets a satisfactory explanation for. I guess if I had then we probably would have died.

But I've generally found that instincts are things you really should pay attention to, especially when it comes to danger. Your mind is very good at putting together a lot of subtle little hints that you don't consciously notice, and when you get the feeling that something isn't quite safe then ninety percent of the time you'll be right. That smell made me uneasy, and however much I might try to reason it away, I decided it was better to be safe than sorry.

Jesse was asleep in the pilot's chair in the cockpit; it was the most comfortable place on the whole ship, but nobody grudged him that.

Most of the time he didn't have much to do other than let the autopilot do its thing, but now and then he did have to make a minor course correction or something similar.

"Jesse, wake up," I whispered, shaking his shoulder.

"What?" he asked, sounding irritable. I guess he was tired, but I couldn't just go back to bed and pretend nothing was happening.

"I think something's wrong," I said.

"What kind of a something?" he asked, sitting up and rubbing the sleep out of his eyes while he tried not to yawn.

"I don't know. I got up to get a drink of water a few minutes ago and I could have sworn I smelled something burning back there," I said.

"Burning? Was there any smoke? Any fire?" he asked.

"No, just that smell," I said.

"What kind of fire did it smell like? Wood? Plastic? Something else?" he asked.

"Plastic, I think. Something really harsh and bitter and heavy," I said, and Jesse chewed his bottom lip for a second.

"That doesn't sound too good, Tyke. I better check a few things," he said, turning to the computer screen in front of him. He quickly typed in several commands which meant nothing to me and then scanned a readout.

"Anything?" I asked.

"Maybe. I'm getting weird signals when I try to run a diagnostic scan on the engines and the life support systems back there," he said.

"What do you mean by weird?" I asked.

"Just what I said. Weird. Like impossible kind of weird. It's telling me the water purifier is working at five thousand percent efficiency right now, for example," he said.

"Dang, boy. You should yank that puppy out and see if you can duplicate it," I said dryly.

"Yeah, no doubt. But it's also telling me we've got only 18 millibars of air pressure inside the cabin, which I *know* isn't true or we'd all be dead. It also thinks the temperature in here is a little over four hundred degrees, and it's telling me we've only got 23 percent thorium left inside the fuel cell. That can't be right, either; no way have we used that much fuel. Something strange is going on," he said.

"Yeah, but what?" I asked.

"I've got a nasty little suspicion," he finally said.

"What is it?" I asked.

"I don't even want to say until we check. Come on, Tyke," he said, getting up from his chair and heading back to the rear of the *Susie Q* where I'd noticed the smell was strongest. He tiptoed through the cabin to keep from waking anybody, and when we reached the bathroom he shut the door behind us so he could switch the light on.

It didn't work.

"What's wrong with the light?" I asked.

"I don't know, but I suspect the same thing that's wrong with the sensors. Here, there's a flashlight in the first aid kit; we'll use that instead," he said. He rummaged through the kit and found the flashlight by touch, switching it on and handing it to me.

"Hold on to that and give me some light," he said, going to the wall behind the door. There was an electrical access panel there, as there were at various other points throughout the ship. It was held on by metal clips, and Jesse quickly pried them open with his fingers and pulled the access door loose.

He was rewarded with a cloud of pungent black smoke that made both of us cough, and he quickly covered up the hole again and replaced the clips. Then he silently returned to the cockpit and shut the door.

"So what's wrong?" I asked. He looked grim, and I knew it had to be something bad.

"This is not good, Tyke. The electrical system is on fire," he said.

"But how can that be? There hasn't been any fire on board," I said.

"It doesn't matter. It must have been caused by the laser hits while those jets were after us. It's not a fire like you think, though; it's just a slow, smoldering kind of thing that'll eat its way along the insulation of the wires inside the walls," he said.

"So what do we do about it?" I asked.

"We don't do anything about it. There's no way to put it out. We can't reach half the areas where it's probably already burning, and even if we could we'd end up ripping loose every electrical system on board. When things like this happen, then you either land or you die. It'll start shorting out electronic components as it moves along, and we'll gradually lose all the various systems. I don't know how much longer we'll have life support, or engine control, or *anything*. Any of it could go at any time," he said.

"How long do you figure we have?" I asked.

"There's absolutely no telling. It could be five minutes or five hours or anything in between for all I know, but I can guarantee you it won't be much longer than that," he said.

"We'll have to go back to Mars, then," I said.

"I doubt we can. We're already too far out to make it back before we burn up," he said.

"Is there anywhere else we can land?" I asked.

"Phobos or Deimos, maybe. But I don't see what good *that* would do us. There's no air down there for us to breathe, and no food or water, either. Even if we wore our space suits, we'd run out of air in only a few days at the most," he said.

"Well... maybe if we killed the electricity to the ship and removed all the oxygen, it might suffocate the fire and then we could keep going," I said.

"We might put out the fire that way for a little while, but it wouldn't help. The electrical system is already full of places where the insulation has burned off and left bare wires. Sooner or later something would short out and start burning again, and it probably wouldn't take all that long, either. If we keep going then eventually we'll either lose power completely and turn into a derelict, or else those smoldering wires will start a real fire somewhere and we'll get roasted alive," he said.

"Which moon is closest?" I asked.

"Deimos, at the moment," he said.

"Then land on Deimos and maybe we can radio somebody to come get us. There are still several more XR's parked at Hilo, you know. It's not like it would be a dangerous mission for them or anything; we're completely out of Colonel Burns' reach up here since he doesn't have any spaceships. We could put out the fire like I suggested and then rewire the life support systems so we could live out of the *Susie Q* while we waited. If the folks back home knew we were at a fixed point on the ground, they'd always be able to find us even if we lost radio contact," I said, and he sighed.

"All that is more complicated than you think, Tyke, but I guess we might as well try it. There's no other way we'll ever make it out of here alive," he said.

"All right, then. Let's go for it," I said.

He didn't answer me, just turned back to his console and started reconfiguring the flight path and whatever else it was he needed to do.

Chapter Eleven

Deimos is the smaller of Mars' two moons, only about eight miles in diameter and not even big enough to be completely shaped into a ball by gravity. It's big enough to be more or less rounded, true, but the shape of it sort of reminds me of a potato, or maybe a lumpy rock which has been worn smooth by flowing water in a creek bed. The name means Terror, and under the circumstances that was an uncomfortably appropriate moniker.

It took us not quite two hours to reach it, and by that time the fire was obvious; the air was full of foul haze. We'd already woken up the others and told them what the situation was, and Brandon instantly ratified our plan as soon as he understood the facts. He also told us to depressurize the cabin immediately to stop the damage as soon as possible, so we all put our space suits on and Jesse bled air away into space till we were sitting there in hard vacuum. That cut off oxygen to the fire and prevented any more immediate damage, but nearly a third of the sensors and systems had already gone crazy by then. Jesse couldn't trust the information the computer was giving him and had to calculate trajectories in his head and fly the ship on just a wing and a prayer, so to speak. I'd always known he was good at math, but that was a feat which surely ought to have earned him a place next to Euclid and Pythagoras among the ranks of the greatest mathematicians of all time.

But he did it, bringing us to rest on an endless plain of dark gray soil. It had a dull, rough texture and it was strewn with pebbles and dust that varied in color from nearly black to silvery-white. It sort of reminded me of ground-up charcoal mixed with bone meal.

"Well, here we are," Danielle said, staring out at the flat landscape. Well, I *say* it was flat; it really reminded me of standing on a flattish mountaintop, actually. Not because we were really parked on one, but because the horizon fell away so quickly that it looked like that. There were actual mountains to the west; not very tall ones, but at least they broke the monotony just a bit.

In fact, the only really interesting thing to be seen was Mars itself. It was *huge,* taking up a massive section of the sky almost directly overhead. Go outside at night and hold a beach ball at arm's length and you might get some idea of how big Mars looks from Deimos. It was hundreds of times bigger and brighter than any full moon on Earth, flooding the surface with reddish light. It was technically the middle of the night in the spot where we landed, but Mars was so bright it seemed almost like daytime.

Jesse had to get to work on the wiring immediately, and since I didn't know anything about that sort of thing I was politely asked to please stay out of the way while other people worked.

Those of us who didn't have any technical skills went outside and nosed around a bit when we first got there, mostly out of idle curiosity. I didn't even pay attention to the fact at the time, but since I was the first one out the door I suppose I can lay claim to the honor of having put the first human footprint on Deimos. I'm not sure how much of an honor it really is to put the first footprint on such a little pebble of a world, but such as it is, I did. I thought to myself I should have planted a flag in the dirt and claimed the place for Hawaii. It would have made an awfully incongruous addition to our little kingdom.

I laughed a little.

"What's so funny?" Danielle asked.

"Nothing. Just losing my mind, that's all," I said.

"Hmm... well, they say the first step to recovery is admitting you have a problem," she said. She was joking, of course, so I laughed again.

"I'm surprised I have a mind left at all, after this little adventure," I said.

"Me too," she agreed.

"So what do you want to do, beautiful? I mean, here we are in this remote and romantic spot, with such an incredible view, and not even any homicidal soldiers to try to kill us," I said.

"Let's take a walk, then. We can always follow our footprints back to the ship," she said, and I nodded. The deep soil and lack of atmosphere on Deimos meant we left really obvious boot-prints everywhere we went, and there was no wind or anything else to erase them.

So we walked across the dark gray plain as far as the western mountains, and I suppose if we'd wanted to we could have walked all the way around the world in about a day's time. But in spite of Deimos being such a small place as far as diameter goes, it still has a surface area of not quite two hundred square miles, roughly comparable to the size of a city like Tampa. Most of it is blanketed with that same thick gray soil, but here and there are a few craters and some scattered hills.

We had plenty of time to explore the place over the next few days, such as it was. We took to calling the steep hills to the west the Mountains of Terror, I guess to enliven the place a little. Deimos is a far cry from the most beautiful or exciting locale I've ever seen, but sometimes you have to take what you can get.

Jesse and the others practically gutted the *Susie Q*, ripping as much wiring out of the walls as they could get their hands on. A lot of it turned out to be fried, so they tossed that aside and reconnected as many systems as they could, laying the wire along the edges of the floor and everywhere else they could find a spot for it. The whole interior of the ship looked like it was strewn with multicolored spaghetti by the time they were done, and even then they had to sacrifice quite a few systems. We had no engines, and mighty few sensors. But we did have life support and communications, and I guess those were all that really mattered. It was sort of like having our own little ratty apartment. A small and very cramped one-room apartment full of ripped-out insulation and exposed wiring, packed with eleven people who had to stay inside most all the time and with only a single bathroom. Imagine that, and you might catch a glimpse of why even the uninteresting landscape of Deimos seemed so attractive in comparison.

But the great outdoors had its own set of risks. The gravity is only about a thousandth as much as it would have been on Earth, which for all practical purposes is almost nothing. I would have weighed something like 190 pounds on Earth, dressed in my space suit. On Deimos, fully suited up, I weighed a whopping three ounces; which is roughly the same as a tennis ball.

That meant we had to creep along carefully and be cautious not to jump or run. Deimos' escape velocity is only about 11 miles per hour, and it's easily possible for even an average human being to run faster than *that*. Even a really hard jump was fully capable of sending somebody flying out into space, never to be recovered.

We did have fun with the gravity sometimes, though. We invented a game called reverse bungee-jumping, where we tied a thousand-foot cord firmly to a stake driven into the bedrock so it wouldn't come loose, and then tied the other end to ourselves. Then we'd jump straight up and go flying into space like a rocket till we were a thousand feet high, and then the cord would jerk us up short and we'd seemingly hang there motionless for several seconds before we slowly, slowly began to fall. Then we'd steadily pick up speed as we plummeted back to the surface, till we were moving at a pretty good clip near the end. There's no atmosphere on Deimos to slow you down and thus no terminal velocity, so that meant we kept accelerating till the very last second. It took a little over seven minutes to reach the ground, if my watch was right, and when we hit the dirt it felt about like jumping off the top of a kitchen counter might have felt on Earth. Enough to twist an ankle or knock the breath out of you if you were careless, but not enough to really hurt you even then, especially since the dirt was fairly soft. It sort of reminded me of jumping off the cliffs at Lake Boscovich on the Moon, except we could do this even on dry ground.

I confess I did keep my eyes shut most of the time, for which Jesse and Hunter usually laughed at me.

"Aw, Tyke, that spoils half the fun if you can't *see* anything," Hunter said.

"Humph. Y'all do your own thing and I'll do mine, okay?" I said.

"Whatever you say, fraidy-cat," Hunter said, rolling his eyes. He was only kidding, of course, but even if he'd been serious it still wouldn't have changed my mind.

But other than bungee-jumping or mountain climbing there wasn't a whole lot to do on Deimos except sleep or look at Mars or maybe sit around in the *Susie Q* and talk, and all those things started to get awfully stale after a while.

We did stay in contact with everybody back home during the whole thing, of course, in spite of the twenty minute time delay between responses. Several of the grubs were supposed to be fixing up one of the remaining XR's and sending a mission to retrieve us soon, if we could only sit tight and wait on them. There was no reason to think we couldn't, since the *Susie Q* had plenty of food and water and there were no enemies at hand. As long as we didn't go crazy and start killing each other from cabin fever then we ought to be fine.

Alas, it wasn't to be.

Colonel Burns could overhear all our plans, of course, since all he had to do was listen in on the radio frequencies we used. Nor had we cared much if he did, honestly, since there was nothing he could do about it anyway.

Or so we thought.

But whatever his other traits might have been, I don't think the Colonel took kindly to being humiliated. We'd humbled him in front of his soldiers by coming to Mars right under his nose, conducting a successful rescue mission, and then escaping in spite of his best efforts to stop us, and now the whole colony at Phoenix knew we were safe and headed back home soon, even though we were right on their very doorstep. That must have galled him to no end.

I think I mentioned before that lasers don't have an infinite range, because of dust particles and whatnot. That's true as far as it goes, but it does depend somewhat on how strong the beam is and what kind of environment you're in. Colonel Burns had some powerful lasers stashed away in Phoenix, as we knew to our sorrow from the battle at Tharsis Tholus. The atmosphere had thickened and crept upward since then, but there were still plenty of high mountains on Mars where the air was practically nonexistent. Mount Olympus is the tallest of them all, of course, so I don't imagine it's any coincidence that that's the one Colonel Burns chose for his plan. He must have been foaming at the mouth for vengeance even if it wouldn't benefit him any other way, because three weeks after we first arrived on Deimos and only six days before we were due to be rescued, he finally had his weapons set up and in position to attack us again.

We never suspected a thing until he started firing on us.

I suppose it must have been hard to aim very accurately from that distance, but his soldiers sure did give it their best shot. All of a sudden we found ourselves surrounded by huge red beams nearly three feet across, hitting the ground like raindrops and fusing the dirt into puddles of molten glass that splashed everywhere. That was enough to snap all of us out of our mid-afternoon doldrums.

"Attack! Get out of the ship!" Brandon yelled, and then for a little while it was all confusion as we struggled to get our space suits on and scrambled out the air lock.

There was no way we could fight back against something like that, so we scattered most ignominiously in all directions, like rats escaping from a sinking ship. Danielle and I managed to stay together by gripping hands tight, but in all the confusion I couldn't have guessed what happened to everybody else.

I know I saw at least two people get vaporized by laser beams, even though I had no idea who they might have been. We didn't dare go faster than a brisk walk, either, for that same reason I mentioned earlier about flying off into space. I saw *that* happen to somebody, too, who forgot the rules out of momentary panic. I had to keep an iron grip on my own nerves so I wouldn't do something fatally insane like that myself. And if you think it's easy to take a leisurely stroll through a battlefield where people are getting fried to ashes all around you and every cell in your body is screaming for you to run, then you should try it sometime.

Eventually we found ourselves hiding in a pile of rocks somewhere on the upper slopes of the Mountains of Terror, looking down on a scene of utter devastation.

The lasers had stopped by then; I guess either because Colonel Burns was satisfied he'd killed us all or because we'd finally moved out of range. It so happens that Deimos is a very speedy little world, revolving around Mars roughly every 30 hours. That's just barely outside the level of a synchronous orbit, of course; that is, an orbit in which a moon moves at the same speed as a planet rotates, and consequently remains in the exact same spot in the sky at all times for an observer on the ground. As it is, Deimos appears to move very, very slowly across the Martian sky, taking 2.7 days from one moonrise to the next. What that meant in practical terms was that the spot where the *Susie Q* rested was only within range of Colonel Burns' lasers for roughly three hours whenever Deimos was directly overhead from Mount Olympus, and that wouldn't happen again for several days.

I didn't know all that at the time; I just knew the bombardment had stopped, and I tried to calm my beating heart while debating with myself whether it was safe to give away our position by using radio or not. The radios in our suits were nowhere near as strong as the one on the *Susie Q*, of course, and for all practical purposes they shouldn't have been detectable for more than a few miles at the most. But the ghastly memory of what I'd seen during the attack was still very fresh in my mind, and sometimes fear will make you do things which are not entirely rational. I finally decided to keep on the safe side, and put my faceplate up against Danielle's so she could hear the vibrations when I spoke.

"Are you okay?" I asked.

"Yeah, I'll live," she said, trying to make light of it.

"I think we're safe here for a little while, as long as we don't use radio," I said.

"But what about the others?" she asked.

"I don't know," I admitted.

"Did you see that one person fly off into space? That was horrible," she said.

"Yeah, I saw it," I said, wishing I knew of some way to erase that image from my mind forever. The ones who got vaporized by the laser beam had been even worse, but I wasn't sure if Danielle had seen that, and if she hadn't then I definitely wasn't going to share it with her. It was bad enough that I had to remember it myself.

"Whoever that was is probably still alive out there, just drifting in space and waiting to suffocate," she said.

"Hush. Don't think about things like that," I said. I didn't want to think about it myself, especially since I knew there was absolutely nothing we could do to help.

"What else could I possibly think about right now, after we just saw it happen?" she asked bleakly.

"Whatever is true, whatever is noble, whatever is right, whatever is pure, whatever is lovely, whatever is admirable. If anything is excellent or praiseworthy, think about such things," I murmured, and she sighed.

"Saint Paul, and yes I know all that. But there doesn't seem to be much out here which is lovely or noble right now, Tyke," she said.

"No, but I tell you what. Let's pray for that poor grub for a minute, whoever he or she might be. It's all we can do, but it's a lot more than nothing," I said.

"Yeah, that's true," she agreed.

So that's what we did, right there in that rocky valley in the middle of what had to be the most forsaken place I'd ever visited, and you know, I think it did take some of the weight off our hearts from what we'd seen, at least a little bit.

"Come on, beautiful; I think the attack is probably over now. I haven't seen any lasers for at least an hour," I finally said when we were finished.

"Where are we going? Back to the ship?" she asked.

"Yeah, I figure anybody else who survived will head back that way after they decide it's safe. Don't you?" I asked.

"Yeah, probably. Not sure what we'll do when we get there, but we'll see," she said.

We slowly clambered down out of the hills and headed back the way we came, soon discovering that the silvery-gray plain was nothing like itself when we got there. Instead of dirt, it was now covered with a brittle crust of greenish-black glass that I could feel crunching under my boots in the places where it was thinnest. In other spots it had cracked on its own as it cooled, leaving razor-sharp edges we had to avoid lest we slice a hole in our suits. They were supposed to be built to hold up to all kinds of abuse like that, but there was no reason to push our luck.

When we got back to the *Susie Q* itself, we found a fused and melted ruin; not much more than a lump of metal and glass and plastic. Inside there were all our supplies; all our food and water, all our air and protective gear that we needed to survive.

Colonel Burns had gotten his vengeance after all.

"How long do you think we can make it, with the ship like that?" Danielle asked, staring at the wreckage.

"I guess it depends on how much we can salvage. I know it looks bad, but you never can tell," I said.

"What I'm asking is, what if we can't salvage anything at all?" she asked.

"Well. . . in that case, we've got enough air in the tanks on our suits to last us about three or four days," I said.

"The rescue team can't get here that soon," she pointed out.

"No, not quite," I agreed.

"So what do we do, then?" she asked.

"We do everything we can and hope for the best," I said.

Chapter Twelve

Within a few hours the remainder of us had gathered together on the glassy plain, minus the three members we'd lost to Colonel Burns' attack. Two had been vaporized by laser fire, and then there was the one who'd drifted off the surface from trying to run. Jesse and Brandon showed up safe and sound, but it didn't take too long to figure out that Hunter was among the missing. There was no way of knowing whether he'd been burned to a crisp or lost in space, and to tell the truth I wasn't sure which was worse or if I even wanted to know at all. I wished we'd left him at home, rather than let him come to such an end as that.

Of course, it was most likely the same end we'd all be facing in a few days or so; his only honor was in going a little sooner than the rest of us.

"We have to try to salvage whatever we can. If we can only make it till the rescue party gets here on Saturday then we might still pull through," Brandon said, and nobody disagreed. I'd calmed down enough by then to realize it was safe to use the radios in our suits, so nobody had to listen to vibrations anymore. We all stood there and watched silently while Jesse used a hand laser to cut his way into what was left of the *Susie Q's* cabin, awaiting the verdict on whether we'd be able to survive or not.

There were only seven of us left at that point; me, Danielle, Jesse, and Brandon, and then the ones from the Redoubt: Nona, the girl who wrapped my ankle that first day. Leo, an electrical engineer from Tennessee. And then last of all Buzz Trewick, the young ranger. I was beginning to wonder if the whole mission had been worth it after all, for such a meager return. Three grubs, at the cost of Hunter's life and untold anguish, and that was if we made it home with no more losses than we'd already suffered.

Then I thought about what Brandon always liked to say about saving the whole world when you save a single life, and I was ashamed of myself for being so hard hearted. My grandpa Cody used to say that magnanimity is the most beautiful thing there is; the courage to cast aside yourself for love of another, the scorning of selfishness in all its myriad forms and disguises. Daddy and even Brandon have told me many times how much I remind them of Cody, but in my heart of hearts I think he was a better man than I'll ever be.

Then my wry musings were rudely interrupted by a crackle of static from my radio.

"Is anybody there?" a voice cried. It sounded hoarse and desperate, whoever it was, and I glanced around without thinking. Deimos is one of those annoying worlds where radio won't work unless you've got a clear line of sight to the person you're talking to, and there was nobody in view that I could imagine would have said such a thing.

"Who's there?" I asked, beating everybody else to the punch.

"Is that you, Tyke?" the voice asked, and then through all the hoarseness I recognized him.

"Hunter?" I asked, in utter stupefaction. It was like suddenly getting a voicemail from someone who's dead.

"Yeah, it's me," he said, and even though I'm sure at any other time it would have embarrassed him to no end to know we were listening, I could hear him sobbing. I guess from sheer unvarnished terror, but I decided the kindest thing I could do was pretend not to notice.

"Where are you, buddy?" I asked, in the calmest and most soothing voice I could muster.

"I'm somewhere up in space. I don't know where exactly but I'm still close to Deimos I think," he said, calming down a little.

"Don't worry, then. We'll find a way to get you back," I said, dearly hoping that wasn't just a comforting lie. In the meantime, Brandon hadn't been wasting time.

"We've got a fix on his position, Tyke. He's in low orbit around Deimos, about five thousand feet altitude. He must not have had quite enough energy to escape completely," he said.

"Did you hear that, Hunter? You didn't fly all the way out into space; you're in.orbit around Deimos. That means you're safe for now. How are you fixed for air?" I asked.

"I've got about eighteen hours left," he said, and I privately cursed. He'd never make it till the rescue crew arrived.

"All right, then. That's plenty of time for us to figure something out," I said, like it was nothing more complicated than clipping fingernails. In reality I had no idea how we'd ever get him down from up there, let alone within eighteen hours.

"How?" he asked, and that put me in an awkward position.

"I'm not sure yet, buddy. We'll have to think about it," I finally admitted.

"I think I've got his orbit plotted, Tyke. He'll pass over this spot every three hours and nineteen minutes, but we'll only have radio contact for about half an hour out of that time. Tell him when he drops over the horizon he won't be able to talk to us again till 4:29 pm, Hawaii time. Tell him to synchronize the timer in his suit so he'll know when he comes back in range," Jesse said.

"Did you hear all that, Hunter?" I asked.

"Yeah, I heard him. I've got the timer set now," he said.

"Time's almost up," Brandon warned.

"Okay, buddy. Looks like you're about to drop over the horizon. Keep your chin up; we'll still be here as soon as you circle back around. Maybe we'll know something by then," I said. Hunter never answered me, so I guess he must have slipped out of range sometime while I was talking.

"So. . . any ideas?" I asked, turning to face the others. The silence from all sides spoke volumes.

"I have one," Jesse finally said, although he didn't sound too enthusiastic about it.

"So spill it," I said.

"Well. . . you remember how we did the reverse bungee-jumping thing when we first got here? If we could patch together a long enough piece of cord, and if we could aim just right, then maybe one of us could go up and grab him and pull him down. He's only moving about ten miles an hour. It'd still be a pretty hard smack when he ran into you, but I think you could hold him if you gripped really tight," Jesse said.

"We'd have to time everything almost perfectly to make something like that work," I said doubtfully.

"Yeah, we would. And it'll be dangerous, too. Hunter is zipping along up there almost a mile above the surface. If somebody stops him and they both start to fall, they'll hit the ground pretty hard. It's gonna hurt, Tyke, maybe even pretty bad if they landed wrong," Jesse said.

"Like how much?" I asked.

"It'll be about like falling off a ten foot roof. Sometimes people walk away without a scratch, and other times they get bones broken. Like I said, it just depends on how they land. But it'll also depend on what size the person is who's doing the falling," Jesse said.

"I didn't think that was supposed to matter. Everything falls at the same speed in a vacuum," I pointed out.

"Yeah it does, but that's not the problem. Momentum is the problem, and that's a direct function of mass. A marble and a bowling ball will both fall at exactly the same speed, that's true, but which one do you think would be easier to stop? The more mass somebody has, the more momentum they'll have, and therefore the more energy it will release and the more damage it will do when they hit the ground. Simple physics, unfortunately," Jesse said.

I knew what all this was leading to, without even needing to ask. As I've mentioned before, Jesse is a big boy; not fat, but tall and muscular. He weighs almost half again as much as I do, and so does Brandon for that matter. Danielle is smaller than me but she's also not as strong, and from what Jesse had said I knew this was a mission which would take every ounce of strength possible. The three remaining grubs had been in low-gravity conditions on Mars for too long, and that inevitably saps away your strength and muscle mass after a while, even if you exercise regularly.

No, it was pretty obvious that all the telltale hints pointed directly to *me,* whether I liked it or not. And I *didn't* like it, not one little bit, but then on the other hand I couldn't leave Hunter to die up there, and I couldn't ask someone else to put himself in more danger than I would have been in myself for the same job. I shook my head and wondered how it always seemed to happen that I was the one who got picked for the crazy stunts like that.

"I should be the one to go get him, then. I'm the smallest and the strongest, so I've got the best chance of coming back with him and not getting hurt too bad in the process," I said.

"I wouldn't ask, Tyke; not if there was any other way I could think of," Jesse said.

"He's my friend too, Jesse; I don't mind," I said.

"All right, then. Let's see how much rope we've got," Jesse said.

We had plenty of cord, actually; it was used for all kinds of things, and we only had to make sure to cut it off at the proper length so I wouldn't go flying out too far.

"All right, there we go; five thousand, one hundred and fifty-three feet. That should be exactly right," Jesse said.

"Good enough. We've got to go somewhere else besides here, though. It'll kill us if we land on all this glass when we hit the ground," I said.

"Yeah, I already thought of that. We'll have to go a little bit west of here till we get back onto plain old dirt again. And there's one other thing, too," Jesse said.

"What's that?" I asked.

"You might need to move around a little bit while you're up there, if you're not quite in position to catch him or something like that. We've got a harness you can wear for that; it pushes you along by releasing jets of pressurized CO_2 from bottles. But I warn you, don't use it any more than you absolutely have to. It's the only one we've got, and there's no way to recharge it at this point," Jesse said.

So that's what we did, hiking about two hours away till we were on a kind of slab-like plateau in the Mountains of Terror where the dirt felt nice and thick under our boots. We left the grubs behind to salvage as much as they could from the ship while the rest of us were busy trying to rescue our lost boy; if we didn't come up with some extra oxygen pretty soon, then it was liable to be a short reunion even if our crazy plan succeeded.

As soon as we reached the plateau, Brandon took a thick steel rod and drove it deep into the ground so it wouldn't come out, and tied the end of the cord to it while Jesse sat and murmured under his breath as he did speed and trajectory calculations. The computer on the *Susie Q* was a melted lump of wreckage, so Jesse's brain was the only tool we had for figuring out time and distance problems, no matter how fiendishly complex they might be. And even though Jesse could crunch numbers in his head the way Mozart could play the piano, I'd be lying if I said it didn't make me uneasy having to depend purely on his mental skills, no matter how extraordinary they were. Especially when I knew he could only estimate some of the numbers he had to use.

But eventually he got up and marked off two lines in the dirt with the toe of his boot, and shoved another metal rod in the ground pointing up at the sky at an angle. Then he came to get me.

"All right, Tyke. Start out here on this first line, then run to that second one and jump as hard as you can, exactly in the direction that rod is pointing. I know you won't be able to match it exactly but do the best you can and then adjust your position with your CO_2 jets after you get up there. It'll take you exactly seventeen minutes and forty-three seconds to reach the end of your rope, and then you'll have at least a minute or so before you fall more than a few inches. That gives us a little bit of loose time to play with, but not much. You'll have to start running at exactly 4:26 if you want to be at the top of your arc when Hunter comes overhead, so when I yell go, you better go. Got it?" Jesse asked.

"Yeah, I've got it," I agreed.

"Good. You better get in position, then; there are only a few minutes left before you'll have to start," he said. I nodded, quickly taking my spot at the first line and checking one more time to make sure the CO_2 harness was securely buckled in place and the tether line was firmly tied around my midsection. The last thing I wanted was to have it come loose and end up joining Hunter in the sky rather than pulling him back down.

"Be careful, baby, and good luck," Danielle said, and put her arms around me. It's awfully difficult to hug somebody in a space suit, but I did the best I could. My chronometer said it was 4:24, so it was almost show time. Danielle went to stand on the sidelines with Brandon and Jesse, and it felt crazily like one of those summer track meets we used to go to a few years ago when Jesse and I were in junior high. If I closed my eyes, I could almost smell the jasmine and camellia that used to grow beside the practice field.

But that was long ago and far away, and Deimos might as well have been in a totally different universe than Clearwater High in the great state of Florida.

Then Jesse yelled *"Go!"* and I took off running. That's hard to do when there's so little gravity because you have hardly any traction, but I leaned down low and did my best to keep my momentum headed forward for as long as possible. Then I reached the metal stake and shoved off from the ground as close to that direction as I could.

I shot off the surface like a bullet with the cord trailing after me, and before I knew it I was hundreds and then thousands of feet above the dark gray hills. I had to keep my eyes open this time whether I liked it or not; I had to be ready when I got to the top of my arc and saw Hunter coming. Nevertheless, I kept my gaze locked on the chronometer so I wouldn't have to look down and see how terrifyingly high up I was, and three minutes into my flight I guess Hunter must have come back into radio range again.

"Is anybody there?" he asked, and I was glad for another distraction. He sounded a lot calmer than he did the first time, and that was good to hear.

"Yeah, we're here. We're coming to get you," I said confidently.

"What did you figure out?" he asked, and so I told him all about the plan to meet him up in space and grab hold of him as he flew by.

"Are you sure that'll work, Tyke?" he asked, sounding doubtful.

"It ought to, as long as we time everything just right. Keep your eyes open and be ready to grab hold of me, too," I said.

"I will," he said.

Before long we were close enough that I could see him, first as a tiny glint of light and then rapidly getting larger. He was slowly rotating head over heels as he moved forward, which must have been disorienting to say the least. But of course there was nothing he could do to stop it.

He was no more than two thousand feet away when the cord finally ran out and jerked me to a stop, knocking the breath out of my lungs for a second. Then I hung there seemingly suspended in space; so far, so good. I had time to adjust my position a bit with the CO_2 jets, and then I was ready.

Hunter was on top of me almost before I knew it, and even though ten miles an hour may not sound like much, it's faster than you think. Try grabbing hold of somebody while they run past and you'll get some idea of how difficult it was. He literally flew by, and even though I did manage to grab hold of his leg, it got torn out of my grip almost instantly. Then he was hopelessly out of reach while I drifted along behind him.

"Did you get him?" Jesse asked urgently.

"No, I got his foot for a second but I couldn't keep hold of him," I said dully, feeling like a complete failure.

"Well. . . don't worry about it. He'll come back around again in a few hours and we'll try again," Jesse said.

"But I'll fall before then," I said.

"Yeah, you will. But you'll be back on the ground a long time before it's time to go back up to meet Hunter again. I'll have to recalculate everything since you probably slowed him down a bit, but that only means we've got more time, not less," Jesse said.

"I know *that*. I was worried more about breaking a leg or something when I hit the ground," I said.

"If you do then I'll go next time, Tyke. We've only got fourteen more hours left before he runs out of air up there," Jesse said.

"I know," I sighed.

It took me about eighteen minutes to crash, and just as Jesse had predicted, it hurt like the devil. I smacked into the dirt and bounced and rolled till I came to rest in a groaning heap of bruises against the base of one of the bigger boulders at the edge of the plateau.

"Are you okay, baby?" Danielle called by radio, and I groaned again.

"I feel like I just jumped off a diving board into an empty pool, but I guess I'll survive," I said.

"We'll be there in just a minute if you'll wait for us," she said.

I certainly didn't feel like running to meet them, but I did get painfully to my feet before they arrived. There was nothing twisted or broken, it seemed.

"You did slow him down a little when you grabbed his foot. He won't be back overhead again till 9:14 next time," Jesse said as soon as they got near. That was still a little over four hours away according to my chronometer, and I welcomed the chance to rest a little while before I had to make another flying leap. But the hours passed all too quickly, and soon enough I was standing at the line again, ready to try it a second time. Jesse had already readjusted the lines and angles to match the new reality.

Hunter never said anything or answered our calls even after he should have been within range, which concerned all of us at first until I actually made it up to the top of my arc again and saw him. He was moving noticeably slower than last time when he finally appeared in the distance, even though he was rotating much faster. I could only guess that he'd passed out at some point from the constant spinning; your semicircular canals don't like that kind of thing very much, as anybody who's turned around and around in a circle for just a few minutes could tell you. I could only imagine what two or three hours of such a thing might do to somebody. The poor boy probably stood a good chance of being cross-eyed for the rest of his life after he woke up from an experience like that.

The rotation made it a lot harder to grab hold of him, I have to say that much. But I was ready for the force of our collision this time, so when he smacked into me I threw my arms and legs around him and really *gripped*.

He almost got torn out of my grasp for a second time, and I think the sudden transfer of momentum practically dislocated my left shoulder and pulled both arms out by the roots, but in spite of that I managed to hold on to him, barely. Then we were both moving along as one unit at a reduced speed, still nauseatingly spinning, and before long I started to feel the cord tighten around my midsection as we pulled against it.

Fifteen minutes later we hit the ground with agonizing force, and Hunter did get ripped loose then, but I was in too much pain to care. My back felt like a mass of white hot fire, and I had a headache the size of Jupiter from smashing my head against the inside of my helmet. There's not supposed to be anything sharp inside those helmets, just in case of that very kind of thing, but I must have hit something hard enough to cut me anyway, because I felt a trickle of blood running down my forehead.

The others had surely seen us crash, and I knew they'd be there soon to give us whatever relief they could, but in the meantime all I could do was lie there and groan.

Chapter Thirteen

It seemed like a long time before anybody arrived, although I know it couldn't really have been more than a few minutes at the most. Then Danielle was there beside me with her faceplate up to mine.

"Are you okay, baby?" she asked, her voice full of concern.

"I think maybe I broke something," I said, and I meant to say more but it hurt too much to talk. It even hurt to *breathe,* but I couldn't stop doing *that,* of course.

"What hurts?" she asked, all businesslike then.

"Everything," I said, and she sighed.

"That doesn't help me, Tyke. I need specifics," she said, and I tried to disconnect from the pain long enough to figure out exactly where it was coming from, at least.

"My lower back and my ribs, mostly; I think on the left side. It's not quite as bad now as it was when I first hit, but it's still pretty bad," I said.

"I imagine so. We'll have to carry you down to the *Susie Q* before we can do anything, though; Brandon's already headed that way with Hunter," she said.

"What's wrong with *him?*" I asked.

"He threw up inside his suit and we think he choked on it, for one thing. We don't know what it might have done to him when he hit the ground because he's not awake to tell us, and Brandon can't do anything to help either one of you because he can't get his hands on you. Apparently he's got to have actual skin contact," she said.

"Can't get that through a space suit," I mumbled.

"No, you can't. He's hoping we might be able to rebuild the cabin of the *Susie Q* enough to let us go inside there and get our suits off, but I have my doubts about that," she said. I had my own doubts about it myself after seeing the condition the *Susie Q* had been in, but I didn't say anything.

Just about then, Jesse arrived.

"I'm fixing to try to pick you up, Tyke. If anything hurts too much let me know," he said, and I made a noncommittal kind of grunt.

Jesse tried to be careful; I know he did, going as slow and easy as he could with slipping his hands under my back. But when his left hand brushed the wrong spot it ignited another explosion of pain.

"Stop! That's too much," I said, gritting my teeth.

"Sorry. Let me try a little bit different spot," he said. He did, and even though that hurt almost as bad I kept my mouth shut about it.

It had been a long time since anybody had had to carry me anywhere; in fact I think the last time had been when Chris carried me up to the top of Mount Bradley when I had radiation poisoning on the Moon. But that had been almost four years ago, and it felt strange to have to endure a repeat of the experience now.

About an hour later we emerged onto the glassy plain, and then crunched our way across the sharp crust for another forty-five minutes till we reached the remains of the *Susie Q*. Then Jesse was able to put me down on the ground again, and none too soon from my point of view. As gentle as he tried to be, any movement at all was painful.

The grubs had been busy during the hours while we were occupied with retrieving Hunter, and there was a small pile of salvaged items off to one side. Including at least two air tanks, I was happy to see. Jesse and Brandon went to join them as soon as they disentangled themselves from Hunter and me, and Jesse at least kept up a continuous chatter about what they'd found and how it could be used. That was mostly for my benefit I'm sure, but I appreciated it.

"I think I can get the air filter to work on manual control and reroute it through the airlock, with just a smidgeon of luck," Jesse said after a while.

"The airlock is still working?" I asked, surprised.

"Well. . . no, not really. The outer door is more or less melted shut, but the inner door still opens," he said.

"So how does that help us, then?" I asked.

"It means we've got at least a small area we know is still airtight, that's what. If I can finagle everything to make the air filter work, then it'll give us a place to stay so we won't have to use up our bottled air," he said.

"Um, Jesse, are we thinking about the same airlock? There's no way we can cram eight people into a space that small," I said.

"I admit it'll be tight, but there's more room than you think. It's six feet square; we measured it just now," he said.

"That's still not much," I said.

"No, but I think we'll at least have room to squeeze all of us in there, even if all we can do is stand or sit," he said.

"That'll be fun," I said dryly.

"It's only for six more days, Tyke, and if it keeps us alive then I'm willing to put up with a lot worse than that if I have to," he said.

"Yeah, I guess you're right. Better see what you can do, then," I said, resigned.

"I'm working on it right this very minute. I *think* it's gonna work, but we won't know for sure till we get everything hooked up," he said.

He kept talking while he and the grubs fiddled with wires and components, and when they finally finished up with everything it *did* work, sort of. Not very efficiently or well, but enough to give us some breathing space at least. None too soon, either; not a single one of us had more than a few hours worth of air left at that point.

So we piled into the air lock and shut the door, crowded shoulder to shoulder as we sat on the floor with our backs up against the walls and tried to find the most comfortable position we could. We didn't have room to take our space suits off since there literally wouldn't have been anywhere to put them, but we did take off our helmets and let them rest in our laps.

As soon as we got our helmets and gloves off, Brandon quietly put his hands on my head and wiped away my broken rib or whatever it was that I had. I could feel it when it happened; a brief surge of warmth in my side and then a sweet lack of pain for which I blessed him in my heart a thousand times. Then he did the same for Hunter. I think Hunter might actually have died if he hadn't; he'd inhaled some of his own vomit while he was unconscious, and that almost certainly would have given him a fatal case of pneumonia if nothing had been done about it.

But again, nobody seemed to notice. Brandon was so incredibly subtle and unobtrusive about the things he did that usually even the people he touched didn't realize what he'd done for them. There wasn't a single one of us in the room that he hadn't healed at some point during the expedition, some of us more than once, and yet Danielle and I were the only ones who seemed to know it. I silently marveled at how stealthy he could be, and wondered if I ever would have noticed anything myself if it hadn't been for glimpsing what he'd done with Hunter in the canyon. I was inclined to think not.

On the other hand, Uncle Philip likes to say that nothing ever happens by chance, so maybe it was fate that I stumbled around that boulder and saw him when I did. Considering everything he'd told me, that wasn't totally unbelievable either.

Then I put aside my idle speculations and decided it didn't really matter either way. Brandon Stone was surely a riddle wrapped inside an enigma, as they say, but nevertheless I was awfully glad to have him around.

An airlock is not the kind of place you want to have to share with seven other people in space suits for almost a week, I promise you. We started calling it The Can because that's exactly what it felt like; eight people living together inside an oversized tin can. That alone would have been bad enough, but there was another reason why the name was appropriate, too. I can't use adequate language to describe it without being what Aunt Joan would call ungentlemanly, but I'll just venture to say there were no bathroom facilities and then let your imagination supply the rest. It was something like living permanently inside one of those extra large portable toilets they have at fairs and on construction sites sometimes, and by the end of the week conditions were so fetid and foul that it was starting to make people sick, me included. Brandon could only do so much; he could make us well again if we started to get deathly ill, but he couldn't change the conditions that were causing the problem in the first place.

But I guess you can endure almost anything for a little while, and even if those six days felt more like six centuries before it was all said and done, the Last Day finally arrived.

When we crawled out of The Can on Saturday afternoon, stinking and haggard and unspeakably filthy, I'm sure the grubs from Kona were shocked at the state we were in. I'm equally sure the stench would have struck them stone-cold dead if they could have smelled it. As it was, one of them actually fainted when we got back to the *Melinda May* and stripped our space suits off. I'm not joking; the dude literally passed out from the smell. I never would've believed it if I hadn't seen it with my own eyes.

Our rescuers hadn't been able to land on the plain of fused glass, so they'd touched down on that same flat plateau in the Mountains of Terror where we'd launched the mission to retrieve Hunter. It took us about two hours to walk that far, and in spite of being kind of stiff and sore from sitting still for so long, I think all of us were thrilled to finally get a chance to stretch our limbs and actually *move* for a change.

It was when we first went inside the *Melinda May* and took our helmets off that the dude fainted, and to be fair the rest of our rescuers looked pretty green themselves. It didn't take them long to make up their minds to abandon ship for a couple of hours and poke around outside while we showered and changed clothes and got as clean as humanly possible again. I don't think any other shower in my entire life has ever felt so good as that one did, either before or since.

But none of us wanted to linger in the vicinity of Mars any longer than we absolutely had to, so as quickly as possible we finished up with our scrubbing so the grubs from Kona could tolerate our presence without swooning. Then we left Deimos without sparing it a second glance. As far as I was concerned, if I never saw the place again it would be too soon.

It took us a week to get back home, and we spent most of that time recovering from our adventures on Deimos. It was a pretty uneventful journey for the most part, and even though I was glad we'd at least been able to save three grubs, I was still relieved that the whole messy business was over. Colonel Burns seemed like an even wickeder character than Colonel Bartow had been, if such a thing were possible. I was glad we'd seen the last of him.

"Are you ready to get home, beautiful?" I asked Danielle, about a day before we were due to land.

"You better believe it. I think I've had my fill of adventures in space," she said.

"Yeah, me too. But hopefully this is the last one we'll ever have to go on," I said.

"I hope so. I'd kind of like to settle down and live a normal life for a change, at least for a while," she said wistfully.

"Oh, babe, there's no such thing as a normal life," I teased. That was one of my dad's favorite sayings, and I'd gradually picked up on it myself after a few months of his company.

"Okay then, smart aleck. I want to do some normal *things* for a change," she said.

"Like what?" I asked.

"Well. . . I don't know, maybe cook supper at home now and then, you know. Milk the cows. Go to church. Give Josie a brother or a sister to play with next year. Maybe go walking on the beach with my husband without having to wonder if he might get killed on a secret mission to Pluto next week," she said wryly.

It wasn't like Danielle to be so moody, and I wondered what was up.

"Is something wrong, babe?" I asked uncertainly, and she sighed.

"No, not really. I think this trip has worn me a little bit fine, that's all," she said.

"Yeah, I know it's been pretty rough sometimes," I agreed.

"I keep thinking about those poor grubs who drowned, and the ones that got lasered on Deimos. Makes me wonder what if that had been you, I guess," she said.

It was hard to know what to say to that, because of course it very easily *could* have been me. I couldn't promise her nothing bad would ever happen, and she knew it as well as I did. Nor could I promise that I'd never have to go on another dangerous mission again someday.

"I'm sorry," I finally said.

"It's not something to be sorry for, Tyke. I'm glad we had a chance to save Buzz and Nona and Leo, and I'm glad we both could be a part of that. Really I am," she said.

"Then what's bothering you?" I asked.

"I think it's mostly just that I want two different things which are incompatible with each other, that's all. I don't know if I can explain it so you'll understand, but I'll try. See, on the one hand I'd like for you to stay home all the time and keep safe and live a quiet and simple life with me and never do anything more dangerous than walk barefoot on the beach. I can't have that as long as you keep going out on missions like this. You understand?" she asked.

"Yeah, I get that much," I said.

"Okay, well, the flip side of that coin is this. If I actually ever *got* that, it would mean I'd also have to give up all the things I love the most about you. I'd never get a chance to see how brave and brilliant you can be in the midst of danger, or how kind you can be when something bad happens. There'd be nothing to let it show. You can't see how strong a branch is unless you try to break it, and that's what my problem is. I want to see the strength without trying to break the branch, and that's impossible. I can't have both. I'm trying to have my cake and eat it too. Does that make any sense?" she asked.

"Uh. . . not really," I confessed, and she laughed a little before letting her breath out in another long sigh.

"I didn't think you'd understand. Don't worry about it, baby; it's just my own little personal dilemma. You can't really help me with it," she said.

"Are you sure?" I asked.

"Yeah, I'm sure. Maybe I'll figure it out on my own one of these days," she said.

"Maybe I should take up some kind of extreme sport that looks really dangerous even though it isn't," I joked, trying to lighten the mood. I guess it must have worked a little at least, because she smiled.

"Like what?" she asked.

"Oh, I don't know. Bungee-jumping, maybe? There are plenty of tall bridges and cliffs without even having to leave Hawaii, and beside that I already learned how to do it on Deimos, sort of," I said. The idea was horrifying even to contemplate, actually, but if that's what she needed me to do then I'd grit my teeth and shut my eyes and give it a try if I had to. But she only laughed.

"We both know you'd hate that, Tyke," she said.

"I might learn to like it," I lied.

"I love you for offering, but really. . . no. I told you it's two incompatible things; there's no way to force them both together. I'll just have to think about it awhile and try to strike a balance I can live with, that's all," she said.

"Well. . . whatever you need me to do, let me know," I said.

"That I most surely will," she agreed.

That was all we said about it at the time, but it troubled me nevertheless, all the more so because there was nothing I could do about it. Just as she herself said, what she wanted was self-contradictory and therefore impossible. Even God Himself couldn't have given her what she wanted.

Uncle Philip asked us a rhetorical question one time at church, about whether God could create a rock so big that He couldn't lift it. That's supposed to be a logical snare, because no matter how you answer it you're forced to end up saying that there's something God can't do and therefore His power isn't infinite. But the question isn't quite what it seems. The answer (inasmuch as it even has one) is definitely "no", because of course God can't do anything which is self-contradictory. You could call that a limitation on His power if you like, but you're really just playing games with words. You may ask miracles of Him, but not nonsense. In the same way, it's quite easy to ask questions He can't answer. God could no more tell you how many inches are in a gallon than I could have; not because it's a limit on His wisdom but because the question is meaningless.

People tend not to like that idea of impossibility; I know I don't. We like to think that given enough time and ingenuity that a way forward can always be found, that all problems can eventually be solved. But the sad and unfortunate truth of the matter is that sometimes they can't.

Nevertheless, I thought about it a lot for the rest of the trip home, fruitlessly trying to think of a solution even though I knew there wasn't one. Danielle never said anything else about it, but I knew her well enough to know that she hadn't forgotten about it.

When we finally landed in Kona and disembarked on that well-remembered airstrip, there was a cheering crowd of hundreds of grubs to welcome us home. I don't think I'll ever get used to that kind of thing, but it does make you feel kind of special, I have to admit. Brandon and Philip planned on having a memorial service the next day for those who didn't make it home, but in the meantime everybody wanted to rejoice for those who had.

So Nona and Leo and Buzz were quickly carried off by old friends for celebrations all over town, and I suppose it would have been ill-mannered if the rest of us hadn't attended. So in spite of the fact that all I really wanted to do was go home and rest for a while, I forced myself to make the party circuit and make an appearance most everywhere at least for a little while. Jesse and Hunter scooped up Leah and Veronica and those four stayed out dancing and celebrating till the wee hours of the morning from what I heard the next day, but then of course they all *enjoy* that kind of thing.

Danielle and I excused ourselves as soon as we could graciously get away with it and went home, and I'm not sure about Brandon. I didn't see him at any of the parties, so maybe he got called away for something more urgent.

Chapter Fourteen

A few days after we got home, Brandon came to me with a serious look on his face.

"We've got a problem, Tyke," he said, getting right to the point. My heart sank as soon as I heard those words, but somehow I stayed calm.

"Oh? What is it?" I asked, like it wasn't anything to get upset about.

"I'm afraid Colonel Burns was busy while he had the *Susie Q*. My informant in Phoenix just sent word that there were three trips to Earth between December 8th when the ship was first captured, and January 25th when we took it back. Colonel Burns transferred 42 elite soldiers to a secure location here on Earth, as a kind of long-term sleeper cell I guess you could say. An insurance policy just in case the *Susie Q* got wrecked or recaptured or some such thing," Brandon said.

"Where are they?" I asked immediately. We'd have to mount an attack on that cell at once.

"I don't know. The only thing my informant could tell me was that it was a place Colonel Burns ordered built way back when all this first started; a kind of back-up plan just in case Mars and Venus didn't pan out," Brandon said.

"Yeah, the Defense Forces are big on back-up plans," I said wryly.

"You can't blame them for that, Tyke. Everybody knows it's good sense not to put all your eggs in one basket," Brandon said.

"So we have no idea where they went?" I asked.

"Well, it would have to be somewhere within the bounds of the Southern Command; Colonel Burns wouldn't have had authority to issue orders outside his own bailiwick, and besides that I'm pretty sure he would've wanted his refuge close by, just in case he needed it suddenly. Back in those days nobody knew exactly when or where the plague would first strike, let alone how fast it would spread," Brandon said.

"That's still a big area," I said doubtfully. Southern Command had included everything south of the Ohio River and as far west as Oklahoma; that was a big chunk of ground to cover, especially if you didn't have the faintest idea where to start.

"It would be, but it so happens we do have a few clues," Brandon said.

"Such as?" I asked.

"They didn't take any space suits or biohazard gear with them," he said.

"But they wouldn't need any, if they were inside a secure facility. And besides that the facility itself might have had some equipment like that for them to use," I said.

"You're not thinking, Tyke. They still would have needed suits just to make it from wherever they landed to the airlock letting them into their facility. They wouldn't dare walk unprotected anywhere on Earth, not even for a few steps. Too many dormant Orion spores lurking out there, just waiting for a fresh victim with no immunity," Brandon said.

"So what does that mean, you think?" I asked, puzzled.

"I think it means they went somewhere on Earth where there are no spores to have to worry about," Brandon said.

"But there's nowhere. . . " I said, and then trailed off. There *was* somewhere, if I hadn't been too thick-headed to see it.

"You mean the ocean?" I asked uncertainly.

"Well, not the ocean *per se,* not like a ship or anything; that would have been too obvious and too unreliable. I think they probably built some kind of facility down on the bottom, out of reach of prying eyes and safely away from birds and seals and such," Brandon said.

"Maybe," I said. That was still a lot of area to cover; the Southern Command had a coastline that reached all the way from Louisiana to Virginia.

"Let's try to reason it out the way they would have. If you and I were selecting a site for some kind of facility like that, what criteria do you think we'd use?" Brandon asked.

"Um. . . deep enough to be out of reach of storms and nosy locals, at least for the most part, but no deeper than necessary because of structural and engineering issues. As close to Atlanta as possible. Preferably in warm, clear water with some steep cliffs and good sturdy bedrock to build on, since that would simplify construction and cut maintenance costs," I said.

"And considering all those things, where would you build an undersea facility?" Brandon asked.

"Florida, at the outer edge of the continental shelf. Probably on the Gulf side and up toward the north," I said immediately.

There was a reason I was so definite, even though I hadn't thought about it in a long time. You see, it so happens that the outer edge of the West Florida Shelf is home to the largest drowned coral reef in the world. A long time ago when sea levels were three to four hundred feet lower, Florida was surrounded by a huge coral reef even bigger than the Great Barrier Reef in Australia, but as the ocean deepened it gradually drowned and died. But the dead remains of it are still there, if you care to go down and look. I'd been out there dozens of times while I was at the Academy, because even in its fossilized form it's still an area of extremely high biodiversity which is a critical ecological support region for the entire Gulf of Mexico. Most of it had been strictly off limits as a marine habitat reserve for nearly a hundred years for that very reason, but certain kinds of scientific and educational expeditions used to be allowed sometimes, with advance permission.

Anyway, it creates a massive bulwark at the edge of the continental shelf, and not incidentally it was an almost ideal place for building a facility such as Brandon was talking about. Colonel Burns might have had other criteria besides the ones we'd used, of course, but in the absence of any other information, the West Florida Reef was high on my list.

"Yeah, that's what I thought, too. We might be wrong, but I think it's the first place we should look," Brandon agreed.

"But how? Even if we limited ourselves only to the Reef and only to the section north of Tampa Bay, that's *still* a huge area," I pointed out.

"That's true, but all we can do is start at the northern fringe and work our way southward. I'm sure the facility is cloaked and camouflaged in every way possible, but no matter how careful they were there are still telltale signs if somebody knows what to look for. There'll be radio leakage when they try to communicate with Colonel Burns, for example. It'll be coded and we won't be able to read it, but that doesn't matter; it might give us a fix on their position if we're vigilant," Brandon said.

"It's also possible there are still some records of the facility in the computers at Southern Command. Jesse and I found a lot of good stuff about the colonies on Mars and Venus in there," I said.

"That's a good idea, too. Why don't you see if you can find anything in the database, and in the meantime direct one of the satellites to keep its eyes peeled on the eastern part of the Gulf to see if it can detect any radio emissions," Brandon said.

"No problem," I agreed.

"Good," Brandon said.

I immediately got to work, assigning one of the remaining communications satellites to focus on the eastern Gulf of Mexico until further notice, to see if it could detect any radio signals coming from that region. Then I went back into the database at Southern Command and started rooting through the files again.

I came up empty on the file search, unfortunately, so either they never kept any records of it, or they destroyed them, or else the records were kept in some other computer that I didn't have access to.

I did a little bit better with the satellite. Five days after focusing on the Gulf, it alerted me to a very faint radio signal coming from a point right where the Reef should have been, about a hundred miles southwest of Apalachicola at a depth of not quite three hundred feet.

It was on Saturday morning when I discovered the signal, and my father was there in the lab with me for our usual weekly visit. Brandon hadn't wanted to tell too many people about the crisis quite yet, but he left it up to my discretion whether to tell any given person or not. I figured Daddy could be trusted, so I wasn't too awfully concerned if he found out about what was going on.

"Find something?" he asked, when the computer beeped unexpectedly. I'd set it to alert me immediately if the satellite reported anything, and I went at once to see what it had found.

"Yeah, I think so. Maybe an old NADF facility under the Gulf," I said.

"Really? Any particular reason you're looking for something like that?" he asked, and so I proceeded to tell him about Colonel Burns and the trips back to Earth and all that while I read.

"And you said this signal is coming from the West Florida Reef?" he finally asked.

"Yeah, looks like it; a section called The Pinnacles," I said.

"That worries me, Tyke. The tachometer is still down there somewhere on the bottom of the Gulf, you know. I'm not saying that had anything to do with why they'd construct a base down there, but it sure does make it easier for them to look for the thing if the thought ever *did* cross their minds," he said.

"I hadn't thought of that," I said, frowning. I'd never seen a tachometer myself, but I'd heard plenty about what they could do, both from my parents and from Uncle Philip and Aunt Joan. It was a device which allowed the user to view events in the future, and even to travel there under certain very limited circumstances. The last thing we needed was for one of *those* to fall into the wrong hands.

"No reason why you should have, but as soon as you mentioned the Reef that's immediately what I thought of," Daddy said.

"Do you think it would have survived this long?" I asked uncertainly.

"I don't know. It was built to be waterproof just in case, but after sixteen years at the bottom of the sea; who can tell? That's how long it's been since your mother and I dropped it there after the *Lusitania* sank," he said.

"Maybe we should go look for it ourselves, even if Colonel Burns never thinks of it at all," I said.

"I'm not sure about that. In some ways I'd almost rather it sat there on the bottom of the Gulf till it corrodes away," Daddy said.

"Why?" I asked.

"Because knowing the future isn't always a good thing, that's why. It causes a lot of problems," he said.

"Yes, but it can also save a lot of people. You and me and everybody else in this town are only here because of that machine. At least in a roundabout kind of way. Aunt Joan wouldn't be here if she hadn't used it against Dr. Garza. Uncle Philip wouldn't be here if he hadn't followed Joan and brought Mama along with him. *You* wouldn't be here if you hadn't slipped up with a screwdriver and activated it at the wrong time, and therefore I never would have been born in the first place. You never would have seen the plague coming in time to warn anybody, either. Without that, Colonel Burns never would have known to order the colonies built on Mars and Venus, which would have meant no grubs for Brandon to bring back here. Mrs. Weiss never would have had time or money to develop her XR plane so the rest of us could escape to the Moon. Not to mention that you and Mama would have died when Colonel Bartow rammed the *Lusitania,* just like he meant for you to. The human race would probably be extinct right now, if it hadn't been for that tachometer," I reminded him.

"I know, I know. I'm not saying it's all bad. Just that it's dangerous, that's all," he said.

"That's true, too. But I think we can both agree we don't want Colonel Burns to get hold of it," I said.

"No, definitely not," he said.

"That's mostly what I'm talking about, just scooping it up for safekeeping. Not necessarily to use it ourselves," I said.

"You'd have to ask Uncle Brandon and see what he thinks, but I guess you have a point," he said.

"Is there any way we could detect it that you know of?" I asked.

"Yeah, it should be fairly easy to detect. It's a constant low-level source of neutrinos, so as long as you've got some equipment to pick up on *those* then you ought to be able to find it," he said.

"Where exactly is it located?" I asked.

"Thirty miles west-southwest of the marina at Treasure Island; that should get you close enough to pick up the signal, if there's still anything to pick up, that is. The water ought to be about a hundred feet deep or thereabouts, with a sandy bottom. In fact the tachometer is probably buried who-knows-how-deep in sand by now. If you find it you'll most likely have to do some digging," he said.

"That's not a problem, I don't think," I said.

"It might be more of a problem than you think. It won't be like digging in dirt. The edges of the hole will crumble under their own weight and keep falling in, so you'll be digging more of a crater than a hole. It'll mean having to move a lot more sand and having to move it a lot farther away," he said.

"All we can do is try," I said, shrugging.

"True enough. Just don't expect it to be easy, that's all," he said, and I laughed.

"Oh, trust me, that's one thing I *never* expect," I said.

Nor did I. Even before I said anything to Brandon about finding the radio signal, I knew we'd need some kind of submersible if we intended to check it out, and those are hard to come by. Subs had been one of the few places where people could seal themselves off and avoid exposure to the Orion Strain, and most of them had been seized for that purpose, either by their own crews or by others.

Not that it helped for long, of course; they ran out of food or fuel after a few months, or somebody inadvertently carried spores inside while trying to escape, or something like that. We'd been searching ever since we got back from the Moon and never found a single survivor that way, more's the pity.

But it *did* make it awfully hard to locate any kind of working sub. There were several naval facilities in and around Tampa Bay, but I didn't have the slightest idea whether there were any submarines docked there. The NADF didn't share that kind of information with the general public, and I'd never been terribly curious, to tell the truth.

It was easy enough to find out by riffling through the files at Southern Command, of course, and it turned out there were five subs in port at the Tampa Naval Yards when the plague struck. It was too much to hope for that any of them would still be there, and my guess was confirmed when I zoomed in with the visible satellite and saw nothing but empty berths where the files said the subs were supposed to be.

By dint of long and patient searching I finally found one late that afternoon, though not quite the kind I'd envisioned at first. There was a tourist place down in Fort Myers called Gator World which specialized in wild animal safari-type excursions both on land and sea, and they had a small tourist model with larger-than-usual windows which was meant for observing manatees and whales and things of that nature. At first I worried that it might not be up to the job; it had no airlock, no heating system, and no exterior lights.

Not to mention the fact that those big pretty windows *really* concerned me. Glass can never be as strong as steel, no matter how thick it is, and the pressure at three hundred feet depth might turn out to be too much for those windows to handle. The Gator World sub was made for short daytime pleasure cruises of no more than a couple hours or so, in relatively shallow water, and the conditions we might have to put it under were a lot more extreme than it had ever been intended to have to withstand. No doubt that was precisely why it was still sitting there in its berth and hadn't been stolen in the first place. But since it was apparently the only game in town I finally decided it would have to do.

Then I went to see Brandon.

He lived in a modest little bungalow surrounded by palm trees and bougainvilleas, on a quiet street across from the football field at the high school. He could have picked something a lot bigger and fancier if he'd wanted to, I suppose, but that wasn't his nature.

April Lemley answered the door when I knocked, which sort of surprised me. I didn't know her all that well except as the girl who sculpted that bronze statue of me which stands in front of the university, and what she was doing at Brandon's house I didn't have a clue.

"He's around back, Tyke, if you want to walk around the side of the house. I'm just about to head home, myself," she said.

"Sure," I agreed, and thought no more of it as I headed around back where she'd told me Brandon would be.

He was lying in a hammock strung up between two palm trees in the back yard when I got to the back fence, with both hands behind his head and bare feet crossed at the ankles while he gazed up at the clouds. He had that faraway look in his eyes that he gets sometimes, and I hated to interrupt him.

But I had to, so I opened the gate and made sure to scuff my shoes on the ground and rattle a few branches so I'd make some noise.

"Come on back, Tyke. What can I do for you?" he asked, glancing at me and then returning his attention to the sky.

"Uh. . . April said this is where I could find you," I said, as soon as I got close enough to speak in a normal voice. There were a couple of wicker chairs sitting here and there in the yard, so I grabbed one and took a seat.

"Did she? I thought she'd already left," he said.

"She was just leaving when I got here," I said.

"She comes over here now and then to fix supper for me and sometimes talk awhile if she's not too busy. Says I'm alone too much and it's not good for me. She's a sweet girl, but we're just friends," he said, answering the question which I hadn't actually asked. I wasn't quite sure what to make of such a situation, but I figured it was really none of my business anyway.

"Well. . . I think I found us a sub," I said, getting to the point.

"Did you?" he asked.

"Yeah, it's in Fort Myers. Not quite what I was hoping for but I think it'll do," I said, and proceeded to tell him all about what I'd found. He only nodded.

"Yeah, I think it'll do. We'll have to get started as soon as we can. It'll be another stealth mission against Colonel Burns' soldiers, of course, so the same basic set of selection criteria still apply. I'd like to have the same people as before, as long as you're all willing. Except for Danielle, anyway," he said.

"Why not her? Did she do something wrong?" I asked, surprised that he'd say such a thing.

"Not at all. I didn't mean to imply that I didn't want her to come or that she wouldn't be useful. What I meant was, she *needs* to stay home for a little while. You're having a boy this time, you know," he said absently, as if it were the most ordinary thing in the world.

"Huh?" I asked, too shocked to think of anything else to say.

"Just what I said. I felt him, there in the cave by the river that night. A second soul, bright and clear," he said, and I couldn't think what to say to that, either. Chris and Emily had just announced they'd be having their third child sometime late in the summer, but in spite of our talk on the way home, Danielle and I hadn't really meant to have another one *quite* so soon. He was a surprise of the first caliber, to say the least. Not that surprises are bad things, of course; they're just. . . well, surprising, that's all.

"Does she know?" I asked, sort of inanely.

"Not yet, I don't think. But that's why she won't be going along on this particular mission, and it may be that the two of you decide that you should stay home yourself for a while. Otherwise I wouldn't have said anything at all," he said.

"I don't know what I'll do," I admitted. Brandon had just cast the whole issue in a radically different light, and I was still trying to figure out all the ramifications.

"It's all right. We still have a few days for you to think about it," he said.

"Will he be healthy?" I asked diffidently. I suppose that's a question everybody wonders about, but I had more reason than most to be concerned. All of us had been exposed to a lot of ionizing radiation over the past few months out in space and even on Mars itself, not to mention long-term carbon dioxide toxicity and a dozen other environmental hazards I could think of. Let alone the anti-sleep medicine we'd all taken and that almost certainly fatal laser shot Danielle had gotten in Phoenix. None of that was good for a very small baby.

"I can't tell you about the future, Tyke. I see only what is and what ought to be. He's fine for now, if that's any comfort to you. He has auburn hair like your grandmother, and he likes the sound of water falling over stone," Brandon said, and I laughed a little at that. I'm not even really sure why; partly for simple heart's ease and partly for the incongruity of the whole thing, I suppose. I mean, honestly, how many times in the history of the world has it happened that the father is the first one to know about something like that? Much less knowing that the kid had red hair or that he liked the sound of falling water, or even that he was a *he* at such an early date, for that matter.

"What else can you tell me?" I asked, curious. It was incidentally fascinating, all these little details.

"Maybe you should wait and get to know him when the time comes," Brandon said gently, and I decided I could live with that.

"Okay, then," I agreed.

"In the meantime, I need to get ready. Your Aunt Joan is having a dinner tonight to which she specifically invited me," he said, sitting up in the hammock.

"Didn't April come over to cook tonight?" I asked.

"She did, but that was before I knew about the dinner. It's all right, though; she just gave me a rain check for another day," he said.

"All right. I'll see you later, then," I said, and that was that.

Chapter Fifteen

I walked home from Brandon's house lost in thought. It was impossible to doubt what he'd told me, but I could only imagine how Danielle would react when I got home and told *her*. She'd either laugh at the oddity of it like I had, or she'd worry, or she might even say or do something completely unexpected. She was awfully good at surprising me sometimes.

She was watching an old movie on TV when I got home, but as usual she met me at the door with a kiss and a hug as soon as she heard me come in. She looked tired, but before I could ask her what she'd been doing she had something to say.

"Philip and Joan invited us over for supper tonight, if you want to go take a shower and everything before we go," she said.

"Oh, okay. What time are we supposed to be there?" I asked.

"About six. You've still got an hour or so," she said.

"Who all's supposed to be there?" I asked.

"Jesse and Leah, Hunter and Veronica, me and you, Chris and Emily, your mom and dad, and I think maybe Brandon. Plus all the kids, of course," she said.

"Sounds like a regular party going on over there tonight," I said.

"Well, not really. Just family members, that's all," she said.

"I guess I better get ready, then. I'll be back down in a few minutes," I said, and then trotted upstairs to have a quick shower and put on some slightly more respectable clothes.

"Where are Josie and Derrick?" I asked when I got back downstairs.

"They're with your mom and dad. I asked them if they'd like to baby sit for a little while this afternoon and of course they said yes. We'll bring them home after the dinner party," she said.

"Of course," I agreed. Mama and Daddy never passed up an opportunity like that. They'd be having their own new baby in just a few months, but for now they still had to borrow ours, as Mama liked to put it sometimes.

"So how was your day? Find out anything interesting?" she asked, and I thought to myself that that probably had to rank right up there with the most stupendous understatements of all time.

"As a matter of fact I did," I agreed.

"Oh? What was it?" she asked, and I really couldn't help myself, I started laughing again in spite of all my determination to play it cool.

"What's so funny?" she asked, smiling herself but obviously clueless.

"I'll tell you, but I warn you it's kind of strange. You remember that talk we had on the way home from Deimos, when you said you'd like to give Josie a brother or a sister next year?" I asked.

"Yeah, what about it?" she asked.

"Well. . . it looks like she'll have one, long about September," I said.

"What on earth are you talking about?" she asked.

"We're having a baby, beautiful; a little boy with red hair who likes the sound of falling water," I said. Danielle was looking at me with the strangest expression on her face, like she couldn't decide if

I was playing some elaborate practical joke on her or if I'd lost my mind.

"It's true, I promise. Brandon told me," I said soberly.

"And how would *he* know such a thing?" she asked.

"He said he could feel him, that night when you got lasered outside the jail in Phoenix. He didn't say anything about it because he thought it was better for us to find out on our own," I said, and she furrowed her brows while she digested that.

"So why did he say something *now*, then? I've been starting to wonder a little, these past two weeks or so; it's not like we wouldn't have found out pretty soon anyway," she said.

"Well. . . that's got more to do with the other thing I found out today," I said.

"Which is?" she asked.

"It looks like I might have found the place where Colonel Burns' soldiers are holed up. I picked up a faint radio signal coming from the West Florida Reef, about a hundred miles southwest of Apalachicola. I also found a working sub in Fort Myers, so it looks like we'll have to mount an expedition against that place as soon as we can. We don't want to give them any more time than we have to; you never know what they might do," I explained.

"I see," she said.

"I'll stay if you want me to," I said softly, and she seemed to think about it for a few minutes.

"What does Brandon think? Does he need you to go?" she asked.

"I don't know. He didn't actually say," I admitted, and she sighed.

"Then let's ask him tonight, if he comes to the dinner. I'd rather you stay here if possible, of course, but not if it would jeopardize the mission or put the others in greater danger. That would be selfish," she finally said.

"So what if he says he needs me, then?" I asked.

"Then I'll make do, one way or another. I always do," she said.

"That you do," I agreed, and pulled her close.

"I know it's got to be done; Colonel Burns is a menace to all of us and to everything we're trying to build here. I won't let him destroy this place if there's anything I can do about it. I took the selfsame Avenger's oath that you did, to fight evil to the utmost of my strength. Sometimes that requires sacrifices, and not always easy ones," she said.

"I knew there was a reason I loved you," I said, and brushed her cheek with the back of my hand. She grasped it in her own and kissed my fingertips.

"Likewise, my love. But if it turns out that you have to go, then I want you to promise me three things," she said.

"Anything," I said staunchly.

"Don't even want to hear them first?" she asked, smiling a little.

"I trust you," I said simply.

"Well. . . I'll tell you anyway, since you can't keep them if you don't know. Number one, be as careful as you can. I know people say that kind of thing so much it hardly even means anything anymore, but I'm serious. Don't take unnecessary risks," she said.

"All right. That's fair enough," I agreed.

"Second, do whatever you can and whatever *is* necessary to finish this mission for good and all. Do your best to make certain the sacrifice is worth it," she said.

"I promise that, too," I said.

"And finally. . . think of me every night when you sleep, and I'll think of you too, and that will make us feel a little closer, I think," she said.

"You could never be farther away than right here in my heart," I said.

"Nor you," she said.

We arrived at Philip and Joan's house a little early, but then of course one of the main reasons for having a dinner party in the first place is so people can socialize. The house was packed with people and kids were underfoot everywhere, almost like it was Christmas or Thanksgiving. I hadn't actually stopped to think about it till that moment, but as I glanced at all the passing faces I realized everybody there had been together since the very beginning; survivors of the good old days at Lakeside Station or sometimes even before that. We were a tight little group after all we'd been through together, and at this point every last one of us was indeed related to Philip and Joan either by blood, marriage, or adoption.

Well. . . everybody except Johnny Weiss, that is. He was still the odd man out, not quite a part of us the way everybody else was. I wondered if he hadn't wanted to come to the dinner, since I couldn't imagine Aunt Joan neglecting to invite him, even if only out of kindness.

But then I saw Brandon in earnest conversation with Philip, and promptly forgot about what Johnny might have been doing that evening. I excused myself to hurry over and join them. Normally I wouldn't have interrupted, but these were far from normal times.

"The man of the hour himself. We were just talking about you, Tyke," Philip said, turning his head to look at me as I got closer. He gave me a bone-crushing hug and then turned me loose.

"Good stuff, I hope," I said, when I could get my breath.

"Well, yes, in a way. Brandon's been telling me you found a possible NADF base out there on the West Florida Reef and he thinks we should launch a mission against it immediately," Philip said.

"Yes, sir. I'd have to agree with that," I said, nodding.

"Unfortunately so would I," he said.

"So who all is going?" I asked.

"That depends. Have you discussed things with Danielle yet?" Brandon asked.

"Yeah, we discussed it. She said she'd like me to stay, but not if it would cut down on the chances of success or make things more dangerous for the people who did go. So she wanted me to ask you for an honest opinion about whether you need me or not," I said, and Brandon nodded as if that were exactly what he'd expected to hear.

"I've considered the matter as carefully as I can, and even though I'm sure we *could* do without you, I can't deny that you'd probably be an asset to the mission. You're the only person available who's ever actually visited the Reef or who has any kind of direct knowledge about it. It's impossible to say for sure, of course, but you never know when that kind of insight might turn out to be critical," Brandon said.

Well, that was as fair and balanced an opinion as I could have asked for, and I suppose he was right about how firsthand information concerning the reefs might turn out to be vitally important at some point. So as much as I didn't like it and as much as I knew Danielle wouldn't like it, the fact of the matter seemed to be that I needed to go.

I sighed.

"Count me in, then," I said.

"Good. Hunter and Jesse have already agreed to come along, too," Brandon said.

"So what time do we leave for *this* little expedition?" I asked.

"We're still discussing that, but it should probably be as soon as possible," Brandon said.

"I think it'll be day after tomorrow," Philip said.

"Why specifically then?" I asked.

"No particular reason, except that tomorrow is Sunday and I'd like for the four of you to be in church so we can all pray for you," Philip said, and Brandon nodded.

"Certainly," he agreed.

We didn't talk about the mission anymore during supper. Aunt Joan had gone all out and cooked a couple of roast hens; a rare treat indeed since our chickens still weren't all that numerous yet. I think that alone would have made the party a smashing success.

So everybody was jolly and seemed in good spirits, and as I've said before, happiness is an infectious thing. In spite of the looming danger ahead, it was hard not to laugh and joke along with everybody else.

It was near the end of the meal when Hunter tapped his glass with a fork.

"There's something I'd like to tell everybody," he said, speaking up for the first time.

We were still sitting around the table in the dining room, even though most of us were done eating by then. Hunter had never had a reputation for talking very much at large gatherings like that; he was the youngest person at the table by several years, and until rather recently he and Veronica both would have been relegated to the kids' table to help Tommy and Amie and Molly look after the littler ones. I think he probably still felt a little bit overawed to be counted as one of the grown-ups, so I was curious what could have prompted him to offer a comment unsolicited like that.

"What is it, Hunter?" I asked.

"Well. . . I know it may seem a little soon to some of you, but Veronica and I have decided to get married," he said.

I wasn't especially surprised, as long as those two had been together. I glanced quickly at Philip and Joan and saw that both of them were smiling, so I could only assume Hunter and Veronica had spoken to them privately ahead of time. My guess was soon proved correct when Philip stood up and held up his glass.

"Hunter and Veronica came and asked our blessing last week, which we were happy to give. They wanted to tell everybody themselves, so that's why we organized this little get-together tonight. I'm sure all of you will want to congratulate them in person, but for now I'd like to offer a toast to my beautiful daughter and the son of my heart. God bless you both," Philip said, and raised his glass. We all did likewise, to cheers of acclamation, and I suppose the surprise really *did* make it sweeter.

"So when's the big day?" Danielle asked, when the chatter had settled down a bit.

"Not till November. Mama and Daddy said we had to wait till our birthday," Veronica said.

I couldn't help thinking that was awfully wise of Philip; telling them *no* would have caused problems, but making them wait for eight more months gave them time to make sure of what they really wanted, with no harm done if they changed their minds in the meantime. I guess Philip has always been perceptive that way, but it's only been the past two years or so that I've started to notice how sharp he truly is. I didn't say anything about the way he graciously finessed what could easily have become a very thorny situation, but my respect for him went up another little notch that night.

"So it'll be the eighteenth?" Danielle asked.

"No, it'll be the twenty-third, I think. The first Saturday afterwards," Veronica said.

"Will it be at the mission church?" Danielle asked.

"Yeah, that's what we'd both like. I'd like for Johnny to play the music if he's willing," Veronica said.

"I'm sure he'd be glad to. Where *is* Johnny tonight, anyway? I would've thought Joan would have invited him," Danielle said.

"She *did* invite him, but she couldn't tell him the secret of course. So he said he was busy tonight and to save him a piece of chicken if we liked. He doesn't really care much about anything except his music, you know. Especially not when he has to socialize a lot," Veronica said.

"Yeah, I know. But I wish he could've been here anyway," Danielle said.

"Me too. But I'll save him a piece of chicken, at least," Veronica said, and they both laughed.

My attention started to wander a bit after that, so I didn't notice anything else the girls might have said about the wedding, or Johnny, or whatever else they ended up talking about. That kind of conversation tends to make my eyes glaze over after a while, to be honest. Talk to me about science or metaphysics or some *subject*, at least; then I'm fine for as long as you want to keep going. But commonplace chitchat I can only tolerate in small doses, unfortunately. I recognize it as a misfortune that I don't like such things; it makes it harder to connect with people and keeps me from getting to know certain individuals at all. But it's a trait I can't seem to change.

After the table was cleared we all went to the deck which looked out across the broad expanse of Kailua Bay to the ocean, and then sat around to socialize a while longer. But little by little people began to excuse themselves and head home, and I was beginning to contemplate doing the same thing when Philip came by my chair.

"We need you to stay a little bit after everybody leaves, if possible," he said in a low voice, and I kind of shrugged a little.

"What was that all about?" Danielle asked after he walked away. She was sitting right beside me, but she must not have heard what he said.

"He wants us to stay a little bit after everybody leaves. Not sure why," I said.

Eventually there was no one left except Jesse and Hunter, Philip and Joan, and Danielle and I, so I guessed Philip must have wanted to have an Avengers' meeting. Well, Brandon was still there, but then of course he almost counted as a seventh member, sort of.

"I'm sorry to keep everybody late like this, but I'm not sure if we'll have another opportunity to sit down and discuss the upcoming mission before Monday morning gets here. We won't be long, but I did want to go over a few things," Philip said.

"Are there any kind of actual plans set up yet?" Hunter asked.

"Yes, but there are all kinds of logistics that still have to be worked out. We have to handle this situation with the utmost care. Not only because of the danger involved, but also because we don't want any of Colonel Burns' soldiers to escape. That would defeat the whole purpose of the mission," Brandon said.

"Gotcha," Hunter said meekly.

"What we have in mind is for fifty of my best soldiers to set up a base camp at the old airport in Saint Petersburg, to monitor the situation and be ready to take appropriate action if necessary," Brandon said.

"Such as?" I asked.

"Such as immediately attacking any enemies who appear to be escaping, for example. Or to provide quick backup if it turns out we need some, which is a very real possibility. In the meantime they'll also be trying to raise and repair a bigger and better sub for us to use in the future, and also to recover the tachometer if that's feasible. If nothing else, those projects might allay suspicions if the soldiers inside the facility notice that something is going on. You might call those projects a distraction, even though both of them are legitimately important in their own right," Brandon said.

"Why not just hit them head on with everything we've got and wipe them out?" Hunter asked.

"We can't do that. Colonel Burns isn't stupid; I'm certain that facility is armed to the teeth and well-prepared to withstand almost anything we could throw at it, short of a nuclear bomb. Besides which, I'd prefer not to have to kill them unless absolutely necessary. And for that, our best hope lies in stealth," Brandon said.

"So what do we do when we actually get to the facility?" I asked.

"Part of the reason we're here tonight is to figure out that very thing, Tyke. In a general kind of way this will be a sabotage mission. Our task is very simple; to capture or kill every soldier loyal to Colonel Burns. Under no circumstances can we allow even a single one of them to remain alive and free on Earth. That may sound harsh, but it's the brutal truth. The survival of every living soul in Kona is at stake. If Colonel Burns ever gets a foothold on Earth again, he'll destroy this place and everyone who lives here, by any means necessary. To him, anyone who won't submit to his absolute authority is a subversive element, a dangerous threat to the survival of humanity. He'd never think twice about killing every last one of us if he got the chance," Brandon said.

A certain kind of gloom hung over all of us at those words, and I wished with my whole heart that Colonel Burns would simply leave us alone. I knew he never would, but I couldn't help wishing, you know.

Chapter Sixteen

"I have one idea for how we might attack the place, if we can make a quick trip into Tampa to get something," I finally said.

"Such as?" Brandon asked.

"Well, you know how they used breeder gases to help terraform the atmosphere on Venus and the Moon, right?" I asked.

"Yeah, I know," Brandon said.

"Well, I thought we might introduce some kind of gas like that into the atmosphere of the facility. It'd have all the air in such a small enclosed space converted within a few minutes at the most," I said.

"But how would that help matters, Tyke? If you converted all the air and left them with no oxygen they'd still die. We might as well just nuke them and get it over with in that case," Jesse pointed out.

"I know it couldn't be anything like *that*, Jesse. I was thinking about something else. You see, all mammals have the latent ability to go into hibernation, with the organs shut down and metabolism almost at zero. Then they don't need to eat or drink, and they don't even have to breathe for several hours. It can be triggered by inhaling the right concentration of hydrogen sulfide. All we need is something to peg that level inside the facility and it'd knock them out like flies. Then we could go in and carry them all out with no sweat," I said.

"It sounds good in theory, Tyke, but are you sure something like that could be made to work in real life?" Brandon asked skeptically.

"Yes it can. We analyzed a case study back at the Academy in one of my biochemistry classes where they did something almost exactly like that," I said.

"But who on earth would know how to make a breeder gas anymore? That's pretty complicated chemistry," Jesse pointed out.

"That I'm not sure of, but I know Colonel Burns did business with a company called Gentech in Atlanta when he had the breeder gases produced for Venus. There might be some information there. I also know that several of the grubs right here in Kona are chemists, which I'm not. Surely at least one of them might know something about it, don't you think? Or at least know where to look?" I asked, and Brandon frowned.

"Maybe," he said.

"Wouldn't it be worth finding out, at least?" I asked.

"We can ask, and if it seems feasible then we'll give it a try. The only thing that worries me is losing the element of surprise. If our first attack fails then it'll put them on guard, and then we may not have any choice but to bomb them after all," Brandon said.

"Do we even *have* a nuclear bomb?" Jesse asked.

"We most certainly do. I intend to take one along with us just in case it turns out to be necessary," Brandon said.

That silenced all of us, even though we knew it might turn out to be an unavoidable necessity.

"So what do we need to do now?" I finally asked.

"Nothing at the moment. Just be ready to go at the airport at seven o'clock Monday morning. We'll figure out the rest between now and then," Brandon said, and I could only hope that somehow this time would be the end of it all.

Monday morning dawned bright and clear, like mornings in Kona usually do, and we all left promptly at seven to squeeze in as much daylight as possible.

It turned out there was only one atmospheric chemist among the grubs at Kailua Kona, but he readily agreed that it shouldn't be any problem to design a breeder gas for catalyzing hydrogen sulfide, as long as he had the proper facilities to work with. It took quite a bit of scrambling to locate such a place, but we did eventually find a lab right across the bay in Sarasota which had all the necessary equipment.

The plan was for Jesse, Hunter, Brandon, and I to head out for Fort Myers to fetch the sub, while a handpicked cadre of grubs (including the chemist) headed for Saint Petersburg to set up the base camp and support facilities for our two-pronged assault. The idea was to have the breeder gas and the nuclear device ready to go by the time the rest of us were able to retrieve the sub.

Brandon had imposed an absolute radio blackout from the moment we took off unless it was a desperate emergency, since any kind of communication among us might alert Colonel Burns or his flunkies that something was afoot. At all costs we had to avoid putting them on guard.

That meant no communication with anybody back home, either, which made for a pretty dull flight. I was too keyed up to read or listen to music or anything like that, but there was nothing else to do except pace the floor and pretend to talk to Brandon or Hunter about whatever came to mind. Even then I was too distracted to keep up much of a conversation, so most of the time we spent in silence.

It was a little bit better once we got to Fort Myers. The Everglades had already started to reclaim huge swathes of the vacant city, and it wasn't at all easy to pick our way through streets that were choked with tropical vegetation. They were downright impassable in several places, which meant we had to get out and clear a path with machetes and hand lasers before we could get through at all.

Gator World itself was about a mile south of town at the edge of the sea, and it was in pretty sad shape, I have to say. Part of the entrance sign had blown down at some point, and as usual everything was heavily overgrown. But nevertheless we soon made it through to the windowless barn-like building where the sub was kept, finding our way forward with flashlights since it was almost impenetrably dark inside.

But the *Manatee* was still there, floating serenely at a wooden dock with wheelchair ramps for easy access.

"Do you really think this old tub will still run?" Jesse asked skeptically.

"I don't see any reason why not. But all we can do is try it and see," I said.

It was immediately obvious that the *Manatee* had been a tourist vessel. Purely aside from those big picture windows that lined each side, the plush red cloth seats and soft carpet would have given *that* much away, I think. I don't imagine most working subs can boast their very own pricey Coke machines and snack dispensers, either. There were twenty seats, arranged back-to-back down the middle in order to give the best view out the windows, a set of restrooms and an engine room in the back, and a small control area up front where the pilot and the hostess were supposed to sit.

Jesse wasn't really all that familiar with undersea vehicles, but we reasoned that at least some of his piloting skills ought to transfer. They were both discontinuous 3-D environments with similar steering requirements, and he was used to having to deal with light and pressure changes from space. In any case, he was the best we had; none of the soldiers from Mars or Venus had any naval training either.

The door was wonderfully quick and easy to seal up; I suppose so the day-trippers wouldn't get claustrophobic while they waited to get in and out. As soon as we were sure the watertight seal was properly engaged, Jesse sat down in the pilot's chair and started fiddling with buttons and switches.

"Seems like she's in top-notch condition, surprisingly," he admitted after a while.

"That's good to hear," I said.

"She's rated for no more than two hundred and eighty feet in depth, though. How deep are the Pinnacles, Tyke?" Jesse asked.

"Um. . . the base is about three hundred, and the tops are about two forty, give or take a little," I said.

"That's not good. It's never smart to exceed your pressure rating, especially not with all these windows to have to worry about," Jesse said.

"Do you think they'll crack if we go down to three hundred?" Brandon asked.

"I'm not sure. They might hold up or they might not; I don't know how much leeway the designers built in. It'll *probably* be okay, but I'd hate to find out the hard way exactly how far we can push her," Jesse said.

"We shall see," Brandon said, and that was all we said about it.

Jesse powered up and gradually eased us out of the berth into deeper water. The *Manatee* gave no trouble, and for a while I could almost imagine we were really on a tourist excursion to look at fish and corals.

It took several days to creep our way northward along the coast, and then we had to put ashore at base camp for another three days while the grubs went over every inch of the *Manatee* with a fine-toothed comb, making sure there were no hidden problems that might trip us up at a bad moment. We loaded enough food for a week, scuba gear, various weapons, and any other equipment we could think of which might be useful in a pinch, not to mention they installed an airlock. The *Manatee* already had desalinization equipment to produce its own fresh water; a feature which surprised me but which I was glad to note.

Just before we left, our chemist friend brought us a small aluminum canister full of gas, which he handled like it might explode at any second.

"Do *not* spill this. There's enough gas in there to poison half the people on this base before the wind could disperse it," he warned, with the most serious look on his face you could ever have imagined.

"There's nothing we could do to counteract it?" I asked. I was a little scared by the thought of it, honestly. No matter how careful you may be, accidents can always happen to anybody.

"No there isn't, except to get fresh air. Most people would probably recover within a few hours to a few days, of course, but in the meantime it would throw a major monkey wrench into our plans and severely jeopardize our mission here. Believe me, it would *really* be best not to spill any in the first place," he said earnestly.

"I'll do my best," I said, and he nodded.

"Now, here's how this will need to be handled. There are actually two gases inside this container. One of them contains sulfur atoms attached to a catalyst which is designed to split water molecules. That gas will instantly react to produce hydrogen sulfide when it comes in contact with water vapor, but not until then. Availability of hydrogen from the water molecules is the limiting factor in that reaction; that's why the hydrogen sulfide won't reach poisonous levels. It'll be just enough to induce hibernation without killing anybody, as long as our estimates of the relative humidity inside the facility are roughly correct," he said.

"And the other gas?" I asked, eyeing the canister.

"That one works similarly, except that it will bind with the oxygen in the atmosphere instead of the water vapor. It's designed to convert oxygen into carbon dioxide. Neither of these is a true breeder gas; they're strictly self-limiting, just in case. Just remember that after you open this canister inside an enclosed area, everybody will either hibernate or die from suffocation," the man said.

With that final ominous warning, the man offered me the canister. It was about the size of a can of beans, triple-sealed and glistening brightly in the sun. I took it gingerly, wondering if maybe my brilliant idea might not be such a great plan after all.

The grubs hadn't managed to find the tachometer yet, but they *had* been able to raise and repair one of the naval subs at the Yards, giving us an additional undersea vehicle to add to our little fleet. As soon as he heard that, Brandon ordered them to monitor the Pinnacles closely for a signal from us that it was safe to approach and pick up the (hopefully) hibernating soldiers. It wouldn't have been wise for them to go anywhere near that area until we'd finished doing our job. The *Manatee* was small enough that it could slip around unnoticed, but we couldn't do that with a huge vessel like the *Lorelei;* the neutrino emissions from her nuclear reactor alone would give her away from a hundred miles off.

After this little adventure was over we had every intention of keeping the *Lorelei* for future needs, even though we all knew it would take weeks at the very least before a skeleton crew could get it moved from Saint Petersburg to Kailua Bay. The canals in Panama and at Lake Nicaragua were long since defunct since the plague struck, so that meant we'd have to take the old-fashioned route, all the way around Cape Horn at the southern tip of South America. Even at top speed, that's a really long way for a sub to have to travel. I couldn't help being glad I wouldn't be asked to go along on *that* trip.

"You know something I just thought of?" Hunter asked as we walked back to the *Manatee.*

"What's that, Hunter?" I asked.

"None of those dudes down there in that base are immune to the Orion Strain. If we go down there without making sure we're not carrying any spores then we'll kill them," he said, and at that we all stopped in our tracks.

"You're absolutely right; I can't believe we forgot about that," Jesse said.

"It's easy for us to forget about it at this point, since it can't affect us anymore. But I guess that does leave us with a really serious question, now doesn't it?" Brandon said.

"Which is?" I asked.

"What do we do with those folks down there if we capture them? We can't keep them on Earth even if we wanted to, not unless we gave them the vaccine," Brandon said. His tone of voice suggested that he wouldn't even consider such a thing as *that*, and I was in full agreement with him. But it did leave us with a serious problem.

"Maybe we could leave them on the *Eastern Star*," Jesse suggested, referring to the oil rig where we'd first lived after coming back to Earth. It was eighty miles offshore from Tampa and safely out of reach of Orion spores, or at least it *had* been; I wasn't so sure it still would be.

"I'm not sure about that, Jesse," Brandon said, furrowing his brow.

"We could make sure they didn't have any biohazard gear or even a boat. Seems like a good place to me; they'd be safe, but they'd never escape," Jesse said.

"So you think. But people are really good at finding ways to do really hard things, especially when they've got plenty of time to think about it. Besides which, in another fifteen years or so the spores will be mostly gone except for in cold places. Then there wouldn't be anything stopping them from floating to shore on a piece of plastic foam if they had to. We wouldn't be containing them forever if we put them on one of the rigs; only for a few years at the most. Then if they were able to find or steal a space vehicle they could easily bring down Colonel Burns' entire army on our heads," Brandon said.

"They might not be safe there anymore in the first place. I've already reconstituted eleven species of birds in the past few years. None of them have spread this far yet I don't *think*, but you never know. They might carry spores on their feathers," I pointed out, and Jesse shrugged in defeat.

"So what else do we do with these people, then?" he asked.

"We could take them back to Mars and drop them off," I suggested, even though I didn't much like the idea.

"No, absolutely not. It would be suicidally stupid to put any kind of space vehicle within Colonel Burns' reach, even for an hour. Or Colonel Bartow either, for that matter," Brandon said. He sounded absolutely firm about that much, and I decided it wasn't worth arguing about. After all, he had a point; I'd seen more than once how crafty Colonel Burns could be. Then inspiration hit, and I laughed.

"What's so funny?" Hunter asked.

"There's one place we can take them where we'll never have to worry about them ever again, but we don't have to come within a million miles of Colonel Burns," I said.

"And that is?" Brandon asked.

"We can drop them off on the Moon. There are no spores on the islands up there; I know that for sure. We can leave them on one of those for a while, and then if they find a way to the mainland after fifteen or twenty years it won't matter anyway," I said.

"But we can't leave them on the Moon, Tyke. You always told us it'll run out of air soon because the gravity is too low and it lets the atmosphere leak away into space. That was the whole reason *we* couldn't stay there, remember?" Hunter objected.

"Yes, but it won't be unbreathable for at least eighty or a hundred years yet. I doubt any of them will live long enough to have to worry about thin air. We'll keep an eye on them with the telescope, and if it turns out they have any kids up there then we can always go rescue the younger ones later if we need to," I said, and the others were silent for a while, digesting that.

"I guess that could work," Brandon said at length.

"Well, in the meantime don't we really need to focus on capturing them first?" Hunter pointed out. And since that was after all good sense, we all got moving again.

I was relieved when the *Manatee* slipped below the waterline, since I felt a little bit safer carrying around that dangerous little canister of gas. The idea that you're holding something in your very own hands which has the power to kill people if mishandled is kind of a sinister thought. I consoled myself with the thought that even if some kind of accident happened while we were underwater then at least we had scuba gear close at hand so maybe we wouldn't have to breathe the stuff.

We diligently irradiated everything inside the ship with hard ultraviolet to cleanse it of any spores, and then it was time to head out.

Chapter Seventeen

Most of the Gulf normally has very clear water, especially around western Florida, and that simplified our journey a little bit since Jesse didn't dare use any kind of navigation which might give away our position. He had to do things the old fashioned way, with manual controls and only his eyes and a compass to guide him. That wasn't too hard as long as the water was clear and the weather was good, and since it wasn't hurricane season we had every right to think there wouldn't be any problems of *that* nature at least.

Nor were there. We glided north across the white-sand sea bottom, the better to conceal our approach just in case anybody happened to be looking.

We approached the Pinnacles late that same evening after leaving Tampa Bay, and we had no trouble at all seeing them through the clear water. They reminded me of a mesa out in the desert, rearing up in sheer and sudden cliffs from the otherwise pancake-flat plain, and then more or less flattish on top. The entire reef is almost three quarters of a mile long but only about five hundred feet wide, stretching along the old Pleistocene coastline in a narrow ribbon about the same height as a six-storey building. Not really very big, perhaps, but still pretty darned impressive when you see it from below.

We were far enough down that the light had faded to a deep and royal blue, making the whole world look strange and alien. It reminded me a little bit of Venus, if only the sands had been black instead of white and the sun had been a blazing holocaust of fire above our heads. Down there we couldn't even *see* the sun, except as a vaguely lighter patch up on the surface. So far we hadn't encountered any problems because of the pressure at that depth, but I knew without asking that Jesse was still uneasy about it.

He took us quietly into a cleft near the top of the mesa which was big enough to conceal the *Manatee*, and there he stopped.

"So what do we do now?" he asked, and that was indeed a good question. We'd detected faint radio signals coming from the Pinnacles several times during our journey there, and we'd managed to fix their position down almost at the southern end of the reef, on the northeast face where the cliffs were steepest. Now came the really hard part of the mission.

"We'll have to leave the *Manatee* here and then see what we can find out on foot with the scuba gear. Then we'll move on from there," Brandon said.

"But how? We can't just go up to the front gate and knock on the door," Hunter said.

"Nor do I intend to try. What I'd like to do is find a place where we can cut through the wall of the facility and get inside without alerting them," Brandon said.

I guess Hunter must have thought it might sound disrespectful to ask the same question twice, but Jesse had no such compunctions.

"How do we do that, though?" he asked.

"We'd have to build a small airlock of our own, so we don't cause flooding. But I'm afraid it might be hard to find a place like that. Tyke, what's the structure of this reef like?" Brandon asked.

"Well. . . it's a reef, you know. Calcium carbonate for the most part, along with some silicates also. I guess you could think of it as a loose mixture of chalk and glass, fairly soft and easily fractured, full of caves and empty space," I said.

"And therefore not very strong, correct?" he asked.

"It wouldn't be my first choice as a building material, no. At least not compared to granite or some other really tough rock like that. It wouldn't hold up very well over the long haul," I said.

"So it probably wouldn't be stable if you tried to dig a lot of holes in it?" Brandon said.

"Well. . . I wouldn't think you'd want to do any more drilling than you had to. You'd be risking a major collapse, either immediately or later on. I'm sure everything could be shored up and stabilized as construction went on, but you still have to dig the hole first before you can do anything with it," I said.

"Okay, so what I'm thinking is that they wouldn't want to make a lot of holes through this crumbly rock for antennas and vents and all those type things. They'd want to use the same opening for as many different functions as possible, right?" Brandon said.

"Maybe, but how does that help us? It just means there won't be as many openings for us to find. Seems like that would be a bad thing," Jesse said.

"It's not *entirely* a good thing. But they still have to have openings for things they wouldn't want to put near the airlocks, like radio antennas or sewage and coolant outflows. If those things are all bundled together in one place then maybe the opening would be big enough for us to use," Brandon said.

"I see," I said. It was a halfway decent idea, actually, if our guesses were right. But as usual, the devil would unquestionably be in the details.

"I can try to detect any thermal irregularities; that should tell us where the coolant outflows are located. We don't have the equipment to test for water quality," Jesse said.

"Go for it, then," I said, and he turned back to the *Manatee's* computer to tap in a few codes. It didn't take him long to get a readout.

"Nothing that stands out enough to be worth mentioning, guys. Sorry," he finally said.

"They must have shielded it somehow. I should have expected that," Brandon said.

"Well, rats. Is there anything else we could check for?" Hunter asked.

"Not that I can think of," Jesse said, and Brandon could only shrug. I knew he hadn't given up because he was still lost in thought, and I was trying my darnedest to come up with something myself.

Maybe it's true what Brandon said about how knowing too much can hinder your creativity sometimes. However that may be, it was Hunter who finally came up with the solution to our problem.

"This place is made out of metal, isn't it?" he finally asked.

"Yeah, I'm sure it is. Why do you ask?" I asked.

"Well, I got to thinking. Couldn't we check the magnetic field?" he asked.

I knew what he was talking about; magnetic metals cause small but detectable local fluctuations in the earth's magnetic field; little deformities, so to speak. Especially when you've got pure metal involved, and even more especially when there's a lot of it. Unfortunately, there was a major problem with that plan.

People who don't know any better (like Hunter), tend to assume that *all* metals are magnetic, but they aren't. In fact, out of all the metals in the universe, there are only three which are: iron, nickel, and cobalt, and none of those are common building materials anymore. Most structures are made of aluminum nowadays because it won't rust and it's also lighter and cheaper. But it's also completely non-magnetic, and that's why it never would have crossed my mind to think of checking the local magnetic field.

But on the other hand, iron isn't *completely* obsolete as a construction material, so it was possible that certain parts of the facility might still contain some. It was worth a try, at least. With a bit of luck, we could have the *Manatee's* computer build up a magnetic resonance image of all the iron inside the Pinnacles and overlay it with a bathymetric image of the rock itself. That ought to tell us exactly where the facility touched the surface at any and all points.

"You're a genius, Hunter," Jesse said, turning eagerly back to the computer.

The *Manatee* didn't have the most powerful computer on the planet, of course, nor the most sensitive magnetic detectors for that matter. But they ought to be sufficient for the purpose, if we gave them enough time.

"How long will it take before we get some results, Jesse?" Brandon asked.

"Just a second; it's giving me an estimate right now," Jesse said, and then he sighed.

"What is it?" I asked.

"Looks like it'll take this slowpoke computer about five hours to analyze all the data," Jesse said.

"Well. . . a little patience never killed anybody," Brandon said.

And with that we had to be content.

In the meantime we weren't idle, of course. We went out and explored the reef, just in case the magnetic analysis didn't pan out.

I'd never been to that particular section of the reefs before, but it looked very much like what I remembered from other areas. Walls of pale knobby stone, pockmarked here and there with holes of various sizes and depressions full of sandy grit. But nothing much alive, except for the fish. There were lots of *those,* at least, of all shapes and sizes and colors. The tops of the Pinnacles are about a hundred feet deeper than most recreational divers like to go, so they'd never been a popular spot for visitors. Especially not when there were shallower, prettier, and much more interesting things to see within a day's drive or so. The reefs that once surrounded the entire Gulf may be mostly dead nowadays, but you can still find bits and pieces of them still living, in the Florida Keys and at the Flower Garden Banks offshore from Galveston. I'd been to Key Largo to visit the one down there on a field trip once, but of course that wasn't the kind of trip the Academy could arrange very often because of the distance.

Still, I remembered it very well, and if I closed my eyes I could easily imagine what the Pinnacles must have looked like, way back in its glory days. It gave me a wistful kind of feeling, especially when I looked at the place as it was in the present. I guess it's true what they say about how nothing lasts forever, but I've often wondered why such an obvious fact as that should make the heart ache. You'd think loss and change would be things we're so accustomed to that we'd never blink an eye at them, wouldn't you? It's rather like finding a fish which is constantly surprised at the wetness of water or a man blind from birth who keeps complaining about the dark.

And yet we do it anyway, and nothing seems to cure us of it. I suppose Philip would have said it's only the yearning for heaven, the place where all things endure forever.

So much philosophy, just from a dead reef.

I didn't have much to do during our little excursion except to ponder those kinds of things. We couldn't talk to each other since we still weren't using radio, so our only method of communication was via hand signals. You can convey a certain amount of information that way, but not enough to hold a conversation. That left me with a lot of time to think.

Brandon took the nuclear device with us and planted it deep inside one of the many holes in the reef where hopefully it wouldn't be noticed. There was no chance of an accidental explosion; it could only be detonated by means of a remote-control mechanism which was safely back home in Kailua Kona. If our mission failed, then we'd have no choice but to give up and push the button. The bomb was only about the size of a briefcase, but I knew all too well that it packed a vicious punch for something so small. That bomb was capable of utterly destroying the Pinnacles and everything inside them, leaving nothing but a mile-wide crater like the one in Memorial Park in Tampa.

It would also create a huge tsunami which was liable to devastate the entire shoreline of the Gulf from Florida all the way around to

Campeche, very likely wiping Clearwater completely off the map in the process. I don't think I'm overly sentimental, but the thought of utterly destroying my home town was hard to stomach, you know. Even though we hadn't lived there in years, it still carried a lot of memories. For that reason among many others, I dearly hoped the hydrogen sulfide worked and we never had to detonate that bomb.

We didn't find anything particularly interesting until shortly before it was time to head back to the *Manatee,* and then Jesse came across a metal antenna sticking up out of the rock. He motioned for us to come over, and soon we were all looking at the spot. It was an almost completely flat area on top of the reef, covered with rippled sand which reminded me of the shelf-plain far below us at the bottom of the cliffs. It was kind of unusual since most of that region was made of lumpy rock, but it gave me an idea.

I swam down next to the antenna to sweep sand away from the base of it with my hands, and sure enough I soon uncovered a metal surface about two inches under the grit. As soon as the others saw it they moved in and started clearing sand themselves, and before long we'd unearthed a smooth aluminum square about six feet wide, with the antenna projecting from the southwest corner of it.

Then Brandon signaled for us to cover it back up and return to the *Manatee.*

"That may be our way inside," he said, as soon as the water began to drain from the airlock. I didn't even have my mask off yet.

"You think so?" Jesse asked.

"Hopefully. We can cut our way in with the hand lasers, and I'm sure there's an access path to let people reach that antenna and whatever lines and equipment are needed to support it," Brandon said.

"Then what are we waiting for? Let's get started!" Hunter said eagerly.

"Not so fast, kid. Wait a little bit for the computer to finish imaging everything, so maybe we'll know for sure what we've got to deal with. Then we'll see," Brandon said.

"Oh, okay," Hunter said.

"Don't worry; it'll happen sooner than you think," Brandon said, a little more kindly.

The *Manatee's* computer had already finished running its scan by the time we got back from our expedition, and we were rewarded with a ghostly gray image of all the iron and steel inside the Pinnacles. There wasn't much of it, I'm afraid; a few bolts and structural members, and here and there some part which I couldn't identify. We couldn't glean many details from such sparse data except for the rough size and shape of the facility, but under the circumstances that was good enough. We did discover that metal touched the surface at three places; a large airlock on the northeast face, a smaller one on the southwest, and then the antenna which we'd found up top. There appeared to be a tube or passageway of some kind leading from there down to the main part of the facility, but that was only a guess.

"All right, boys; I think it'll work. Let's get started," Brandon said, looking at the model.

The first thing we had to do was to build a temporary airlock next to the antenna to keep water out. That isn't really so hard; you just have to create an airtight chamber which is strong enough to hold up to the pressures involved, with a door so you can get in and out and a tough pump. I'd seen it done after the hull breach on the *Alabama,* and more recently on the *Manatee.* It's mostly a matter of choosing the right materials and making sure you don't leave any holes or weak spots which might give way at a bad time.

We'd brought metal and other materials with us specifically for that purpose, and Jesse moved the *Manatee* right next to the workspace so we wouldn't have to struggle with hauling heavy pieces of sheet metal over long distances. Then we wasted no time getting to work. Lasers don't work quite as well underwater as they would in air or space, but we managed well enough. When we finished we had an ugly but usable airlock, and that was all that mattered. Brandon motioned for us to go inside, and as soon as we did he shut the door and sealed it behind us. It would have been dark as the inside of an elephant's belly in there if Jesse hadn't switched on his headlamp, since we hadn't had time or materials to install such frills as lighting.

But he did, and soon the pump was running and gradually emptying the chamber of water. I had to manually release air from a compressed tank to make up the difference, since the whole idea was to match pressure inside the facility. Well, that and keep our rickety lock from having to withstand any more force than absolutely necessary. Catastrophic failure is what they call it when an airlock collapses from the strain of too much pressure, which is a nice way of saying you'll get instantly crushed like a tin can under a sledgehammer.

Jesse and I used to smash empty aluminum cans against our foreheads sometimes to prove how tough we were, back in the days when we were still young and silly enough to think stuff like that looked cool. But I don't think I was ever silly enough to think it would be cool to get crushed inside the can myself, not even when I was in junior high.

My momentary reverie was interrupted by a sound like somebody sucking the last bit of a drink through a straw, and I glanced down to see that the pump had finished emptying the chamber of water. We couldn't quite get it all, of course; there was still about a quarter inch of liquid sloshing around our feet. But that was good enough to suit the purpose.

We hunkered down and got to work with the hand lasers again, cutting a hole in the floor just large enough for a person to slip through. The metal was several inches thick, like a ship's hull, and it was no easy business to slice through it. There was a sudden whistling suction of equalizing pressures when we finally punched through, but I must have judged the difference pretty well because it wasn't anything major. As soon as we had the hole cut open, we all four slipped down inside the facility one by one.

We were finally inside.

Chapter Eighteen

We found ourselves in a cramped room full of wires and electronics gear, most of which I wouldn't have recognized even if somebody had told me what it was. There was a spiral staircase leading straight down through the rock below us, and since there was no other way to go, that was obviously the way we had to use.

We all had our masks off by then, even though we still kept them handy. We'd have to put them back on again as soon as we released the breeder gas into the atmosphere, unless we wanted to end up knocked out on the floor ourselves.

"Should we go ahead and release the gas since we're inside?" Hunter whispered.

"No, not yet. Let's make sure there are no gastight doors between here and the main part of the facility before we do that. But we can go ahead and break two of the seals. That way we can get it open in a hurry if we need to," Brandon said, also whispering.

It sounded like a good plan, so I took out the little canister and carefully twisted the seals open, leaving only the last one. Then we headed down the spiral stair, Brandon in the lead and me right behind him, with Hunter and then Jesse bringing up the rear. We all had lasers, of course, even though I hoped desperately that it wouldn't come to a fight. The whole purpose of all this cloak and dagger business was to save lives, not to destroy them. Otherwise we could have simply nuked the facility as soon as we found out about it and never had to worry about the matter.

The staircase seemed to go on forever, although of course I know it couldn't have. We tried to step lightly to keep from rattling and clanging against the metal frame, so maybe that's partly why it seemed to take so long. But we did eventually reach the bottom, and sure enough, there was a steel bulkhead door down there. I suppose it was a safety feature just in case the antenna region ever developed a leak, but it would definitely have stopped the breeder gas cold in its tracks. Maybe not forever; watertight isn't quite the same thing as gastight, after all. But long enough to wreck our carefully calibrated plan.

There was a wheel we had to turn to get the heavy door unsealed before we could open it, and that was a dicey proposition since we didn't know what was on the other side. I could vividly imagine it leading directly into a large control room with a dozen armed soldiers who'd notice movement the instant the wheel started to turn. In that case there was no telling what they might do. But on the other hand, turning the wheel a millimeter an hour in the hope that it wouldn't be noticed might easily backfire too.

Sometimes you have no other choice but to base a decision on incomplete information, unfortunately. Or sometimes no information at all, as in our case. I hate having to make blind guesses like that, knowing the results could be disastrous. But as I said, sometimes you simply don't have any other option. Brandon grabbed hold of the wheel and started to turn it, slow enough to make as little noise as possible but still at a pretty fair clip, gambling that there was no one on the other side to see.

That particular gamble we won; the door swung open on well-oiled hinges to reveal a control room indeed, but there were no soldiers lounging around as I'd feared. Instead the place seemed deserted, although it couldn't have been completely; some kind of readout was scrolling quietly across a large computer screen on the far wall.

Then I noticed a single grub sitting in a chair with his back turned to us, apparently oblivious to the fact that we'd entered the room. The control room seemed to be a central location from which passageways radiated out like spokes on a wheel, from the little that I could tell.

Then Brandon tapped my shoulder.

"Release the gas," he said. Well, he didn't really *say* it, he just mouthed the words and I read his lips, but I nodded to let him know I understood. We all had our faceplates back on, so there was no more reason to wait. I unscrewed the final seal on the canister, and even though I knew the gas was a precision tool designed for this very mission, it still gave me a cold shiver as I watched the white vapor begin to hiss out. It disappeared almost instantly as it left the canister, and at first it seemed that nothing had happened. I knew it was spreading swiftly even while we stood there and already beginning to convert the atmosphere into CO_2 and hydrogen sulfide, but for a while the results wouldn't be obvious. According to Jesse, it should take exactly eight minutes and forty-three seconds from the time we released the gas until the time it finished its conversion. That may not sound like much, but you'd be surprised how long eight minutes can seem when you're waiting. We couldn't leave without finding out whether or not the plan had worked, because then we'd either have to call the *Lorelei* to come pick up our unconscious enemies, or else we'd know it was time to go home and detonate the bomb instead.

But it wasn't fated that we should have an easy time of it. Two minutes after we released the gas, another grub walked into the control room from one of the spoke-like passages, carrying what could only have been a cup of coffee. It took a split second for our presence to register, I guess, but as soon as it did he dropped the cup with a cry of alarm, spilling steaming black liquid all over the metal floor.

The open control room was a bad place for any kind of fight, surrounded as we were by open corridors from which enemies could attack us on every side. All four of us knew *that* much, and we were running for cover even before the last drops of coffee had left the cup.

They probably didn't quite dare use high-powered lasers inside a facility like that for fear of punching an irreparable hole in the wall in some place where it might cause serious or even fatal structural damage. Sort of like throwing rocks inside a glass house, I guess you could say, to put a new twist on an old metaphor. But they *did* have stunners, and that coffee-drinking grub must have been incredibly quick on the draw. Before we made it even halfway back to the bulkhead door I saw Brandon stumble and fall unconscious.

The other man at the computer must have hit the alarm even before he reached for his own weapon, because suddenly we were surrounded by the shrieking of an alarm klaxon. Hunter fell next, and then Jesse. I remember thinking those dudes must have been expert marksmen, and then that was the last thought I had a chance to have. I fell to the deck a split second after Jesse and knew no more.

It must have been about thirty minutes later when I opened my eyes; stunner fire doesn't last much longer than that. My head was killing me, just like the one and only other time I've ever been shot with a weapon like that. Maybe not *quite* as bad as that other time; this grub must have been a much better shot than the last one had been, because I could feel the numb spot where he'd nailed me on my hip. That explained the marginally less painful headache, at least, even though it still hurt like somebody had cut open my skull with a rusty knife and then dumped a tray full of red-hot coals inside. A really *big* tray.

I curled up in a ball and suffered in silence till the pain started to fade away after a few centuries. The alarm klaxon was still blaring and that didn't help matters, but finally I recovered enough to open my eyes and get unsteadily to my feet again.

I found myself in the center of a thick brownish fog, and realized vaguely that I couldn't see. I honestly didn't have the sense to think very clearly yet, but I knew well enough that it's nothing uncommon for stunner shots to scramble your brain for a little while, up to and including temporary loss of vision. All I had to do was wait for the effects to wear off. I knew all that, but in the meantime you'd be amazed how crippling it is to be blind.

I listened carefully and heard nothing; no movement, no weapons fire, nothing. I had no way of knowing how long it had been since we released the gas, but it had to have been longer than nine minutes by then. There was no telling how long it might take before the facility's air purifier could restore a breathable atmosphere, nor how long after that before some or all of the grubs started to wake up. They'd be asleep for a few hours, no doubt, but I didn't have time to sit on my hands and wait for my eyes to recover before I did something. The grubs in St. Petersburg had to be notified immediately or else there might not be time for them to get there before the gas wore off.

That was easier said than done, though. I remembered seeing the others fall, so I got down on all fours and started to feel my way across the floor to see if I could find them. I reasoned that they had to still be knocked out or else they would have been the ones who came to find *me,* and therefore they were probably still lying where they fell.

Presently my left hand touched somebody in a wetsuit, and I quickly discovered that his faceplate must have been knocked off when he hit the floor. That explained why he was still knocked out, if he'd been breathing the hydrogen sulfide. I couldn't tell who he was just from touching his face, and I couldn't have seen him even if he'd been half an inch in front of me.

He wasn't breathing, whoever he was, and when I checked his pulse he didn't seem to have one. In any other situation that would have scared me, but in this particular instance I knew his body had been shoved into deep hibernation mode by the gas. He *definitely* wouldn't be waking up anytime soon, so I left him alone and tried to locate the others.

I finally did, only to find that both of them were in similar shape. It must have been only a freak of the way I landed that kept me from losing my own faceplate when I hit the floor, since all three of the others had lost theirs.

I was at a loss for what to do at that point, actually. I didn't have Brandon to tell me what the smartest choice would have been, and I didn't even have Jesse or Hunter to talk it over with. I was all on my own, blind as a bat and stuck in a cave full of people who were at least clinically dead. That's not a good situation, to put it mildly.

Nor could I think of any way to signal the grubs in St. Petersburg to come get us. The tiny radio in my faceplate wouldn't reach that far, and I couldn't figure out how to use the one at the facility when I couldn't see. Blindly pushing buttons on the computer didn't seem like a very smart move.

On the other hand, I couldn't get back to the *Manatee,* either. Our makeshift airlock up on the roof was practically useless till I could reseal the hole we'd made, and that was impossible with no eyes. Nor did I know where the regular airlock for the station might be, and even if I did somehow locate it I wouldn't dare try to find my way back to the *Manatee* from there just by touch.

I sighed and wondered how I ever managed to get myself into such deep holes at times.

But nevertheless the clock was ticking, so I finally decided my best bet was to try to fix the hole in our original airlock. If I could get that one to work, then the *Manatee* was right outside. I crawled in the general direction I thought the bulkhead door should have been and finally found it, and after that it wasn't hard to get it shut and sealed behind me. I didn't dare leave it open just in case I punctured the lock and caused a flood, but I dearly hoped that didn't happen. Then I started climbing stairs, not caring a bit about whether I made noise or not this time.

Everything in that part of the base was small enough and close enough together that I could cope fairly well with only my hands to guide me, even to the point of finding the hole in the ceiling which led back up into the airlock.

Then I was balked by a ridiculous thing. I couldn't remember what Jesse had done with the piece of metal we'd cut out to get inside, and without it I had nothing to fix the hole with. It wasn't inside the airlock, and even though I knew it had to be somewhere in the room with me, I could *not* find it.

Then I thought of one possible solution. A very risky, potentially fatal solution, but the only one that offered any hope at all.

I mentioned earlier that catastrophic failure of an airlock is a really bad thing, and that's true as far as it goes. But all else being equal, it's much harder on your body when pressure suddenly drops than when it suddenly increases. Neither situation is *good,* but on the whole I'd much rather deal with the hazards of compression rather than those of decompression.

What I had in mind was to fire my hand laser up through the hole in the ceiling and hopefully cause a catastrophic failure of that flimsy airlock. What would happen then would be that water would start pouring through the hole in a high-powered jet, quickly filling up everything from the bulkhead door up to where I stood. The grubs had maintained the facility at a pressure of one atmosphere, more or less, and the pressure underneath 260 feet of water is more than eight times as much. That's a lot of pressure differential. It was going to squeeze me hard and it probably wasn't going to feel too good, but as long as I stayed out of the way of collapsing metal and rushing water, I ought to survive.

I hoped.

There was nothing to do but try it, so I tore loose some heavy wire that ran to the antenna and tied myself securely to the wall so I wouldn't get swept away. Then I stood as far to one side as possible and felt for the edge of the hole. As soon as I found it, I pointed my laser up through the opening. Then I pressed the button.

For almost a full second nothing happened, and then almost instantly the water came rushing in, shooting out of the hole like a high-pressure fire hose and knocking me off my feet. If I hadn't been tied to the wall then I would have gotten swept away down the stairs almost instantly. But the wire held, and I quickly pulled myself as far away from the current as I could, climbing up on top of some metal containers in the corner. I couldn't see the water at all, but I could sure *hear* it well enough to give me a vivid idea of what it must have looked like. The torrent was flowing in so fast that I could already feel the pressure starting to rise in the room. It felt like getting compressed from all sides and slowly suffocating, and even worse than that it *hurt.* I felt a sharp *pop* as both my eardrums burst inward, and then almost as quickly as it began, it was over. Pressure equalized, and I was left with two throbbing earaches and a body which felt like somebody had used it for a punching bag.

There's no sensation quite like being blind *and* deaf at the same time, I promise you. All I had left was touch, and that tells you precious little.

There was still air in the room, but it must have been leaking away through the hole as water kept pouring in to replace it. When I ventured out of my corner to test the matter, I found that the current had slowed until it was more like a waterfall than a fire hose at that point, though it was still much too intense for me to even think about fighting it. I had to wait for almost twenty minutes while it filled the remainder of the antenna room and the flow finally stopped.

During that time I finally started to get at least a little bit of my eyesight back. It was still blurry and full of fog and I could barely see a shapeless blob when I held my hand in front of my face. I couldn't have guessed how many fingers I was holding up to save my life, but it was still much, *much* better than nothing.

As soon as the water stopped flowing, I was able to untie myself from the wire and climb out through the hole.

All I can say is, I'm glad I wasn't inside the airlock when the water came in. The steel door itself had been wrenched off its hinges, and the rest of the structure had almost collapsed from the force. I thought again of those aluminum cans Jesse and I used to like to crush against our foreheads, and shivered.

At long last I made it back to the *Manatee,* and none too soon, either; my air gauge said that I had less than thirty minutes of time left in my tank. But that didn't matter anymore, and I gratefully pulled off my faceplate to breathe some semi-fresh air for the first time in hours.

But there was no time to relax, and even though I was practically deaf as a post, I could still talk. I went immediately to the pilot's chair and keyed the radio, sending out the strongest broadcast possible to tell the grubs in St. Petersburg what the situation was and to get to the Pinnacles as soon as possible.

I know they answered because the light beside the speaker came on, even though I couldn't hear whatever it was they said. I interrupted the speaker and told him what happened to my ears and that he might as well not waste his breath talking to me, but I'd get back to him if anything else happened. I guess he must have taken me at my word, because that was the last time the speaker light came on.

The grubs could make the journey much faster than the *Manatee* ever could have, of course; the *Lorelei* was a much faster vessel for one thing, and besides that they didn't have to worry about being stealthy. But even so, it would still be at least two hours before they arrived, and in the meantime I intended to make good use of the time. The pilot's chair was the largest and cushiest spot on the entire ship, so I leaned way back with my feet up on the computer screen, and promptly went to sleep.

Chapter Nineteen

Several hours passed, and by the time the *Lorelei* arrived I was at least semi-rested and I could more or less see again. My ears were no better, of course, but it would take at least a week or so before my eardrums could grow back. In the meantime I'd just have to carry around a notepad and a pen. It was aggravating, but I guess there are worse things.

The grubs had to break into the facility with no help from me, only they used the front airlock and carried out the hibernating prisoners one by one to a specially reserved area aboard the *Lorelei* where they could be kept unconscious by a judicious amount of hydrogen sulfide added to the air in that room.

Brandon, Jesse, and Hunter all recovered without a hitch as soon as they were given fresh air for a few hours. Hunter woke up first and Brandon last, but that probably had something to do with age if I had to guess. None of them felt very well for a few hours afterward, but it didn't seem to have affected them too awfully much.

The grubs carried out forty-two prisoners from the facility; exactly the number Brandon's informant on Mars had told him there should be. We were fairly sure there were no others, since there was really nowhere else for them to go anyway unless they had a specific mission to take care of.

We tried to get them out without exposing anybody to spores; we really did. The grubs took extreme precautions, irradiating all surfaces and even themselves with hard ultraviolet. But somehow we must have overlooked something, because no sooner had we made it back to Saint Petersburg than one of the medical staff on board the *Lorelei* informed me that two of the prisoners were already showing signs of infection. We knew quite a lot about them by that time; their metabolism and bodily functions had slowed down a hundredfold from what would have been normal. Their hearts beat only once every two minutes, and they took a shallow breath only once in several hours. It was incidentally fascinating to poke and prod them a little and see what their bodies were doing. I'd never had a chance to observe somebody in suspended animation before.

But they were still very much alive, and apparently still susceptible to the Orion spores. If the metabolic slowdown held true for all processes then I figured the plague ought to take something like two weeks to actually kill them, rather than the thirty-six hours that it normally took. But living organisms are unpredictable things, and there was really no telling how long it might be till the prisoners succumbed.

I had no choice but to give them the vaccine at that point; I couldn't decently have done anything else. But it did cast a different light on the question of what to do with them, since there was no reason they couldn't stay on Earth anymore.

I was still deaf as a post, so I'd found a pad and pencil on a string and started carrying it around my neck so people could write me notes when they needed to tell me something. It was a cumbersome system, but it worked.

We won't have to take them to the Moon now, Jesse wrote to me that afternoon.

"No, but we probably ought to anyway. They'd be safe enough down here, true enough. But we'd still have to either put them in prison or find somewhere to leave them where they couldn't escape, and I'm not sure there *is* any such place when it comes right down to it. We'd always have to worry about it, at the very least," I said.

Well, true. But if we're still taking to the Moon then at least we can put them at Lakeside Station instead of having to drop them off on the islands, Jesse wrote.

"Yeah, no doubt. They'll be a lot more comfortable there," I agreed, and even though I knew that was true, I couldn't help feeling a twinge of. . . something. I couldn't quite put my finger on what it was, but I felt sort of like you might feel if you heard that drug dealers or criminals were moving into a house where you grew up and had mostly been happy. I had a lot of good memories of Lakeside, and I didn't like the idea that Colonel Burns' flunkies would be living in my cabin and sleeping in my bed, that they'd be using the community center that I helped build with my own two hands and where I first kissed Danielle. I didn't want to share all that with people I didn't like, you know.

I knew it was silly, of course; the Moon no more belonged to me than the universe did. I'd simply lived there for a little while, that's all. But feelings aren't always rational, and even though it didn't make much sense I still couldn't help feeling the way I did.

I suppose Uncle Philip would have told me to have more love in my heart, and no doubt he would have been right. Joan told us a story once about that horrible verse in the Psalms which talks about blessing anybody who will take a Babylonian baby and beat its brains out against the pavement. She told us little resentments and cherished hatreds are just like those babies; they start out small and sweet and seemingly harmless, but whenever we notice one of them we should do exactly what the writer of that psalm suggested. . . bust the little darlings' brains out before they get a chance to grow up and turn into monsters. It'll be a definite blessing if you do.

She and Philip have always had a way of forcing the most bitter truths out of the most unlikely hiding places like that. But then again, I guess that's probably exactly why I remember them so well. So I bit my tongue and killed my resentment, much as I didn't want to.

We'll have to keep them somewhere on Earth for at least a little while, till we can refit another of the XR's to carry that many people. It won't be safe to make more than one trip, Jesse wrote.

"That's true, but where would we leave them in the meantime?" I asked.

We don't have any prisons, and these are elite soldiers who are trained to escape from almost anywhere. We can't risk that, and we can't keep them in hibernation for that long, either; we don't know enough about the long-term effects of what that might do to them. We'll have to leave them on a small island so far from other land that there's no chance for them to escape, and someplace where nobody ever lived before, Jesse wrote.

"Why somewhere nobody ever lived before?" I asked.

Because we don't want them to find a boat or have a chance to build one, that's why, Jesse wrote.

"But people lived almost everywhere till the plague came, Jesse. Where would we find something like that?" I asked.

We'll have to look. Nobody ever lived on several of the remotest islands, and that's exactly the kind we want, he wrote.

"It'll have to be somewhere close by, if we don't dare keep them in hibernation for very long," I said.

We'll find one, he wrote.

There are lots of islands within a few hundred miles of Florida; thousands of them, actually. But unfortunately most of them are fairly close together, and the water is plenty warm enough for a determined person to float and swim his way back to the mainland by island-hopping if he wanted to badly enough. That wouldn't do.

There were very few islands far enough from other land to be absolutely inescapable by swimming and which had been uninhabited at the time of the plague. Such few as there were tended to be harsh, desert-like places with no fresh water available. Humans can't survive for very long in spots like that, which is exactly why those islands had been uninhabited in the first place.

We ended up choosing Clipperton Island, which is way out in the middle of the Pacific Ocean off the west coast of Mexico and which fit all the criteria we were looking for. It had never been inhabited, and there was practically nothing there except sand dunes, a few coconut palms, and a landlocked lagoon full of semi-fresh water. It was basically a bare and desolate patch of land in the middle of nowhere, and that was a perfect location for our purposes.

The plan was to simply leave them lying there on the beach above the high tide line, along with food and water and various tools we thought we could trust them with and things of that sort, including a radio transmitter so they could let us know if they needed anything. They'd wake up in a few hours or so as the hydrogen sulfide wore off, and then they'd have to do the best they could for a few weeks till we could make it back to collect them. I admit I had serious misgivings about keeping people like that on Earth under any circumstances whatsoever, even for a little while; it's generally not very wise to invite a poisonous snake to come live in your house, even if he seems harmless at the time.

There was no reason to stay in Florida any longer at that point, so we left a skeleton crew aboard the *Lorelei* to pilot the sub back home to Kailua Kona while the rest of us headed home more directly. I was ready to be back; it felt like I'd been gone for centuries already, even though I knew logically it hadn't even been two weeks. But my father likes to say that life is measured in experience rather than time, so periods when there's a lot packed in always loom larger in memory than lengthy periods when nothing much happened.

So it may be. All I knew was that I could hardly wait to set foot in Hawaii again, and that was no exaggeration.

There had been five workable XR planes that we'd brought back from Socotra, one of which had been the poor *Susie Q,* now irreparably wrecked on Deimos. That left us with four; the *Melinda May* and three others. But transporting forty-two prisoners in such small ships was problematic at best, especially when those same prisoners were dedicated to capturing at least one of those very ships and probably still hadn't quite given up yet.

The grubs found a way, though. They sealed off the rear half of each cabin as an airtight capsule where the prisoners could be kept, with separate life support circuits so that the atmosphere could be maintained with just enough hydrogen sulfide to keep them unconscious while not affecting the front half of the ship where the pilot and crew would be.

All this took time, of course; nearly three months of steady work before the technicians were satisfied. It was mid-June before everything was ready to go, and by that time quite a few things had happened.

Chief among them from my point of view was the fact that my eardrums gradually grew back and I was actually able to hear again and hold a normal conversation without having to lug around a notepad necklace all the time.

The *Lorelei* finally arrived and cast anchor in Kailua Bay at the end of April, after its epic odyssey all the way around Cape Horn. There wasn't much immediate need for it, true, but I'm sure it'll turn out to be useful sooner or later. In the meantime it sat there next to the pier and didn't require much attention except a little routine maintenance now and then, which the grubs took care of in their unfailingly efficient kind of way. Before long the novelty of seeing it there wore off and it became more or less part of the background scenery, as unremarkable as the palm trees on the beach.

My little sister Melissa was born on the first of June, and my cousin Camber eight days later. I confess I worried a little bit about what kind of name my parents would manage to come up with, after the one they inflicted on me. But Melissa is beautifully ordinary, and I breathed a long sigh of relief for her sake. I don't think parents quite realize how cruel it is to saddle their children with oddball names, and after living with one of those names all my life I do think I'm qualified to have an opinion on the subject.

It was actually Camber who worried me more. It wasn't as odd as *some* names I've heard, but it was definitely unusual. It reminded me vaguely of something that might fit on a race car when I first heard it. But then Philip got to talking about how Camber was an ancient king of Wales and I don't know what all else; he and Joan are awfully picky about names that way and took months to make up their minds on that one, so I don't doubt they had a list of reasons half a mile long. I guess the boy will grow up and learn to either love it or hate it, just like I had to do with mine, but in the meantime he had my sympathy.

Philip and Joan seemed to fall in love with him instantly, though; the way people do when they've been waiting and hoping and praying for something for so long that it hurts, and I was reminded of how Philip used to dote on Callum so much before he died and how he'd never really gotten over that loss ever since. I know that one child can never truly replace another, but after seeing the way those two latched onto Camber I think maybe he'll be a comfort to them, you know.

I hope so.

In the meantime Danielle was just beginning to show a little bit and felt better and more energetic than she had in months, so I was contemplating a surprise for her.

"How would you like to go back to the Moon for a few days, beautiful?" I asked lightly.

"What for?" she asked.

"Well. . . I don't know. To relive some sweet memories, maybe? We could go to Ukert Springs and let the Doctor Fish give us a pedicure like we did that one time. Or have a crab cookout at Trinity Bay or go walking on the beach with a shell full of coconut milk in the Summer Isles. I could even bring along a recording of Johnny playing the *Canon in D* and I could kiss you while we danced, like we did that first time. It'd be awesome," I said, and she smiled.

"That's sweet, Tyke. And I'm sure it would be. But I already have all those things tucked away right in here; I don't have to do them over again to remember," she said, putting my hand just above her heart.

"That's true, but there's one thing I always promised you and never got to do, and this may be our last chance," I said.

"What's that?" she asked.

"I promised I'd take you to the Red Rock Desert someday, during the morning bloom. But then we never had a chance because of the way things happened. I'd love to do that while we still can," I said.

"All right then, you convinced me. I'll let you keep your promise, and I'll keep mine," she said.

"What one are you talking about?" I asked.

"That I'd never let you go back out in space again unless I was with you," she said.

"When did you promise *that?*" I asked, laughing a little.

"I promised *myself* that, after you went to Titan. Neither one of us had any choice in the matter when Colonel Bartow dragged you off to Venus, but you notice I didn't stay home from Mars," she said.

"I didn't think you liked it," I said.

"Oh, I've been through worse. I'm glad it was something we got to share together for a change. But I hope the Red Rock Desert won't be anything but a sweet little vacation," she said.

"It shouldn't be. The prisoners will be asleep the whole time, and then after we drop them off at Lakeside we won't have to worry about them anymore. We can do whatever we like for a few days and then come home. I already talked to Jesse about it a little bit and he said he and Leah might even come along, and maybe Hunter and Veronica if he can talk them into it. He could fly one of the transports, and then the rest of us would be enough to make up the crew and take care of everything. That way we'd have the ship for as long as we wanted to afterward," I said.

"It's a shame Chris and Emily can't come too; then we'd have everybody," she said.

"Yeah, I know, but Emily's a lot farther along than you are. It wouldn't really be a good idea for them to go anywhere right now," I said.

"Well. . . we'll see, then," she said.

And so it was. The six of us formed the crew on the good old *Melinda May,* and Brandon didn't seem to mind if we wanted to volunteer. As he said himself, it wasn't expected to be a dangerous mission by any means. He wasn't going himself this time, saying that he had things to do in Kona which were much more urgent than going on vacation for a few days. But he smiled and wished us a fun time, even though it wasn't his own cup of tea at the moment.

We recaptured the prisoners at Clipperton Island by going back there with helicopters and having the grubs shoot them from the air with tranquilizer guns used for lions and zebras and such. They never had a chance to fight back or cause us any problems; the island was too small and too barren for them to have any place to run or hide. I'm sure they already hated us with a black passion after being left out there in the middle of the ocean for three months, and getting hunted down by helicopter and shot probably didn't improve their opinion of us one single bit.

But it couldn't be helped, and soon enough we had them loaded up like logs inside the hibernation chambers aboard the ships, ready for the last leg of our strange and sometimes quirky journey.

Danielle was sick a lot on the way to the Moon, even with the anti-nausea pills that Joan had thoughtfully sent along for that very purpose. She didn't complain, but I still felt bad.

Nevertheless, the day came when all four planes landed safely on the airstrip at Lakeside Station, and then we had the arduous task of carrying the prisoners into the hangar and laying them down on the floor. Then I had to make a quick trip into the station itself to switch on all the systems.

We left a booklet of useful information for them in the middle of the table where they couldn't miss it; a sort of *Lunar Survival Guide,* if you will. God knows we could have used one ourselves during those first few weeks we lived there. Then the grubs headed home, and the rest of us were left to our own devices.

Getting away from Lakeside before the prisoners woke up was the number one crash priority, and since there were only a limited number of places where the *Melinda May* could land, we dispatched Hunter and Veronica to fly the sole remaining triphibious seaplane and follow us.

After considerable debate, we decided to park the *Melinda May* at the foot of the Fallen Astronaut Memorial on Mount Hadley, since that was fairly far from Lakeside and there was no way the prisoners could have guessed where we went anyway. Jesse changed the computer access codes just in case, even though we didn't expect it to matter.

Then we all six climbed into the triphib and flew off to enjoy our vacation.

It was the height of the morning bloom by then, and the Red Rock Desert didn't disappoint. It was every bit as gorgeous as I remembered, and finally getting to keep my promise at long last and share it with Danielle was a deeply satisfying thing. She was the only member of our little group who hadn't seen it before, and to see uncritical delight in the eyes of someone you love is one of life's sweetest pleasures; all the more so when you know you're the one who caused it to happen.

But the bloom was fleeting as always, and from there we moved on to have a hunt for the blue hamburger crabs at Trinity Bay with a bonfire on the beach, which Hunter and Veronica and Leah had never done before. We climbed the north face of Diamondtop, said to be the most beautiful peak in all the Snowy Mountains, a feat which *none* of us had ever done before. We visited Ukert Springs for a nice little spa treatment, and jumped off the cliffs at Lake Boscovich a few last times. Leah doesn't like things like that and Danielle didn't think it was wise, but the rest of us enjoyed it; even Hunter, once we could convince him that a 1200 foot drop into water wouldn't smash him flat. Even Veronica gave it a try.

We ended up near sundown in the Summer Isles, of course, as if there'd ever been any doubt about where the last days of our trip would be spent. We'd have to spend the entire two-week lunar night there, but that was all right. The cave where we'd spent our last night four years ago was still there, dry and snug as always, and with just a little cleaning and organizing we had it in even better shape than before.

A few days later Danielle and I visited the little pool up on the mountainside where we'd first started to think there might be something more than just friendship between us, and we sat there in the cool bubbly water for a while to watch the incredible lightning displays out over the Sea of Tranquility. It was just beginning to rain a little bit, and now and then the wind would toss the palm trees all around us.

"I love this place," I said after a little while, holding her hand under the water while we watched the storm.

"So do I," she agreed.

"We'll probably never see it again, though," I said wistfully. Trips to the Moon weren't without some level of risk even at the best of times, and it was unlikely we'd ever have a legitimate reason to justify another visit.

"*Que sera, sera,*" she murmured.

"What's that mean?" I asked.

"It means whatever will be, will be. Something my grandma Catalina used to like to say. She was a pure-blooded Spaniard, you know, even after a dozen generations in America. One of those old true-blue aristocratic families from New Mexico who could trace her ancestry all the way back to the *conquistadores.* She almost died when my mother married a *sureño,*" she said, and giggled.

"What's that?" I asked.

"It's a slangy Spanish word for an Anglo Southerner, a hillbilly redneck, I guess you could call it. In his case a Texan, the worst kind of all," she said.

"Why the worst?" I asked.

"Well. . . Spanish New Mexicans have never liked English Texans, and vice versa. Especially the upper crusty ones like she was. So Mama created a scandal when she ran off with one," she said.

"I wonder what your grandma would have thought of me, then. I'm an English Texan, at least by blood," I said wryly.

"Oh, she would've thoroughly disapproved, I'm sure. She would've told me not to hang around with such riffraff," she said, and I laughed.

"Would you have listened?" I asked.

"Not a chance," she said, and kissed me.

We sat up and talked for hours in the rain that night, our conversation ranging all the way from silly to somber. And just like the last time I sat with Danielle in that place, I think the memory of that night will live forever in my heart as one of the happiest moments of my life.

"What do you think we should name the baby?" she asked at one point. It wasn't like we hadn't already discussed that question a million times, of course, but choosing a baby name is one of those topics which never seems to get old.

"Shirley Elmer McGrath," I said, and she laughed.

"Come on, Tyke; be serious," she said.

"What about Tommy Lee, then? That was my grandfather's grandfather's name. He was a famous guitar player and gospel singer at one time," I said.

"We've already got a Tommy in the family so that won't do. Maybe Thomas, though. And what about Levi instead of Lee? That was *my* grandfather's grandfather's name, so that way everything will match up. He was a small engine mechanic," she said, and then it was my turn to laugh.

"Well, hey, nothing wrong with that. Hmm. . . Thomas Levi McGrath. Sure, that could work," I agreed. I remembered what Brandon had said about how Levi Black had been a friend of his, so I figured the old boy must have had a few noble traits besides just knowing how to degrease motors. Even though I knew we'd probably change our minds a hundred times yet before the little guy came along and forced us to settle on something, it was still a fun game to play in the meantime.

But all good things must someday end, and when dawn finally broke across the placid sea we quietly gathered our things to leave for the last time. I collected a little bottle of green sand from the beach as a memento, but that was all.

Then it was off to Mount Hadley and back home, and hopefully this time to a life without fear of Colonel Burns or his henchmen. All six of us had so much to look forward to.

I hardly knew at the time what a prophetic statement that truly was.

Chapter Twenty

As soon as we got back home things settled down to the old routine fairly quickly, and I soon found myself absorbed in the minutiae of advanced genetics again. In some ways it was almost like I'd never been gone.

The repopulation project was still plodding slowly along, though not nearly as fast or as well as I would have liked. I'd managed to revive thirty-nine species of mammals and birds since the day I first started working on it three and a half years ago, a little while after we came to Hawaii. That might sound pretty good at first glance, but when I pondered how many bird and mammal species there had actually been on Earth at the time of the plague then it didn't seem quite so impressive anymore. In fact, even with all possible help and even if I worked at it constantly, I calculated that it would take me something like eight hundred years before I'd have time to restore everything that was lost. That was discouraging.

But it couldn't be rushed, unfortunately; reconstitution of living organisms from nothing but computer code is an exact and demanding science, and it's very unforgiving of mistakes. It requires starting with a living, unfertilized egg cell and bit by bit modifying the DNA inside the nucleus till it matches the computer code, then finally letting it divide and grow. There are all kinds of things that can go wrong at almost any point, and you usually can't tell until it's too late to fix it. I couldn't even begin to count the number of times I'd ended up with nothing but monstrosities which had to be killed in simple mercy if they lived at all, forcing me to start all over again from scratch. It was hard work, on a lot of different levels.

Not to mention the fact that I had no one to help me, let alone replace me, and considering the small number of human beings left in the world, it was quite possible I'd *never* find such a person. I hope it doesn't sound snotty to say it, but you can't just pick any individual off the street and teach him how to do genetic engineering; especially not the advanced kind I was doing. It takes years of study and also a certain aptitude which not everybody has. That really worried me sometimes.

All I could do was try to prioritize which creatures I thought were most important and try to allocate my time accordingly, and pray some kid with a brilliant mind and a taste for genetics would be born while I was still alive to teach him or her what I knew. Otherwise the world was going to remain an awfully empty place for a very long time.

I was pulling some fresh embryos out of the incubator one morning when the phone rang, interrupting my gloomy thoughts. I was working on a type of songbird known as the scarlet tanager at the time; for no particular reason except the fact that I liked them. They were a brilliant red color and had a pretty song, not to mention being an adaptable little creature which could live in many different environments. An important point, if I expected them to survive.

That stage in the process always reminded me of baking a cake, except much more tedious and difficult, of course. But it wouldn't hurt if they stayed in the incubator for a few extra minutes while I answered the phone.

"Yo!" I said, expecting that it was Danielle. She's normally the only person who ever calls me at work, and stuff like that always makes her laugh.

"Yo?" someone asked, and I recognized Brandon's voice.

"Uh. . . yeah, never mind that. What's up?" I asked, embarrassed.

"Well, I'd like for you to stop by the house and see me this evening after work, if you've got time. It won't take too long," he said.

"Sure, I guess so. I'll be done here about five o'clock, probably. Is five thirty okay?" I asked.

"That'll be fine. I'll see you then," he said, and that was that.

I clicked off the phone, kind of curious as to what he might want to talk about, especially considering some of the other discussions we'd had in the past. But in the meantime I had work to do, so I put it out of my mind while I focused on the tanagers for the rest of the afternoon.

They were another failure, sadly; the poor little things came out of the incubator so deformed that I knew they'd never survive on their own. I had no choice but to put them down, and that's always a depressing occasion.

It was close to five o'clock by then and there was no time to get started on something else, so I decided to call it a day. I texted Danielle to let her know I'd be a little bit late, then washed my hands and switched off the lights, making sure the lab was ready to swing into action again first thing in the morning. Then I locked the door and headed out.

It was a warm and breezy day, and I decided to walk over to Brandon's house instead of driving, just to enjoy the sunshine and the view. I tried to ignore April Lemley's statue of me, standing there on his bronze pedestal as I walked past the entrance to the university. The only good thing I could say about him was that at least he wasn't looking at me.

But soon I was past all that, off campus and headed north along Wall Street.

One of the interesting little tidbits that I like so much about Kailua Kona is that it's a walled city; the only one I've ever seen, actually. I'm sure the Hawaii Tourism Commission had something to do with that, back in the day; carefully preserving and extending the old walls as an attraction of sorts. There was an eruption of

Mount Hualalai in 2097 which caused incredible destruction on the entire southwest side of the island, but one of the few redeeming features of the incident was that it allowed Kailua Kona to be rebuilt in a much more historical fashion than before. The place has a pungent atmosphere of Old Hawaii that you simply don't find anywhere else. Everywhere else in the islands might be covered up in luxury resorts and high-priced condominiums, but not here. And for that I'd always been grateful. I'd already seen quite enough of that kind of thing back in Florida; I didn't need an instant replay.

As you might imagine, Wall Street ran right along the inside of the city wall, and fetched me up eventually on the Queen's Highway near the high school. It was a little bit out of my way, but I didn't really mind the extra distance. I like to walk when the weather is nice, which is 98 percent of the time.

I turned left onto Palani Road and finally onto Brandon's street, making an effort to look cheerful when I finally came to his gate. He was out in the back yard again, just like he'd been the last time I came over, only this time he was burning dead leaves and palm branches.

"Come in, Tyke. Grab a chair and I'll be there in a minute," he called, so that's what I did. He stirred the fire till it was arranged to his liking, and then came to sit down in the chair next to me to watch it burn.

"So what's on your mind?" I finally asked.

"Several things, but first and foremost there's something I want to ask you," he said.

"Fire away," I said.

"Do you remember what I told you, that first day after we escaped from Phoenix?" he asked.

"Which part?" I asked.

"Well, all of it, but specifically what I said about the Fountain," he said.

"I remember you said it made you live a long time and never age, and that it gave you the power to make broken things whole, and that it could only be used for the sake of love," I said.

"Good, and do you remember the dream I told you about? The one your grandma Lisa had about you?" he asked.

"You told me she had one, but you never really said what it was *about*," I said.

"Then I think it's time I did. She saw you sitting alone at a lab bench, on a rainy night in a place with palm trees swaying in the breeze. She didn't know your name, or when or where you were, or anything at all about what it meant except that you carried the fate of the world in your hands," he said.

"I see," I said, not sure what else to say.

"I never told Lisa, but this is what God said to me that day. He said a terrible disaster was coming, something of our own doing which would devastate the entire world. But He meant to lift up a champion to make things right again; namely the boy in that dream. You, Tyke," he said.

"Okay, so what's the point of telling me all this *now*? It's over and done with at this point, isn't it?" I asked.

"Not at all. In fact, it's only just now beginning," he said.

"What do you mean, just beginning? Didn't it have to do with finding a cure for the plague?" I asked, utterly perplexed as to what he could possibly be talking about. Brandon had a way of being oblique like that sometimes, but he'd never said anything *quite* so obscure before.

"Look around you. Is the world as it should be?" he asked.

"Well. . . no. It can never really be right again, without the animals. But I'm doing the best I can about that," I said.

"Yes, Tyke; we all know that. But surely you can see that it'll take an awfully long time to finish the job, if things keep going as they are. More years than any of us will live, including you," he said.

"Yeah, I know that. But I don't know of anything else I could do, other than what I'm already doing," I said.

"That depends on how much you're willing to sacrifice," he said.

"I'm not sure what you mean," I said.

"You could do the same thing I did. Drink from the fountain. Then you'd have the power to heal all those deformed embryos that slow down your work, and you'd live long enough to finish all of it, too," he said.

"Me?" I asked, shocked almost out of my seat. Of all the things Brandon might have suggested, that was certainly one I never would have imagined.

"Yes, you. Is it that much of a surprise?" he asked, utterly calm and unruffled.

"I guess I never really thought about it before," I admitted. After the initial shock was over it didn't seem *quite* so outlandish, I don't suppose, but I still had trouble wrapping my mind around such an incredible idea. But Brandon wasn't finished yet.

"This isn't something I came up with on my own, Tyke. It's something you're *meant* to do, if you're willing. It's part of God's plan to restore the Earth from its hurt, and to give these people a leader after Philip and I are too old. I've known it ever since Lisa told me her dream. You weren't ready to hear it before now, but from this point forward you can't walk in darkness anymore. You're twenty-one years old, the number of perfection and completion. Your whole life has been a preparation for this. It all narrows to this one moment in time, and the choice you make right now. Are you willing?" Brandon asked.

"That's a lot to ask," I finally said, when I could find the words to speak.

"Yes, it is. Nobody knows that better than I do, I promise you," he agreed.

That was undeniably true; if anyone knew the cost of such a burden then Brandon most certainly did. My first impulse was to ask him all kinds of things; to start counting the costs and weighing the benefits to see whether it was worth it to me to agree to such a thing or not. But something held me back from starting out down that path. If Joan had ever taught me anything, if Philip's sermons had ever sunk into my heart, if experience had ever shown me a single truth, it was simply this: when God asks a thing, you trust in his love and then do whatever it might be. You don't start playing twenty questions to see whether you agree with Him or not.

I thought about lots of things at that moment, from Brandon's seemingly idle comment about becoming a leader of men back on Barbados to the story Daddy told me about the night he had to throw me into the stormy ocean when I was four years old after God spoke to him. I thought about all sorts of little facts like that, some of which had never meant anything at all to me before. But they did *now*.

"I'm not sure if I could live up to all that," I finally said.

"You'll never be asked to do anything you can't do," Brandon said solemnly.

"Well. . . what exactly *would* I have to do?" I asked.

"Come inside for a minute and let me show you," he said, getting up from his chair and heading for the door. I followed him into the dining room of his little house, where he went to a china cabinet full of various whatnots and started moving things around.

"What are you looking for?" I asked.

"This," he said, reaching far in the back to pull out a small crystal flask of what looked like water. Then we both sat down at the table and he placed the flask in between us. The surface was beaded with moisture like a glass of ice water in the summertime, and as I watched a single droplet slid down to wet the tablecloth.

"What is it?" I asked. I didn't quite venture to pick it up since he'd been so reverent with it, but I couldn't help wondering about it.

"It's water from the Fountain. When I went there to drink, I was told to save this for you. So that's what I've done, ever since I was sixteen years old," he said soberly.

I picked up the flask then, watching the liquid inside glitter like a diamond in the light from the western window. It was cold as ice to the touch, even though the room was warm.

"So what actually happens if I drink this?" I asked.

"You're still young enough that you won't notice much right away. But you won't age anymore; not for at least a hundred years or so, and maybe a little more. Then eventually the effect will wear off and you'll grow old, just like anyone else would. But in the meantime your body will be perfect and beautiful, and so will any living thing you lay hands on. I can't explain what it feels like to someone who never experienced it, but you'll be able to see the brokenness in any living creature, and by your will alone to make them whole. All the things you've seen me do, you'll be able to do also," he said.

"Even the way you know things sometimes?" I asked.

"Maybe. I'm not sure about that part; foresight was a gift I received for a completely different reason, so it may not apply to you. But the rest of it I know for certain," he said.

"I don't know what to think," I said.

"There's nothing to think, Tyke; only a choice to make. If you want to bring life and beauty to a dark and broken world, you should drink. But only if you're brave enough to forsake everything else in the meantime; to keep on living while everyone you know and care about passes away and leaves you behind. To love the world enough, and God enough, that you would give up everything to be like Him. If you have the courage, then drink," Brandon said, nodding his head toward the flask.

That was a scary thought, and for a few seconds I still hesitated. If I drank that water, it meant that someday I'd have to watch Danielle grow old and die, and everyone else that I loved, too. Even Josie, and Camber and Melissa, and my baby son who wasn't even born yet. The cost was almost unimaginable, and no amount of talk about destiny or fate could make me forget that.

I had the choice to refuse, of course; no one would ever know except Brandon, and I knew he'd never mention it. The risk of disappointing him didn't amount to much in comparison with everything else.

I almost said no; I really did. I don't think anyone will ever know how close I came to saying the words. They were right on the tip of my tongue, ready to spill out. But then I remembered something Danielle had said to me, months and months ago, reminding me of the Avengers' oath we'd both taken, and that sometimes it might require heavy sacrifices from both of us.

"I'll have to think about it for a day or two," I finally said, and he nodded.

"Do that. And talk to Danielle; it affects her too. Then come and tell me what you decide," he said.

I was thoughtful and preoccupied on my way back home that night. Maybe it was true what Brandon said, that my whole life up till then had been only a preparation for this single decision that otherwise I wouldn't have had the courage or the wisdom to make. I could see how that might be so, as I reflected back on all the things I'd been through. All of them had been some kind of test, some kind of forced overcoming of a certain kind of flaw in my nature.

And it might also be true that this was the solution to my troubles with the species repopulation project; the key to undoing the terrible harm which had been done. If I could make any creature perfect the first time, then I wouldn't need to spend weeks or months trying to get each one right.

Daddy sometimes likes to say that in the end a man can only say that he is what he does, and maybe that's true. Choices are what make us who we are, little by little over time. The choice Brandon had asked me to make was a major crossroads in my life, and I still didn't know for sure which fork I wanted to take. All I knew for sure was, no matter what I decided, things would never be the same again.

Chapter Twenty-One

I hadn't meant to say anything to Danielle about it, at least not till I had time to sort things out in my own mind first, but she knew there was something wrong as soon as I got home that night. She's awfully perceptive that way.

"What's the matter, baby?" she asked, almost the instant I came inside.

I knew better than to pretend it was nothing, of course, however little I wanted to talk about the whole affair. But I smiled tiredly and tried to think how to explain.

"Brandon told me a lot of things tonight that I don't really understand, that's all," I said.

"That's nothing unusual. What did he say?" she asked.

"He said a bunch of stuff about my grandmother having a dream about me a long time ago and then telling him about it when my dad was still just a baby. I don't know; seems crazy to me," I muttered.

"I wouldn't go so far as to say that. You had that dream about Titan," she pointed out.

"Well. . . yeah, I know that. I guess that's not really the part that bothered me so much anyway," I admitted.

"So what bothered you then?" she asked.

"I don't even know where to start," I said.

"Anywhere you like. You'll have to get around to all of it eventually anyway," she pointed out.

"Well, you know all that stuff he can do, right? About healing things and all that?" I asked.

"Yeah, I remember," she agreed.

"He told me he drank from a holy fountain when he was sixteen years old, and that's why he's able to do all those things. But now he seems to think I should drink from it myself," I said.

"But how would you even know where to find such a thing?" she asked.

"I wouldn't have to. He's got a bottle of that water sitting at home in his china cabinet, waiting on whatever I decide. All I have to do is say yes and drink it," I said.

"So what's the catch? I'm sure there's got to be something you haven't told me yet, or else you wouldn't be so tied up in knots over it," she said.

"Yeah, there is. Did you know Brandon is a hundred and sixty years old?" I asked.

"No, can't say I ever would've guessed *that*. He doesn't look more than early twenties, tops," she said.

"He may not look it, but he is. That's something else the Fountain did to him, to make him live so long and never age," I said.

"Would that part apply to you, too?" she asked.

"Yeah, it would. But that's not all," I said.

"What more could there be?" she asked.

"He also said he thinks he's coming to the end of his years pretty soon, and he believes I'm supposed to lead everybody after he and Philip are gone. He says God told him so," I said.

"That's a lot to swallow," she finally said.

"I knew you wouldn't like the idea," I said.

"That's not what I said, Tyke; I said it was a lot to swallow," she corrected.

"But. . ." I began.

"Hush. I know what you're thinking; about what it means for the future. I can't tell you whether you should do it or not, but I do want you to remember one thing," she said.

"What's that?" I asked.

"You won't be costing *me* anything, if you do this. To still have you like you are now, young and handsome and loving me just as much as always even when I'm old and fat and wrinkly; that's a beautiful thing to look forward to, for *me* at least. It'll be *you* that has to pay the price, my love, not anyone else. That's why I can't tell you whether you should do it or not," she said.

I hadn't seen things in quite that light before, but when I considered it I saw that she was probably right. I might have to watch all the people I loved grow old and die one by one, but the flip side of the coin was that no one would ever have to watch those things happen to *me*. I suppose that should have been some comfort, and if I were a completely selfless and noble individual then maybe it would have been. But unfortunately I'm not.

"You sure do know how to put a different spin on things," I said wryly.

"I call it like I see it, that's all," she said.

"I still don't know what to do," I admitted, and then there was a long pause while neither of us said a word.

"Do you *really* not know what to do?" she finally asked, pulling back a little to look me dead in the eyes. I couldn't fool myself anymore while she was looking at me that way; I've never been able to.

"I know what I *should* do, Danielle. I just don't know if I *want* to or not, that's all," I said.

"Well. . . nobody can help you much with that part, I'm afraid. But think it over, and then pray about it tonight, and we can talk about it some more tomorrow if you like. Brandon didn't give you any deadline to make up your mind, did he?" she asked.

"No, he just said come back and let him know whenever I decided," I said.

"Well, I want you to know that I'll support you, no matter what. But in the meantime there's some food in the oven if you're hungry; I'd like for us to enjoy a quiet evening together for a little while without having to deal with all that heavy stuff," she said.

"That sounds like a great idea," I agreed, and followed her to the kitchen. She'd made steak fajitas, which she knew was one of my favorite things. So for a little while we talked about normal things and enjoyed our simple meal in spite of all the weighty decisions hanging over our heads.

That night I lay wakeful in my bed for a long time, praying for wisdom and then simply thinking. It was a warm night, and I soon pushed aside the monster-skin comforter I'd brought back from the Moon, lying there in the light from the window with nothing on but my boxers. I looked down at my almost-naked body and wiggled my toes in the moonlight, wondering what it would be like to never grow old. Nothing much would change, I supposed; I was near my physical peak, biologically speaking. I might get rid of a few scars here and there, and maybe not have to worry anymore about the long-term effects of Colonel Bartow's meddling with my chromosomes to carve out all the bad stuff.

In fact, if Brandon was to be believed, then I might even be able to fix all those worrisome clip-tags in everyone else, left over from the NADF's genetic surgery program back in Atlanta. Everybody was all right for the moment, yes, but when you meddle with intricate biological systems on such a grand scale you tend to run afoul of the Law of Unintended Consequences. Clip-tags are basically scars, and deeply scarred genetic material can often lead to vicious cancers and things like that after a lot of years go by. It wouldn't affect future generations, which I suppose is all Colonel Burns cared about, but I happen to think individuals matter for their own sake. The pitiless cruelty of sacrificing thousands of innocent people in the name of idealism was still a very fresh and vivid memory in my mind. Up till then there hadn't been much I could do about the lingering after-effects of all that genetic butchery, but drinking from the Fountain might give me more options.

There was so much good I could do, so many broken things I could put right, if only I was willing to pay the price. Then I glanced at Danielle sleeping peacefully in the shadows of the moonlight beside me, and my heart ached at the thought. A wisp of her long dark hair had worked its way loose from the ponytail she usually wore, sliding down across her right cheek as she lay on her side. I gently brushed it away with one hand, and she stirred for a second before settling back to sleep. She was more beautiful than the stars of heaven, more dear than my very heart; how could I ever willingly choose to live without her?

Then a new thought came into my mind, seemingly out of nowhere, and I almost laughed out loud. It was such a blindingly simple and beautiful thing that I could have kicked myself for not seeing it sooner, and suddenly all my doubts and fears about what I'd been asked to do evaporated like vapors in the wind.

"Thank You," I murmured under my breath, and then rolled over to put my left arm around Danielle before I fell asleep in complete contentment.

I didn't say anything about it when we got up in the morning, just in case things didn't go quite the way I planned. But she noticed my chipper mood anyway, I guess.

"You must have made up your mind," she said, leaning on her elbow while she watched me put my shoes on. I'd already finished shaving and brushing my teeth before she ever woke up.

"Yeah, I did. I'm gonna do it," I agreed, and she nodded.

"I thought you would, after you had some time to think about it," she said.

"Are you still okay with it?" I asked.

"Yeah. Kind of wish it was something we could do together, though," she said wistfully. I laughed a little at that, and she gave me a strange look.

"What was that all about?" she finally asked.

"Come go with me and I'll tell you when we get there, beautiful," I said, jumping back on the bed and rolling over to give her a kiss. She had morning breath from not brushing her teeth yet, but I couldn't have cared less. Then it was her turn to laugh a little.

"Well, I'm glad you're so happy this morning, but you'll have to wait till I get ready," she said.

"Sure thing," I agreed, putting my hands behind my head to let her get up and do all her morning rituals. As soon as she finished brushing her hair, I took her hand and left the house with the firm resolve to go see Brandon and make an end.

Or perhaps a beginning, if I chose to see it that way.

Palani Road was morning-silent, still shadowed in places by the huge bulk of Mount Hualalai to the east. And in spite of my good mood, I confess that a twinge of nervousness began to creep up my spine as we walked. I couldn't help thinking an awful lot about how many long and lonely days lay ahead if it turned out I was wrong. I had to keep telling myself not to think about things like that, right up till the second when I found myself standing in front of Brandon's dining room table again. It felt almost like I'd never left, other than the fact that Danielle was with me this time.

"Have you decided?" Brandon asked.

"Yes. I'll do it," I said.

"Has he discussed this with you, my dear?" Brandon asked, looking at Danielle.

"Yes, sir. We both agreed to come here this morning," she said.

Brandon nodded, and then went to the china cabinet to retrieve the crystal flask he'd shown me the night before, placing it on the table in front of us.

"If you want a piece of advice, I'd suggest not telling anyone. I can tell you from personal experience, it'll make life much easier if you don't," he said.

"I remember," I agreed.

"Then go ahead, Tyke. Whenever you're ready," he said. Danielle smiled encouragingly, and I picked up the flask.

"How much of this do I have to drink?" I asked.

"I don't know that there's any certain amount, but you can't save any, if that's what you mean. It's only meant for you," Brandon said.

"No, that's not what I was talking about. But I don't see why Danielle couldn't drink some of it too," I said, and Brandon frowned.

"I'm not sure if that's allowed," he finally said.

"I don't see why it wouldn't be. You said this was meant for me, didn't you?" I said.

"Yes," he agreed.

"Well, she's my wife, you know. We're supposed to be one flesh, aren't we? She's half of me, and vice versa. God Himself said that, didn't He? So if it's meant for me then it must be meant for her, too," I pointed out.

Brandon considered that for a while, with that faraway look on his face.

"You're becoming wise," he finally said, and then smiled in that way which brought light to his deep blue eyes.

"Thanks," I said.

"This is what God has said. Does anyone think I would forget My own word, or that it would ever come back to Me void? Each of you can drink half, according to what you've asked. But as you've asked, so will it be. So long as you both remain together, you'll share the same life and the same gift. But if you go separate ways then you'll both have to give it up completely. Will you accept that?" Brandon asked.

"Absolutely," I said staunchly.

"And you, my dear?" he asked, turning to Danielle. I hadn't known for sure till that very moment what she might say; it was a big choice, after all, for her as much as it was for me. She was quiet for a while, thinking it over I guess. Then she smiled, and I knew what her answer would be even before she spoke.

"Yes, sir," she agreed.

"All right then. But both of you need to understand that there's no turning back. You can't change your mind once you do this," Brandon said.

"We know," I said.

"Then there's really nothing left to say. God bless you and be with you, and guide and comfort your steps for the journey ahead," Brandon said. Before I had time to change my mind, I picked up the flask and popped off the lid.

"All for You," I murmured to God under my breath, and then drank. I don't know what I expected it to taste like, if anything, but it seemed to be only water. Icy cold perhaps, but otherwise perfectly ordinary. Then I handed the flask to Danielle so she could drink the other half. I felt no different than I had before, and I wondered at first whether anything had actually happened.

"How long does it take to work?" I finally asked.

"It's already done. Not everything in the world has to be flashy and dramatic, you know," Brandon said. I guess in a way that was sort of a letdown; I have as much taste for the dramatic as anybody does, but of course I also understood that substance is infinitely more important than appearances. As long as it worked then that was all that really mattered.

"I hope we did the right thing," I said to Danielle not long after we left. I suppose it was a moot point since the deed was already done, but that didn't keep me from being gripped with a sudden attack of second thoughts.

"Starting to doubt me already?" she asked. I knew she was teasing, of course, but I could only smile tiredly.

"No, beautiful; never that. I put my whole life into your hands a long time ago; this is nothing new. If you ever decided to leave me I don't think I'd want to live, anyway," I said.

"Me neither," she agreed, and clasped my hand.

We walked home together like that, and as we followed Palani Road back down to the sea I began to notice things I'd never seen before. Kailua Kona is full of palm trees, of course, and Palani Road is lined with them. I wouldn't normally have paid much attention, but as we walked I felt a vague sense of wrongness from some of them, like something wasn't quite what it ought to be.

"Do you feel that?" I asked Danielle, wondering if I was imagining things.

"That not-quite-right feeling? Yeah, I feel it," she agreed.

One of the "wrong" trees was only a few steps away, and I tentatively placed my left hand against the trunk. I felt it sharply then, no doubt about it. The tree was infested with *Ganoderma zonatu;* a fungus which I knew would eventually kill it. The blight grows silently underneath the bark for a long time before anything shows on the surface, and by that time it's usually too late to save the tree.

It was strange that I'd noticed such a thing from ten feet away and then known what it was without even having to take a core sample for analysis, but I could only assume it had something to do with the water we'd just drunk. Then it came to mind what Brandon had said about making broken things whole.

"Do you think we could fix this?" I asked Danielle.

"Wouldn't hurt to try," she said, putting her hand on the trunk next to mine.

I focused my attention on the tree and willed it to be healthy, and then suddenly it *was*. The blight disappeared under my hands just like it had never been there at all.

"That's weird," I muttered out loud, dropping my hand to my side again.

"Yeah. . . this might take some getting used to," Danielle said, and I couldn't have agreed more.

But even though I could sense wrongness, I soon found that I could sense rightness, too. That palm tree wasn't quite normal after we finished with it; it was somehow *more* than normal, if that makes any sense. It was perfect, down to the last leaf and strand of bark. I could *feel* it.

I felt the same perfection in hundreds if not thousands of places all over town over the next few days, in animals and plants and even people, and I began to realize that Brandon must have been awfully busy ever since he first set foot in Hawaii last year. He'd never uttered a single word about everything he'd touched during that time, but the evidence was abundantly clear for anybody with eyes to see.

It awed me, frankly, and I even began to have a strong suspicion that he might have had something to do with all those beautiful places I'd seen on the isles of Venus. He'd been there for over ten years, after all; that was plenty of time to accomplish a lot.

Over the next few weeks Danielle and I both started to follow his quiet example, touching and beautifying things whenever the opportunity presented itself in such a way that no one would be likely to notice.

He opened up and told us lots of stories about all kinds of things over the next few weeks, and the more I learned the more I started to realize what a hard act to follow he really is. He told us about how he died and came back to life when he was four years old, and how he stood there with my grandparents to consecrate Cadron Pool, and all kinds of things like that I'd never known. But of all the stories he ever shared with us, there was one in particular that I loved most of all.

He told us that long ago the ancients spoke of a place called Elysium, a shining land far away beyond the sea in the west, where the blessed of God live in bliss beneath a blue and cloudless sky. He'd been there himself, he said, long ago when he was young, and that's how he earned the title I think he loves most: Bran the Blessed. It was from Elysium that he brought the water we drank.

Maybe it's true what he always told us, that men live by the stories they hear and that they hunger and thirst after heroes. All I can say is that his tale of that sun-kissed isle in the midst of the western sea touched my heart in a way not many others ever have, and I'll treasure it as long as I live.

At the same time, I couldn't help thinking what a strange coincidence it was that of all the places on Earth we should have ended up in Hawaii; our very own sun-drenched island in the uttermost West. Brandon would say it's no coincidence at all, I suppose; that God planned it that way ever since the day the world was made.

He finished his tale by telling us that above all else, the purpose of our gift is to plant memories of Heaven and to turn men's eyes to God; to show them the Light so beautiful that no one who sees it can ever turn away.

That was something my grandpa Cody used to like to say, too, so maybe that's where Brandon first heard it. All I know is that combined with that story, it planted a passionate fire in my heart to lift up Kailua Kona until it becomes as beautiful as the land of Elysium long ago; a living reminder of Heaven.

I'm not sure if I'll ever be able to live up to all that, but I fully intend to try.

Epilogue
Friday, October 25, 2159

Tomorrow is my birthday.

It's sort of hard to decide how to celebrate it this year, honestly. According to the calendar I'll be 22 years old, but then on the other hand I don't suppose my body will ever really be any older than 21; at least not for a very long time. It reminds me of that old saying about how birthdays are only a number, and I guess in my case that will turn out to be literally true. But it does make it awfully hard to decide how many candles to put on a cake.

Danielle and I haven't told anyone what we did yet; not even my parents or Philip and Joan. For now there's nothing much to give it away, and no doubt for a while we'll be able to slide by without having to explain ourselves. Maybe even as much as twenty years or so, with any luck. But we both know the day will come sooner or later when we won't be able to hide it anymore, and I still can't imagine what we'll say when that moment finally arrives.

No doubt a lot of people would give anything for such a gift, but I confess that even now when I think of the cost, it staggers my heart. Even sharing it with Danielle, the price tag is still awfully high. Sometimes I don't know how Brandon was ever able to bear it.

But it's also true that the gift holds its full share of sweetness, too. One of the first things I discovered was that when I reconstruct creatures these days, I don't have to worry about creating monstrosities that won't live. Now when I pull them out of the incubator and hold their warm little bodies in my hands, it's just like it was with the palm tree on Palani Road. I can feel the way they *ought* to be, and whatever mistakes I might have made in reviving them I can erase by simply willing it so. I've watched, oh so many times, when a mangled bird or small animal came out weak and barely breathing, sure to die and leave me with no choice but to start over again at square one, and then seen it grow strong and perfect as I cupped it in my palms. No light, no weird special effects, nothing like that; just wholeness from brokenness, and life snatched from the very teeth of death.

Sometimes I think about Saint Tycho of Cyprus, the namesake of my namesake, and I wonder if this is how he felt when he saw those dead grapevines come to life again in his own hands. I don't know that I'd call myself saintly, but it may well be that people will someday call me a worker of wonders. I don't even know that I could disagree with them on that part, even though I know it's all God and not me. I'm just as awed to watch it happen as the grubs are.

I can't make something from nothing, of course; I still have to slave over a hot microscope for a lot of long hours to prepare the protoplasm, and there's a lot of old-fashioned skill and hard work involved in nurturing those embryos till they get big enough to handle. But it's a lot faster now that I don't have to worry about mistakes, and I calculated awhile back that if things keep going like this, I should have every species on Earth restored in only about eighty years. Heck, I might even have time to bring back the saber-toothed tiger and the woolly mammoth.

But all that is far in the future, and in the meantime I have a lot of other things to occupy my attention besides finding a good home for a mammoth herd.

Thomas Levi McGrath was born last month to much fanfare, his head covered in gingery fuzz just like Brandon predicted. And even though I never really doubted what he told me, it was still kind of eerie to see it come true with my own eyes. I wonder if the kid will really grow up to like the sound of waterfalls.

I do know that he turned out to be a beautiful baby, strange as it sounds to say that about a boy. And no, I'm not just being a proud daddy, either. It's a very noticeable thing, and sometimes in my heart of hearts I wonder what that might mean. Tommy was still unborn when Danielle and I drank that water. Did he, just possibly, get a taste of it himself? I don't claim to know the answer, but I can't help wondering sometimes.

Chris and Emily had their third child back in August, so along with Thomas and Melissa and Camber that adds up to four new members of our little extended family this year alone. They named him Jonathan, and he's not the last one, either; Jesse and Leah are expecting their second one sometime in the spring, a girl they say they'll name Daisy. Joan always likes to say that an extra kid or two is no more work than the first one; you just throw out an extra baked potato on the table and forget about it. I'm not sure if I entirely believe that, but no doubt we'll find out soon enough.

Hunter and Veronica are still getting married next month, so I'm glad for that, too. They stood the test and waited it out without giving up on each other, which I suppose is exactly what Philip wanted to see all along. Joan likes to say that those two were fated for each other ever since they were born on the same day and the nursery workers put them side by side in front of the window. It's only a joke, of course, but it really *is* strange how things work out sometimes, isn't it?

It'll be a grand occasion, of course; it's not every day that one of the leader's children has a wedding. Philip understands perfectly well that part of his role is to give people a little pomp and circumstance now and then; something magnificent and splendid to revel in and look up to, even if that isn't really his own taste. I'm sure he would have preferred to keep things quiet and simple if he had his own wish, and if I had to guess then I'd be willing to lay pretty good odds that Hunter probably felt the same way. But then of course Veronica thrives on that kind of thing, and she's been in the seventh heaven of delight for weeks.

But other than the buzz of excitement swirling around the wedding and the babies, Kailua Kona is pretty tranquil these days, actually. I have no reason to think it won't stay that way this time; we have no reason to ever go back to Mars or Venus again so far as I know, and all of Colonel Burns' flunkies are safely stowed away on the Moon. With just a smidgeon of luck, we'll actually be free of all that for good this time.

I've gone up to the observatory to watch the grubs at Lakeside now and then, and they seem to be settling in pretty well. I can't listen to their conversations, of course, but they seem as content as anyone has a right to be in that kind of situation. I see them fishing and walking on the beach and seemingly enjoying themselves, and that's as much as I can hope for. They don't seem to have ventured far from the station itself as of yet, but then again most of *us* barely ever set foot outside the station the whole time *we* were there. It takes a certain kind of person to reach for the distant horizon, and not everybody feels that same stirring inside.

But I suppose finding myself concerned about whether they're happy or not is a good sign on *my* part, at least; it means I'm learning to be a little kinder and more loving than I was before, and I'm grateful for that much. I hope and pray it'll make me a better leader someday, when the time finally comes that I have to take up *that* burden. I often wonder if I'll ever feel up to it.

Philip likes to say that a man is naught but a collection of the memories he ponders most, and if that's true then I choose to remember the good and the beautiful things that I've seen and done, inasmuch as I can. Lightning and rain across the Sea of Tranquility. The clasp of N'grumth's cold hand when he pressed his *akiri* necklace into my palm. Golden flowers on the hills of Barbados. The light and the softness in Danielle's eyes when Josie laughs or the baby sleeps. All those things are sweeter than honey in remembrance.

And so in a way all things end where they began, I suppose, with castaways on the Moon and a world almost empty. Maybe someday I'll live to see it full once again of laughing children and wise old greybeards from pole to pole. God knows; I don't.

But in the meantime the future is wide open, and as I lie on my bed next to Danielle and dream of what may be, I don't think I could ever have chosen a better path for myself, to work out the fullness of the promise we all made last year as we knelt in the churchyard. My life has been a bridge between the things of God and the things of science, a link between truth and truth, although it took me a very long time to see that.

I hope it always will be.

The End

Author's Note:

Elysium contains a lot of food for thought, I believe. In this book, Tyke finally grows up and learns his ultimate purpose in life, which he must then choose whether to accept or not. Up till now, our hero has never really considered the possibility that his life might have some deeper meaning below the surface. Finding out that things were always a bit more significant than they seemed causes him to have to rethink a lot of old assumptions.

Most of this story involves unfinished business from *Freedom,* specifically the abandoned soldiers at Tharsis Tholus and what ended up occurring as a result of that. Mars is one of those places which has been used in fiction so often that it's hard to say anything fresh about it. I don't know whether *Elysium* is particularly unique or not since I haven't really read much Martian fiction in a long time, but hopefully it contains a few interesting twists.

The description of the Martian desert is fairly accurate, and I've tried to faithfully describe some of the particular problems that might be involved in terraforming Mars. The gravity, orbital characteristics, and other numbers are real ones, even for Deimos. Details such as the amount of moonlight given by Phobos and the generally dusty and windy character of the planet are all true to life.

The details of the West Florida Reef system are also factual, as are most other things. I made a few minor changes to the real town of Kailua Kona to make it better suit my story, but I figured that was a legitimate thing to do since towns really do change over time and so many things had to be rebuilt after the eruption of Mt. Hualalai which Tyke mentioned. In particular, there isn't a high school located within the town in the present day, and I changed a few other minor details like that, although nothing major.

Hualalai has historically erupted about once every 300 years, with the last time being in 1801. That being the case, a major eruption is indeed highly likely around the time that one occurred in *Elysium.* The results would almost certainly be every bit as horrendous as I described, with major destruction all along the Kona coast and probably a significant number of lives lost.

There were several miracles which took place in this story, which I suppose might seem out of place in science fiction (at least to some people). I personally disagree with that viewpoint since I think it smacks of naturalism, which is an atheistic philosophy having nothing to do with science. Science is simply the search for rules and regularities in nature, nothing more, and in that capacity it has blessed us with many wonderful things. But we should never delude ourselves into thinking it can explain *everything*. Indeed, any event which can't be expected to recur lies outside the bounds of science completely. This is precisely why history isn't a science.

I have never seen any conflict between science and theology. I believe that truth is truth, wherever it comes from, and a wise individual will take care not to be too sure of his own understanding. I take it as a matter of faith that any apparent conflicts are simply a reflection of my own lack of comprehension. Indeed, things like that frequently conceal deeper truths which no one ever considered before, if only we're patient enough to fully investigate them without jumping to conclusions. As the great physicist Richard Feynman once said, don't fool yourself; and remember that you're the easiest person in the world to fool. That warning applies equally well to all of us, unfortunately.

At the beginning of this series, Philip predicted that the world would surely die for lack of love, and that if there were anything to be saved from the ruins then it would only be love that saved them. He turned out to be right on both counts, and in fact that's what this series has always been about; having love for God and for each other, in spite of all that the world might throw at us. To be good and faithful servants under the circumstances we find ourselves facing, whatever those might be.

Will there be any more sequels to Tyke's story? Well, perhaps. There are several characters I think I'd enjoy working with some more, like Jesse and Hunter for example, or maybe even some of the younger kids like Thomas or Camber. But as I've often said, it depends very much on what people would like to hear.

William Woodall
March 3, 2014

Discussion Questions

1. Tyke says that his life has been a bridge between the things of God and the things of science. Discuss this idea. Do you think such a bridge is needed? Explain why or why not.

2. Brandon says that we should never do anything at all which isn't done for the sake of love. Explain what you think he meant.

3. Tyke says that anything which is self-contradictory is absolutely impossible, even for God (such as, it's impossible for Him to create a rock so big that He can't lift it). Discuss this idea. Have you ever wished for something which was self-contradictory in this way? What did you finally do in that situation?

4. Tyke says that it's not very wise to invite a poisonous snake to come live in your house, even if he seems harmless at the time. What do you think he meant by this? Have you ever made friends with someone that you knew it was unwise to associate with, just because they seemed fun or interesting? What happened as a result?

5. Philip says that most moral questions are very simple, and it's usually when we're looking for an excuse to do wrong that we try to make them complicated. Discuss a time when you made this mistake and what happened as a result.

6. Tyke often likes to quote things which Philip and others have told him. Is there a particular person in your life whose wisdom has influenced you? Discuss that person and some of the things you've learned from him or her.

7. Near the end, Tyke faces a difficult choice about whether to accept his destiny and drink the water Brandon offers him, or to keep on with his normal life. If you had been in Tyke's shoes, which choice would you have made? Explain your reasons.

8. On Christmas Day, Danielle says that a grateful heart is happy anywhere, or in other words that thankfulness is the key to happiness. Discuss this idea. Do you believe this is true? Why or why not?

9. At one point, Tyke says that he might have thought slightly better of Colonel Burns if he believed that the man harbored a disinterested love of beauty. Suppose you knew or read about a

very wicked person like Colonel Burns, and then discovered that they also had one or more noble traits also. Would this change your opinion of him or her? Discuss why or why not.

10. The "theme" of a story is the underlying message or messages about life the author is trying to convey. It is the lesson or moral of the story, such as "Love conquers all". What do you think the theme of *Elysium* is? (There can be more than one.)

11. Considering all the places Tyke has visited during this series, which one do you think is most interesting? Which one would you most like to visit yourself? Give reasons for your choices.

12. Brandon often likes to lead missions personally, and has a low opinion of commanders who don't. Do you consider his attitude to be courageous, or do you think it's unwise of him to risk depriving his soldiers of a leader? Give reasons for your opinion.

13. Suppose that you were Colonel Burns and could choose whether to live on Mars or Venus. Which one would you choose, and why? Why do you think Colonel Burns chose Mars?

14. Other than Tyke, discuss your favorite character from *Elysium* and explain why you like (or dislike) this person so much. Give examples of things he/she said or did which you especially enjoyed.

15. Tycho and the other characters make several mistakes during the story, and they aren't always wise. What are some of the mistakes you think they made, and what should they have done differently?

16. Brandon's informant on Mars sympathized with the rebels, but wasn't willing to actually join them herself. What reasons do you think she might have had for this? Are there any circumstances which might lead you to make the same choice that she did?

17. Suppose you were asked to interview any character from this book. Which character would you choose, and what questions would you most want to ask him or her?

18. At one point, Tyke says he might bring back the saber toothed tiger or the woolly mammoth. Consider this. What are some of the risks and benefits of bringing back extinct animals? If you could bring back just one extinct animal, which one would you choose? Give reasons.

The Stones of Song Series
By William Woodall

"There's a thing called magnanimity, or greatness of heart, and to me it's the most beautiful thing that ever there was. It means courage, but it's more than that. It means to cast aside all thought of yourself for the sake of another, like Moses in Gilead or the martyrs who died with a smile on their face. In its own small way it's a reflection of the Lord Jesus at Calvary, and therefore of God, the Light so beautiful that no one who sees it can ever turn away."

So says Cody McGrath, and in many ways that statement is the central theme of this series; the casting away of self for love of another, the scorning of selfishness in all its forms.

These are the stories of the Stone family: Brian, Jenny, Lisa, and Brandon, and some of the people they know and love, most notably Cody. All of them were called for great and glorious things, though sometimes only after great suffering and many mistakes.

Unclouded Day: Brian's life isn't easy. Abandoned by his father, abused by his alcoholic mother, and mocked by his classmates, his only treasures are his beloved little brother and his old guitar. This is the tale of his journey to find the Fountain of Youth, and perhaps to save the world.

Many Waters: Lisa is a small-town waitress with heavy burdens to bear. Cody is a young cowboy with big dreams and some very dangerous enemies. But when the two of them must face down an evil witch who tries to destroy their very lives, it seems that only a miracle can save them.

Bran the Blessed: Brandon hasn't always made the right choices in life, but he's never found himself in quite such deep trouble as this. But even though his life seems ruined forever, Bran still has a high calling to answer. . . if he can find the courage.

* * * * * * *

"I would absolutely, without reservation, encourage you to read this wonderful novel, even if you aren't the fantasy genre type. It was a blessing."
-Sue, Reflections and Reviews

"There are so many nuggets of truth in this book. It's about Heaven. It's about bad things happening for a reason. It's about deciding for yourself what truly matters most in life. It's a really good book!"
-Tattie, Christian Fiction Ebooks

The Last Werewolf Hunter Series
By William Woodall

Zach Trewick always thought he'd become a writer someday, or maybe play baseball for the Texas Rangers. What he never imagined in his craziest dreams was that he'd find himself dodging bullets and crashing cars off mountainsides, let alone that he'd ever be expected to break the ancient werewolf curse which hangs over his family.

But Zach is the last of the werewolf hunters, the long-foretold Curse-Breaker who can wipe out the wolves forever, and he's not the type to give up just because of a few minor setbacks. . .

Cry for the Moon: What would you do, if your family wanted you to become a monster? What if they wouldn't take no for an answer? When 12 year old Zach faces questions like these, he seems to have only one choice; *run*. Thus begins a long search for refuge, and perhaps redemption also.

Behind Blue Eyes: When a stranger kidnaps him from his own back yard, Zach soon finds that the past isn't quite as dead as he might wish. For the time has come at last for him to break the werewolf curse forever; and his family has no intention of letting that happen.

More Golden Than Day: When his girlfriend and then his cousin fall into the hands of the wolves, Zach has no choice but to take on his enemies for a second round. Only this time the stakes are horribly high, and if he fails he may end up losing everything he's ever loved.

Truesilver: When a family of wicked ex-wolves is accidentally awakened, Zach soon finds himself locked in a desperate fight for survival that he never anticipated. And even though he's sworn an oath to fight evil to the utmost of his power, there are times when courage is awfully hard to come by.

* * * * * * *

"If you are looking for a story about a boy who learns valuable lessons about family, love, friendship and God this is the book for you. I recommend this book to a pre-teen or adult. I truly enjoyed this book."
-Rae, *My Book Addiction Reviews*

"I found myself captivated with the story and could not stop reading until I reached the final page. Everything about this story is thought-provoking. Readers of all ages will appreciate this wonderfully told story."
-Jancy, Kansas

The Tyke McGrath Series
By William Woodall

In the year 2154, the world has become a dangerous place. Extremist groups would like nothing better than to wipe out humanity completely, and even the people sworn to defend civilization against such threats have become deeply corrupt and untrustworthy.

When a virulent plague destroys all warm-blooded life on Earth, a small band of survivors clings to life on the partially-terraformed Moon. But fresh dangers lie in wait for the unwary; nor have they left behind all the wickedness in the hearts of men.

Nightfall: When Micah McGrath suddenly finds himself thrust into a dangerous and ugly future after a lab accident, his only choice is to make the best life for himself that he can. But when the secret police get wind of his research into time travel, he soon finds himself in deep trouble indeed.

Tycho: Tycho McGrath is a high school honor student in Florida when he discovers a terrifying secret: a man-made bacterium is about to wipe out all warm-blooded life on Earth within days. The only hope for survival is to flee at once, a plan which carries its own set of unexpected dangers.

Avenger: After spotting an SOS coming from the abandoned Moon, the survivors must organize a rescue mission. But the expedition quickly becomes far more complicated, leading them to the icy world of Titan in search of a holy mountain that no human eye has ever seen.

Freedom: When a cruel and power-hungry military commander on Venus decides to reconquer Earth, the only thing he needs is the formula for Tyke's Orion vaccine. The survivors soon find themselves locked into a bitter battle over the future of mankind, and who will inherit the Earth after all.

Elysium: What began as a simple mission to recover lost comrades in the Martian desert quickly turns deadly when Tyke and the others find *themselves* stranded on the Red Planet, with only the slimmest of chances to make it home again, or to fulfill the destiny which God has in store for them.

* * * * * * *

"Reminiscent of Freedom's Landing, by Anne McCaffrey, Tycho combines the best of traditional space-exploration sci-fi with modern apocalyptic fiction. For any fans of hard science fiction, it doesn't get much better than this."
-Liz, 0H2 Reviews

<u>*Trewick Family Tree*</u>

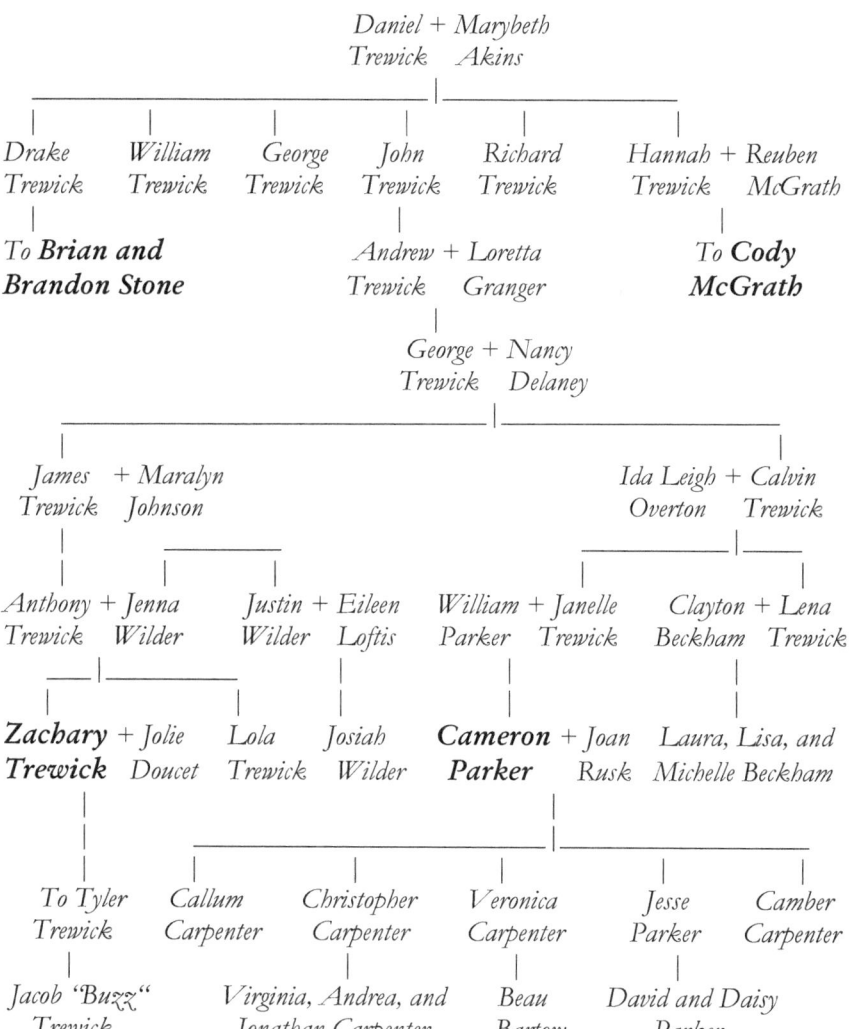

1. *Curse-Breakers are in bold.*
2. *Cameron Parker later changed his name to Philip Carpenter.*
3. *Tyler Trewick is Zach's great-grandson.*
4. *Lisa Beckham's husband is Logan Tygart.*
5. *Laura Beckham's husband is Heath Coates, son of Albert Coates.*

Trewick Family Tree

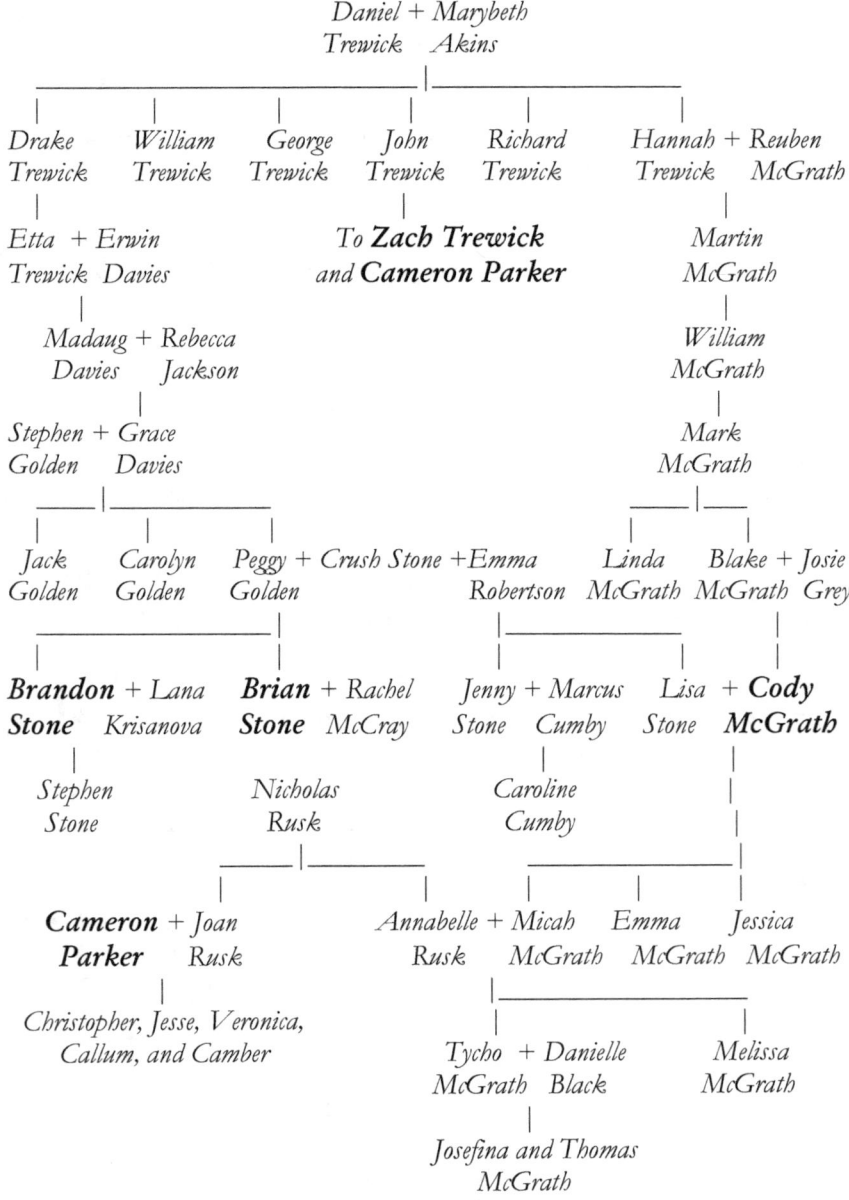

Daniel + Marybeth
Trewick   Akins

Drake   William   George   John   Richard   Hannah + Reuben
Trewick Trewick   Trewick Trewick Trewick   Trewick   McGrath

Etta + Erwin   To **Zach Trewick**   Martin
Trewick Davies   and **Cameron Parker**   McGrath

Madaug + Rebecca   William
Davies   Jackson   McGrath

Stephen + Grace   Mark
Golden   Davies   McGrath

Jack   Carolyn   Peggy + Crush Stone +Emma   Linda   Blake + Josie
Golden   Golden   Golden   Robertson   McGrath McGrath Grey

Brandon + Lana   **Brian** + Rachel   Jenny + Marcus   Lisa + **Cody**
Stone   Krisanova **Stone** McCray   Stone   Cumby   Stone **McGrath**

Stephen   Nicholas   Caroline
Stone   Rusk   Cumby

Cameron + Joan   Annabelle + Micah   Emma   Jessica
Parker   Rusk   Rusk   McGrath McGrath McGrath

Christopher, Jesse, Veronica,
Callum, and Camber   Tycho + Danielle   Melissa
                            McGrath Black   McGrath

                            Josefina and Thomas
                                McGrath

Doucet Family Tree

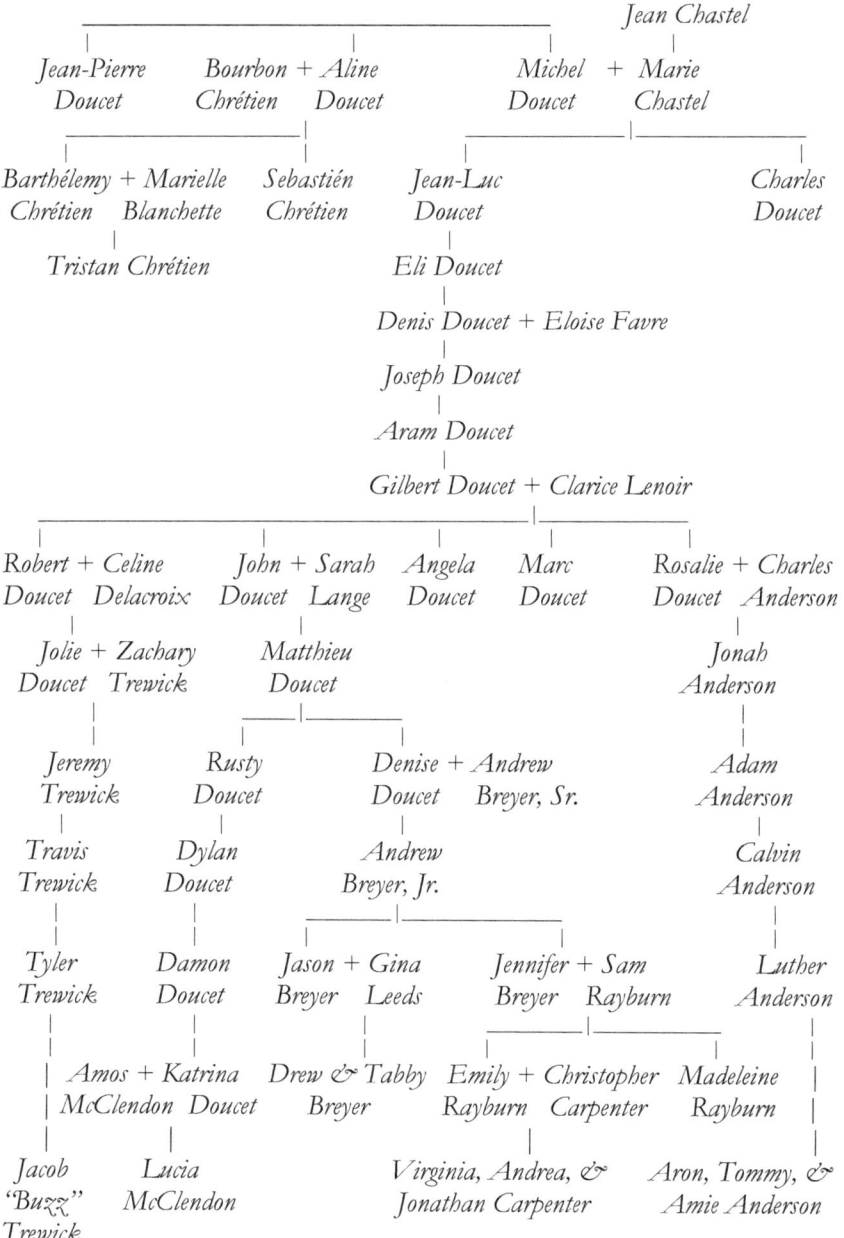

Bartow Family Tree

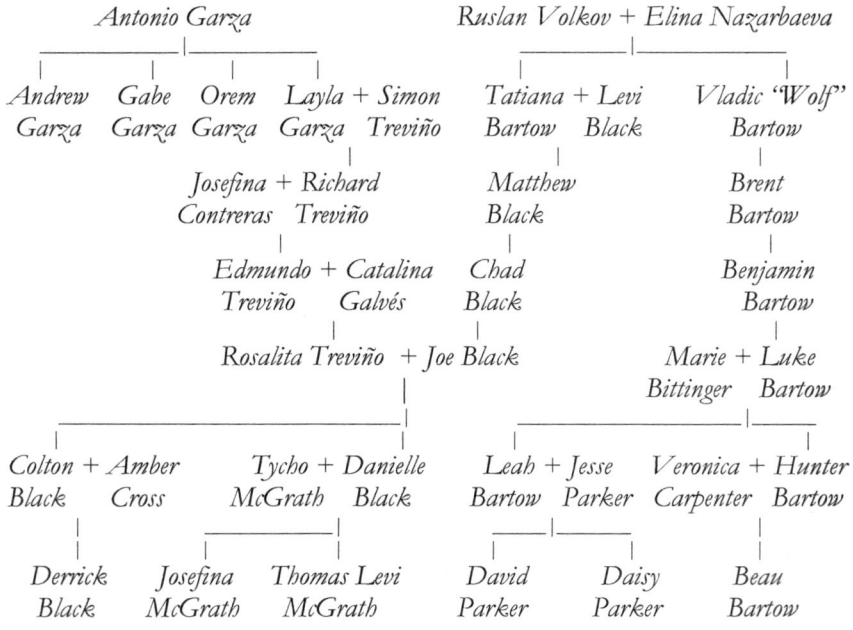

Jones and Golden Family Trees

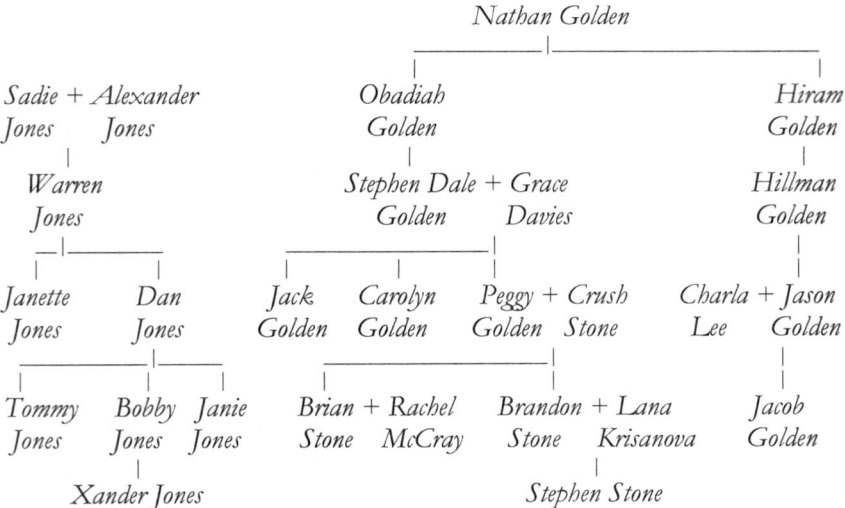

If you'd like to find out more about
The Tyke McGrath Series
and other books, please visit:

William Woodall's
Official Author Website

www.williamwoodall.org

Here you will find:

Free short stories
Discussion questions for teachers and book clubs
Free sample chapters of all my books
Photos of characters and locations for each story
Articles
Interviews
Quotable Quotes
Contact Information
And much, much more!